A sound at the bathroom door made her straighten and whirl around.

Her eyes widened in surprise. "What are you doing here?" she asked. "Aren't you supposed to be—"

But she didn't finish the question. A strong hand gripped her arm and pushed her toward the tub. "Get in the water."

"In the...?" Maribel looked up in confusion and tried to pull away. "You're joking," she said. The situation was too bizarre to be frightening, though her heart began to pound crazily. "And let me tell you," she added with rising anger, "it's not very funny."

But the hands propelled her forward and she wasn't strong enough to resist. She stumbled against the tub and hurt her shins, then climbed in and clutched the nightgown around her hips, feeling ridiculous as water drenched the flannelette and turned it dark blue.

She looked at the familiar face hovering close to hers. "This is some kind of joke," she whispered. "Isn't it?"

At that moment Maribel saw the knife, and realized it wasn't a joke at all.

"Margot Dalton's a writer who always delivers: probing characterization, ingenious plotting, riveting pace and impeccable craft."
—Bethany Campbell, bestselling author of *Don't Talk to Strangers*

MARGOT DALTON

Second Thoughts

MIRA

ISBN 1-55166-421-6

SECOND THOUGHTS

Copyright © 1998 by Margot Dalton.

AUTHOR NOTE

This is entirely a work of fiction. There is no Northwest Substation presently associated with the Spokane Police Department; nor are any of the characters in this book based on real people. Apart from a basic effort to portray the work of an investigating officer with some accuracy, a number of liberties (mostly related to administrative and procedural matters) have been taken for the sake of the story.

Many thanks to Sergeant James Earle of the Spokane Police Department, and to Sergeant L. K. Eddy (retired) of the RCMP for their generous assistance. Any errors or discrepancies in this work are not theirs, but the author's.

1

Snow hissed along the streets, driven by a north wind that swept down into Washington from Canada just a hundred miles to the north. The city of Spokane was weary of winter, tired of icy roads and piles of dirty slush at every curb, of biting winds and frosty mornings and blizzards that sprang out of nowhere.

People were restless and on edge. Crime statistics, especially the numbers for violent crime, began to climb sharply as they always did in the waning days of a long hard winter. The police beefed up patrols and delayed scheduled vacations so they could keep a few extra members on call, and hospital emergency rooms went on full strength.

On a cloudy Tuesday morning near the downtown core, a couple of police cars pulled up in front of an old brick apartment building, disgorging a group of officers wearing dress slacks and topcoats. They hurried across the snow and entered cautiously through the front doors.

Inside, the run-down building was wrapped in an eerie stillness. Nobody walked in the hallways, no doors opened or closed, no telephones rang behind the peeling walls. The only sound was the wind as it whipped at the sagging metal fire escapes outside and set them clanking against the walls.

On the third floor, Jackie Kaminsky and her partner edged warily out of the stairwell with their guns drawn. They exchanged a glance, then began to make their way down the hallway, checking apartment numbers as they went.

"This is it," Jackie whispered, stopping outside a green-painted door.

Close behind her, Brian Wardlow leaned forward to peer at the number on the door, then nodded tightly. "Okay," he muttered. "Let's do it."

Jackie grasped the doorknob with her free hand. It turned easily in her fingers.

"Unlocked," she mouthed over her shoulder. "I'm going in."

She slipped the door silently off the latch, grasped the handle of her gun in both hands and kicked the door open.

"Police! Freeze!" she shouted, crouching in the doorway with her weapon leveled.

The room was empty. Jackie took a deep breath and edged forward a couple of steps, her eyes darting around as she checked the corners.

The place was squalid and littered with empty beer cans. A chair lay on its side near the window, next to a stained plaid couch. Scattered bits of clothing were draped over furniture and thrown onto the floor. The venetian blind hung at a crazy angle from a broken string. Over everything lingered the smell of human misery and decay.

Jackie crept a little farther into the room, conscious of Wardlow moving through the doorway behind her.

She paused to assess the doors leading out of the room. One stood partly open at her elbow and was obviously a closet. She could see clothes on hangers, shoes piled untidily on the floor. Another door, probably leading to a bedroom, was closed. The kitchen was an alcove in the corner, half concealed by a torn plastic curtain. Jackie saw part of a cluttered table, the edge of a sink full of dishes.

"Come out with your hands on top of your head," she called. "Move slowly into the room. We have the place surrounded."

There was no response. The March snowfall seemed loud in the stillness, splattering against the smeared glass. A sagging balcony outside the window creaked with each gust of wind.

Jackie could hear Wardlow breathing raggedly. She glanced at him, the gun still held in front of her.

"I'll take the bedroom," she muttered. "You check the—"

The room erupted in violence. The closet door swung outward and struck her shoulder with brutal force, sending her stumbling forward. At the same time a young woman appeared in the entry to the kitchen, holding a gun.

Jackie regained her balance and faced the woman, conscious of a numbing pain that began somewhere in her shoulder blade and spread down her back. Behind her she could hear the sound of a scuffle, some grunting and a muffled curse from Wardlow. She waited tensely for the sound of a gunshot, but nothing happened.

"Drop the gun!" the woman said.

For a long breathless moment the two women stood facing each other.

They were physical opposites. Jackie was in her early thirties, long-limbed and athletic, with short dark hair, blunt cheekbones and attractive features that hinted at a mixed racial background.

The woman with the gun was small and shapely, barely out of her teens. Masses of blond hair were piled messily on top of her head and her face was pouty, almost childlike. She wore black tights and a long pink T-shirt, and her feet were bare.

Jackie kept her eyes tensely on the girl. "Talk to me, Brian!" she said without turning around. "Where are you?"

There was no response from her partner.

The girl's face twisted with rage and panic. "I told you, drop the fucking gun!" she shouted.

Jackie's mind raced. What should she do? All her training urged her to retain possession of the weapon in her hand. But she had no idea what was happening behind her, or if Wardlow...

In the split second that she continued to hesitate, the girl raised her gun, pointed it directly at Jackie's chest and fired.

Jackie felt a crushing blow that seemed to come from somewhere behind her. The room echoed with the deafening roar of the gunshot, so loud that the walls actually vibrated. She fell to her knees while the harsh smell of gunpowder drifted into her nostrils.

She crouched near the floor, conscious of a confused whirl of activity around her, of shouts and bodies lurching about. Then she crept forward on her knees, wincing with pain, collapsed against the wall and looked up at a ring of faces.

The blond woman stared down at her with detached interest, the gun still in her hand. A man stood at her side, wearing a dirty sweatshirt and jeans, a strip of red cotton bandanna tied around his head. He was young and muscular, with curly dark hair and a couple of days' growth on his cheeks.

"Hey, sorry," he muttered, looking sheepish. "I didn't mean to hit you so hard with that door."

Jackie turned to Wardlow, who was so pale the freckles stood out in sharp relief across his cheeks and nose.

"You're dead," he told her.

"I should've thought about the closet. Jesus, Brian..."

"Dead as a doornail," he repeated.

Jackie glared at him. Her shock was beginning to ebb, replaced by a bracing flood of annoyance. "Go ahead," she muttered, grimacing as she tried to sit up, "rub it in. Who hit me from behind? I feel like I was run over by a truck."

"That was Wardlow," the blonde said. "He jumped on top of you just as I fired."

Jackie stared up at her partner. "What for? She would've shot you, too."

He shrugged and holstered his gun. "What choice was there? She had you on ice, Kaminsky. I had to do something."

Her anger vanished again in a hot wave of embarrassment. "God, I'm sorry, Brian. I just didn't think about the goddamn closet. I could've gotten both of us killed."

"Hey, don't sweat it," he said with an attempt at jauntiness. "We're investigators, right? We're not supposed to be good at all this action crap."

The blonde laughed and knelt beside Jackie, touching her arm. "Are you okay?"

"Sure." Jackie struggled to her feet. "The two of

you were great," she said. "You should get Academy Awards or something."

The younger police officers exchanged delighted grins. "We planned the whole thing before you got here," the man said. "We were hoping we could use that closet to get the drop on you."

"Well, it worked like a charm." Jackie restored her gun to its holster and fastened the restraining leather flap above the handle. Her hands were still shaking badly.

Wardlow watched her for a moment, then moved forward and took her arm. "Come on, Kaminsky," he said. "Let's go. Look, I'll even buy you a coffee on the way back to the office."

Jackie stared gloomily into the depths of her cup. "I still feel like such an idiot," she told her partner. "Not thinking about that closet."

"That's why they make us do these training exercises. Next time you'll see the closet right away." He rummaged through a doughnut box. "Do you want this last one with the crushed peanuts on top? That's your favorite, right?"

"Stop being so nice to me," Jackie complained. "It's entirely out of character, and it makes me feel worse. I could've gotten you killed."

"I wish you'd quit saying that." Wardlow leaned back expansively, his curly red hair glinting under the fluorescent lights. "When are we ever in a situation like that? We always get to the scene *after* the crime, at the investigating stage. Hell, I'll bet you can't even remember the last time you aimed your weapon at somebody in a real-life situation."

But in fact, Jackie could recall that occasion all too

well. It had been in a musty basement on a wet summer morning, and the memory still made her shiver.

But Brian was right. Almost a year had passed since she'd actually drawn her gun on the job.

"I liked it better the old way," she said. "Back when we did all our firearm training on the outdoor range, shooting at targets."

"But outdoor shoots don't replicate the kind of situation cops have to deal with nowadays. That whole apartment setup was probably a lot more realistic. I have to admit," he added, "it threw me a bit when I saw that little blonde holding the gun. It's pretty tough to shoot a woman, even if she's ready to blow you away."

Jackie nodded agreement. "But you know the worst thing?" She pulled the doughnut box across the table and glanced inside, then pushed it away. "The worst thing was the noise. I had no idea how loud a gunshot would be in a small room like that."

"It's really disorienting, isn't it? All the guys say close-quarter shoots are the worst kind of training exercise. Almost impossible to think fast and deal with that gunfire at the same time."

Jackie gave him a wan smile. "Why can't we be like the cops on television? They rush an apartment, take a bullet in the shoulder, blow a couple of people away and then go out for lunch."

Wardlow snorted in derision. "Yeah, right. Actually I'll bet it's a whole lot worse to shoot somebody than to take a bullet yourself."

"Having just taken a bullet—okay, well, a blank—I guess I could agree with that."

"Ever shoot anybody, Kaminsky?"

"Not personally. But I was on patrol with a female officer who did back in L.A."

"What happened?" Wardlow asked.

"We were called to an armed robbery in progress at a liquor store. Two clerks on the floor in a huge pool of blood, broken glass and liquor everywhere, people screaming and hiding behind the shelves, suspects fleeing though the rear door. The other officer fired at them while they were running away down an alley. Shot a kid in the back and nearly killed him."

Wardlow munched on a chocolate doughnut. "So did she go out for lunch afterward?"

"Hell, no. She got debriefed and filed all the paperwork on the shooting, then had to take the rest of the week off and get some trauma counseling before she could go back to work."

Wardlow nodded thoughtfully while Jackie glanced out the window of the coffee shop. The spring storm was passing, and a fitful sun glimmered through masses of clouds.

Her partner finished the last of his doughnut. "Ready to go?"

"I'm getting soft, Brian." She turned away from the window and began to push doughnut crumbs around aimlessly with her fingertips. "I'm not as good a cop as I used to be."

"Look, Kaminsky, don't get me mad, okay? Anybody can make a mistake."

"That's not what I mean. I feel like…"

"What?"

"I don't know." Jackie gave her partner a troubled glance. "Like I'm slowing down or something. I don't have the same edge anymore."

"You're in love," he said comfortably. "It happens."

She continued to arrange the crumbs in a neat little circle. "You know how awful my childhood was, Brian. I never really felt close to anybody until I met Paul. I didn't have any impression that my life was valuable to anybody but me. Now it's all different. I feel like I have to be really careful."

"So? It doesn't hurt for a cop to be careful. In fact, that's rule number one, like Michelson always says."

"But what if I'm being so careful I put you in danger?"

He made an impatient gesture. "Quit worrying about the goddamn training exercise! For one thing they knew we were coming and they had lots of time to make their plan. In real life they probably wouldn't have that kind of advantage. And we knew it was just an exercise, so you weren't running on adrenaline the way you would in a real situation."

"You're not scared to have me for a partner?" Jackie said.

"Only when you get real mean before you've had your coffee in the morning and start swearing at me. Then it can be pretty scary."

She gave him a grateful smile. "Thanks, Brian. I appreciate it."

"Speaking of being valuable," he said, getting up and shrugging into his topcoat, "I'm feeling like a damned bankroll."

Jackie got up with him and, carrying the doughnut box, followed him out to the street. "Why?" she asked. "Has something new happened?"

"Just the same bloody merry-go-round. I have to

go back to court tomorrow, remember? I feel like a walking wallet."

Jackie settled into the passenger seat of the police car while Wardlow got behind the wheel. "I don't see how she can get so much money out of you. It's not like the two of you had kids or anything. And she still has a job, doesn't she?"

"Her lawyer's claiming she can't work because of the stress of the divorce, so I'm required to support her." Wardlow slammed the car into gear and pulled into the midmorning traffic. "What a farce. I catch her in a motel with another man, and *she's* suffering from stress."

"So what does she want now?"

"She's going after alimony and half my pension."

"Half your pension!" Jackie looked at him, appalled. "But you were only married for four years."

"Tell that to the judge." He set his jaw bitterly. "I won't do it. I'll go to jail before I give her a cent of my pension."

"Well, you won't be eligible to draw your pension for years, anyhow," Jackie said, trying to soothe him. "By that time she'll be remarried and the whole thing'll be a dead issue."

"Not if she's managed to get an order in place. God, sometimes I just—"

Jackie's pager beeped. She pulled it out of her bag and looked at the number. "It's Michelson."

"I wonder what he wants."

"Maybe he heard about the exercise and he can't wait to chew me out."

"He's not going to hear about it." Wardlow drove through the underpass below the freeway, sending up sprays of slush and dirty snow. "It's all over, Kaminsky. Nobody's going to talk about it."

She pulled out her cell phone and dialed the sergeant's office.

"Michelson," he said, picking up on the first ring.

"Hello, Sarge. Kaminsky here."

"Hi, Jackie. How'd the training exercise go?"

Jackie exchanged a glance with her partner. "I screwed up big time. Wardlow and I are both dead."

There was a brief silence. "We'll go over it later," the sergeant told her. "Right now I've got a job for you. Where are you?"

"In the car heading back to the substation."

"Good. You can catch this on the way."

"Okay." Jackie got out her notebook. "Go ahead."

"It's a residential break and enter near Corbin Park. Happened overnight, discovered early in the morning when the home owner got off shift. Patrol officers have already responded and the Ident guys are there now."

Jackie glanced at her partner again. "Anything else we should know?"

"There's something a little strange about this one," Michelson said. "Nothing stolen apparently, but some personal effects have been disturbed and the home owner's really upset. Practically hysterical, the patrol says. She's a single woman who claims to have gotten an anonymous death threat. The patrol officers can't get her to open up about what's going on. We were hoping you might be able to get somewhere with her, Jackie."

"I'll try. Where is it?"

Jackie wrote the address in her notebook, hung up

and gave directions to Wardlow. Then she settled back to look out the car window as they headed for the north side and the residential area near Corbin Park.

2

The house was larger than most of the others on the block, and a lot shabbier. It had a weathered, down-at-heel look, like a place that had seen happier times but now was barely holding on.

"You know, I'd really love to buy one of these old houses," Wardlow told Jackie as she hauled her brief-case from the back seat.

"What for?"

"It'd be fun to do what your boyfriend does for a living. Fix up a big old house and restore the place to its former glory."

"So when would you do all this?" she asked. "During your spare time?"

He ignored the sarcasm. "Look, Kaminsky, it's a dream house." He beamed with enthusiasm. "Original clapboard and shingle, two full stories and a third-floor attic with big dormers. And all that shrubbery around the windows... Are those lilacs?"

"How would I know?" Jackie went down the walk and mounted the steps. "I grew up on the mean streets of L.A. I can hardly tell a pumpkin from a sunflower."

"Well, they're both yellow." This earned Wardlow a rueful grin.

Jackie rang the doorbell and waited, gripping her

briefcase. The door was opened cautiously, and Jackie was briefly taken aback at the woman who stood there.

She couldn't tell in the half light if the woman was young or middle-aged. She had coal black hair that was parted in the middle and fell in dark curtains on both sides of her face. Her eyes were huge and light gray, ringed heavily with makeup, but her lips were pale, almost white. The look on her face was one of cool inquiry.

"Police," Jackie said as she and Wardlow displayed their badges. "I'm Detective Kaminsky and this is Detective Wardlow. We understand there's been a break-in?"

The woman moved aside languidly, allowing them to enter. In the musty glow of the hall lamp, Jackie realized that their hostess was very young, probably just a teenager. She wore a translucent red silk dress over a black body stocking and hiking boots. A small gold ring flashed in her left nostril.

"Are you the home owner?" Jackie asked.

"My grandmother is," came a voice from an open door at one side of the hallway.

Jackie turned to the new speaker. He was a boy of about twelve with a thick brush of blond hair, a round earnest face and chubby body. His eyes were reddened from recent tears. He walked into the foyer, his thighs rubbing together as he did so. Jackie felt a quick rush of sympathy, wondering if kids at school teased him for being fat.

"What's your name?" she asked, since he seemed willing to provide information.

"I'm Gordie Lewis." The boy toyed nervously

with his T-shirt, pleating and twisting the fabric in his fingers. "This is my aunt Desirée."

"Aunt?" Jackie looked at the girl, who couldn't have been more than eighteen or nineteen at the most.

"His mother is my half sister," Desirée said. It was the first time the girl had spoken. Her voice was low and expressionless. "Same father, different mothers."

Jackie got out her notebook. "Can I have your full name?"

"Desirée Antoinette Moreau." And with that the girl glided toward another open door at the end of the foyer and disappeared.

Gordie, meanwhile, looked as if he might be about to cry again, and Jackie turned her attention to him. "My grandmother's really upset," he said. "Like totally freaked-out."

"What's your grandmother's name?"

"Granny's name? Uh, it's Maribel. Maribel Lewis." Gordie sniffed loudly, then rushed on, "She works at a place for old people out in the Valley. It's called Pleasant Acres. She works at night, and the house was all messed up when she came home this morning."

"So do you and Desirée both live here in this house, Gordie?"

The boy shook his head. "We live down the street with my mom in a basement apartment. Granny called us this morning when she found the mess, so Desirée and I came right over."

"What's your mother's name, Gordie?"

"Christine Lewis."

Jackie recorded all this information, along with his home address and phone number, while Wardlow left the foyer to check out the living room.

"Look, Kaminsky," he said from the doorway.

Jackie moved over beside him to survey the wreckage of a room that no doubt had once been painfully neat. Some of the sofas and chairs still had their crocheted antimacassars rigidly in place, and others were covered with protective layers of plastic. But all the drawers in the big oak sideboard were pulled out and upended, their contents scattered.

Two bulky photograph albums had been ripped to pieces, and a sea of pictures littered the floor. Smiling faces of little children, wedding parties, long-ago family picnics and graduations, all lay strewn across the fading carpet.

Jackie looked down at Gordie Lewis who still hovered at her side. "Granny says they must've got in through the back door," he said in a voice that trembled with fear. "There's some other cops out there looking for fingerprints and stuff."

"And where's your grandmother?"

"In the kitchen. This way."

Gordie seemed somewhat comforted by the level of police interest in him. He led the way importantly to another room where a woman sat at an arborite-topped kitchen table clutching an empty coffee mug.

She was trim and well-groomed, probably in her early fifties, with hair that was permed and tinted a defiant shade of red. She wore a white nylon pants uniform and nursing shoes, but her outfit was brightened by big red-and-yellow dangling earrings and a red cardigan. At the moment her makeup was badly smeared, dark rivers of mascara running down her cheeks.

Jackie was briefly taken aback by the woman's expression. She'd seldom witnessed a look of such naked terror.

Desirée was lounging against the counter and seemed faintly amused. Jackie ignored her and seated herself across the table from Maribel.

Wardlow, meanwhile, moved outside to join the fingerprint techs on the back porch, Gordie following in his wake.

"Mrs. Lewis," Jackie began, "I'm Detective Kaminsky and—"

"They're going to kill me," Maribel whispered. "They said they would, and now they've come right into my house."

"Somebody's been threatening you, ma'am?" Jackie asked.

"I don't know. They sent me a letter. Such a horrible letter..."

"Did you keep the letter?"

"Yes." The woman lowered her head, and the bright plastic earrings clattered incongruously. "I was... I was afraid to throw it away, in case they—"

"May I see it?"

Maribel Lewis raised her ravaged face again, looking horrified. "Oh, *no*," she whispered. "No, I could never ever show that letter to anybody else. It's too...filthy."

Jackie felt a twinge of impatience, but let the issue rest for the moment. "Has anything been stolen?"

"I don't think so. I couldn't bear to look, but Gordie thought nothing was missing. They were...just after the pictures."

"Any specific photographs, do you think?"

"Family pictures. They went through all the drawers looking for pictures."

Jackie glanced at the pale girl by the counter. Desirée returned her gaze.

"Do either of you have any idea who might have done this?" Jackie asked.

Desirée shook her head vaguely as if the identity of the perpetrator was of absolutely no interest to her, and looked out the window at the backyard.

Maribel Lewis stared down at her folded hands. They were hardworking hands, rough and corded with heavy blue veins.

Jackie got up after a moment, closed her notebook and went outside to check on Wardlow. He stood next to Gordie, watching the police technician.

A windowpane on the back porch had been smashed, allowing the intruder to reach inside and release the lock. Broken glass lay scattered across the back steps and on the brown lawn and shrubs, glittering in the sunlight.

The technician dusted fingerprint powder all along the door frame and around the break in the glass, then snapped photographs. His assistant appeared at the corner of the house, a fresh-faced young trainee lugging a big silver case, full of camera equipment.

Desirée wandered outside, moving soundlessly in spite of her heavy boots. She paused on the step to favor the younger policeman with a distant smile.

Wardlow moved closer to Jackie. "There's stuff scattered around in a few other rooms apparently, but no fresh prints on the glass at point of entry, or on any of the drawer fronts that were handled."

"A professional job?" she asked.

"Somebody wearing gloves, at any rate. No sign of theft or damage so far, except for the broken window."

Gordie edged nearer as if trying to overhear their conversation, while Desirée kept her bored gaze fixed on them from the step.

"Why aren't you kids in school?" Jackie asked the boy suddenly.

"It's spring break. Everybody's on vacation this week."

"Does Desirée go to school?" Wardlow asked.

"She's in eleventh grade. She goes to Wilcox High."

"That's just down the street, right?"

The boy nodded. Jackie tried without success to picture Desirée sitting obediently at a desk doing algebra problems.

"Look. Here comes a gang of kids," Wardlow said, pointing toward the alley.

Jackie followed his gesture and saw a group of teenagers approaching from the direction of the high school. They were in high spirits, laughing and roughhousing as they approached. There were five of them altogether, three boys and two girls, wearing the usual jeans, plaid shirts and boots. Most of them carried books under their arms.

The young people paused in the alley and looked over the fence at the uniformed police technicians and the two detectives in Maribel Lewis's backyard. After a moment one of the boys detached himself from the group, opened the back gate and came hesitantly up the walk.

He was tall and well-built, with curly blond hair and a square handsome face. Gordie stared up at the boy with a look of hero worship and edged closer to Jackie and Wardlow.

"That's Joel Morgan," he whispered. "He plays football."

Jackie glanced at Desirée and saw what appeared to be avid hunger on the girl's face as she watched the newcomer. It was the first time Desirée had shown any sort of emotion besides amusement and contempt. She masked her expression as soon as she became aware of Jackie's scrutiny.

"Hi," the boy said, approaching Jackie and Wardlow with quiet courtesy.

He ruffled Gordie's hair, making the little boy squirm with pleasure, then looked at the broken glass, the two policemen with their fingerprint equipment and cameras. "Is there…is Mrs. Lewis all right?"

"Her house was broken into last night," Wardlow said. "But she wasn't home at the time. Do you live around here?"

"Just down the block." The boy waved his hand, indicating an imposing brick house on the corner that appeared much better-kept than the Lewis place.

"So you're on your way home right now?"

He nodded. "It's lunch break."

Jackie frowned. "I didn't think there were any classes this week."

"We're taking a seminar in Japanese during spring break."

"Japanese?" Wardlow said.

"A group of exchange students are going to Japan this coming summer. You need to speak a bit of Japanese to get into the program, so we're all trying real hard to learn."

Jackie smiled at the boy and his friends, thinking what a shame it was that her job gave her such a negative view of teenagers. For she saw only the ones who got in trouble, and most were sullen and foul-mouthed. But here was a group of kids who were actually giving up their spring vacation to study Japanese.

"Do you know Mrs. Lewis?" she asked.

"Sure. I've known her all my life. I help out sometimes around here, mowing the lawn and shoveling snow for her, stuff like that."

"Gordie tells me your name is Joel?" Jackie asked, taking out her notebook.

"Yup. Joel Morgan." He glanced over his shoulder at the group in the alley who remained by the fence.

Desirée lingered in the doorway, her huge gray eyes still fixed on Joel's face. He, however, seemed oblivious to her presence.

Jackie recorded the boy's address and telephone number. "Do you know of anybody in the neighborhood who might want to cause trouble for Mrs. Lewis? Somebody who's got a grudge against her or anything like that?"

Joel was silent for a moment, staring down at the broken glass with a worried expression. Finally he shook his head.

"Can't think of anybody," he said. "The Lewises usually keep to themselves, sort of mind their own business, you know? When I was little," he added with a shy smile, "Mrs. Lewis always used to give me cookies. I'd ride down the alley on my tricycle and she'd give me a fresh-baked cookie and send me home. I still remember how good those cookies tasted."

Jackie smiled back at the boy and handed him her card. "Thanks, Joel. If you think of anything else or hear something that might help us, would you give me a call?"

"Sure."

He pocketed the card and headed toward his friends. Halfway down the walk he paused, turned and came back.

"You said this happened last night?" he asked.

Wardlow gave him a keen glance. "Yeah, that's right. Why?"

"And Mrs. Lewis wasn't home?"

"She worked the night shift, found the window broken when she got home."

Joel glanced at his friends as if longing to be gone, then squared his shoulders and turned back to the two detectives. "Well, there's something I saw that might be...that maybe I should tell you."

Jackie got out her notebook again. "Yes?" she said. "What is it, Joel?"

"I was at a basketball game last night. I walked Cheryl home. That's her over there." He gestured at one of the girls by the fence, a slim attractive brunette with a pile of books in her arms. "Then I came down the back alley, heading for my house."

"When was this?" Jackie asked. "Could you give us an exact time?"

"Hey, Cheryl," he called. "What time did you get home last night?"

"Eleven-thirty," she called back. "My dad was watching the news and waiting up for me."

Joel turned back to the detectives. "Cheryl lives about three blocks from here. And I stopped for a doughnut on the way home and talked to some of the guys for a few minutes, so I must have been coming down the alley sometime after midnight. Maybe around twelve-thirty.''

Jackie was scribbling busily. ''And what did you see?''

''I saw a light up there.'' He indicated the third-floor dormer. ''It struck me kind of funny, because I'd never seen a light in her attic before. And it was…like, bouncing around.''

''The light bounced around?''

''Yeah. Like somebody was using a flashlight up there.''

''So what did you think?''

He shrugged and spread his hands. ''Just that Mrs. Lewis was looking for something in her attic. I didn't know she was at work.''

''Did you notice anything else?'' Wardlow asked. ''Any strange cars parked nearby, people hanging around, anything like that?''

The boy's sunny face creased with effort as he tried to remember. ''Not a thing,'' he said at last. ''Sorry.''

''That's okay. You've been very helpful, Joel. Thanks a lot.''

The boy gave Jackie and Wardlow an awkward smile and returned to his friends. The young people moved off down the alley, talking in hushed tones.

Jackie put her notebook away and exchanged a glance with Wardlow. ''So has anybody checked the attic?'' she asked.

''Not that I know of.''

They went into the house and spoke to Maribel Lewis about the attic. Their questions seemed to confuse her.

''The attic? Why are you asking me about that?''

she said. "I never go up there, you know. It's just for storage. I haven't been up there in months."

She led them to the second floor, past a series of rooms that were shabby, but clean and neat. In one of the larger bedrooms, a few drawers were upended and more photographs lay scattered across the floor.

"Those are the attic stairs." Maribel indicated a steep flight of unpainted wooden steps at the end of the hallway.

Jackie and Wardlow stood side by side, examining the dark stairwell. They could see the closed wooden door at the top of the steps. It was latched with a slide-bolt high on the frame.

"I had that bolt installed years ago when my son was a little boy," Maribel said as they studied the lock. "Otherwise, Stanley always wanted to climb up into the attic and get into everything."

"The bolt's fastened from the outside. Our guy can't be hiding up there," Wardlow said.

Jackie released the flap on her holster. "Twice in one morning," she muttered. "Jesus, what a job."

"Let me go first, Kaminsky."

She gave her partner a level glance. "No way. Not this time."

Jackie began to climb the stairs with Wardlow close behind her. At the top of the stairs she took a thin plastic glove from her pocket, slipped it on and eased the bolt back, one hand resting near her gun.

She opened the door cautiously and peered inside. The attic was a single large room, dry and shadowy. Boxes were stacked all around the walls, while rocking horses, sports equipment, used appliances and other bulky things took up most of the remaining floor space.

Jackie flipped a light switch at her elbow. The overhead bulb flickered as Wardlow reached the top of the stairs and stood in the entry next to her.

"Any footprints?" he asked. "The floor should be dusty if nobody's been up here for months."

The attic was floored in splintery hardwood planks, entirely bare of dust or marks. In fact, the wood appeared to have been recently swept. Jackie noticed a broom leaning against the wall next to the door.

The two detectives made their way cautiously through the room, peering behind boxes and into corners, but it was soon clear that nobody was hidden in the attic.

"Mrs. Lewis," Jackie called, "could you come up here, please?"

Maribel appeared in the doorway, gazing around with frightened eyes.

"Does it all look normal?" Jackie asked. "Has anything been moved?"

"I'm not sure..." Maribel hesitated. "Those boxes," she said at last. "I think they were piled over there, beside that old floor lamp. But why would anybody...?"

Jackie followed the woman's gaze. A floor lamp with a broken Tiffany shade stood alone against one wall. She made her way across the room, threading through stacks of cartons.

"There's a piece of paper at the base of the lamp," she called to Wardlow. She knelt and lifted the sheet with her gloved hand, looking at it curiously. It was the sort of glossy paper used for magazines, and the image on it was garishly colored and sexually explicit—a voluptuous woman in bloody shredded garments kneeling abjectly before a naked man with a huge thrusting penis.

The heads of the people in the picture had been covered by smiling faces cut from photographs and pasted neatly in place. The rest of the paper was splattered with dark red stains that looked like blood.

Jackie held the sheet of paper carefully in her gloved hand and took it across the room to show to Maribel Lewis. "Do you recognize either of the people in these photographs, Mrs. Lewis?"

The woman studied the blood-smeared paper and gasped, a hand to her mouth. Her face suddenly looked hollow and old. She swayed on her feet and would have fallen if Wardlow hadn't reached out to support her.

"It's...it's my son," she whispered, looking at the man's smiling face superimposed on the pornographic image. "That's Stanley."

"And the woman?" Jackie asked, watching her closely.

Maribel stared at the pretty blonde in the small cutout. Her face twisted with hatred and angry color flooded her cheeks.

"That's *her*," she said. "My God, I wish that woman had never..."

She turned away abruptly and began to cry, then stumbled out of the room and clattered down the stairs with her hands over her face.

3

Once again Jackie sat at the kitchen table across from Maribel Lewis, who fumbled in her pocket for cigarettes and a lighter. Wardlow had taken Desirée and Gordie out of the kitchen and was questioning them on the glassed-in front porch.

"I quit smoking almost six months ago," Maribel said. "But with all this going on..." She flicked the top of the lighter with shaking hands.

Jackie looked down at the obscene picture, now encased in a clear plastic envelope, and opened her notebook. "You say the man in this cutout photograph is your son, Stanley, Mrs. Lewis?"

"Yes."

"How old is he?"

"Thirty-four."

"And where does he live?"

"He has an apartment out in the Valley. He works at a feed mill east of the city."

"When would be the best time to contact him?"

"Evening, I guess. Sometimes he's home in the evening."

"Okay. And the woman?"

Maribel took a long hungry drag on her cigarette. "That's Stanley's ex-wife, Christine."

"Gordie's mother?"

"Yes. She lives in a basement suite a couple of blocks from here. Gordie and Desirée live with her. She works at a ranch out by Reardan, training horses."

"How long has she been divorced from your son?"

"About eight months. They were married for twelve years. Met on the rodeo circuit. Stanley used to be a champion rodeo cowboy back in his younger days." Maribel blew out a plume of smoke, and her eyes narrowed. "He met Christine when she was just a girl, but she chased him and got herself pregnant. They were married when she was eighteen. Gordie was born a few months later."

"So Christine's about thirty now?"

"That's right." Maribel's lip curled briefly. She tapped her cigarette against the ashtray.

"You don't like her at all, do you?" Jackie asked.

"No, I don't. When she was living here, I nearly went crazy."

"She and Stanley lived here, in your house?"

"Yes, most of the time they were married," Maribel said. "It was hard for Stanley to make a home when he was gone so much on the rodeo circuit, and they had that little baby and Desirée to look after, besides. So I let them stay here. They took over a couple of rooms on the second floor and we had a small kitchen put in up there."

Jackie looked thoughtfully at her notes. "Why did they have to look after Desirée? She's Christine's half sister, isn't she? So where are the parents?"

"That family's just trash. Their father was killed in some kind of rodeo accident years ago when Desirée was small, and her mother ran off. God knows where the woman is now."

"So both your son and Christine moved away from here after the divorce?"

"I couldn't possibly have that woman in my house any longer. And Stanley didn't want to stay here after they broke up, so I lost my son, too. I hardly ever see him anymore," Maribel added, her voice breaking.

"When Christine left, she took the kids with her?"

"They didn't want to go. They wanted to stay with me, but she wouldn't let them."

"Even Desirée?"

"Desirée hates Christine as much as I do."

"Why?"

Maribel shrugged. "She's just a girl, but I guess she knows well enough what that woman is."

"I see." Jackie glanced up. "Could you show me the anonymous letter you received, Mrs. Lewis?"

The older woman's head jerked back and two spots of color appeared in her cheeks again. "No!" she whispered. "No, it's too awful."

"I think you should let me see it," Jackie said patiently. "I don't want to alarm you, but if you've had a threatening letter and somebody's broken into your home, you might be in danger, especially when you're living here all alone. I really think we should check out the letter."

"Gordie and Desirée will stay with me at night whenever I want them to," Maribel said stubbornly. "I won't be alone."

"I thought you were working at night."

"Yesterday was my last graveyard shift for a couple of months. I'll be on straight afternoons now until June."

"Don't you think you should consider the welfare

of the children?'' Jackie said. ''If there's any possibility of danger…''

Maribel stared down at her cigarette for a moment, then got up abruptly and left the room. She came back with a plain white business envelope, carrying it gingerly by one corner, and tossed it onto the table in front of Jackie.

The postmark bore a date about a month old, and the address was printed by computer.

Jackie sighed and put her plastic gloves back on.

Modern technology was a great boon to anonymous letter-writers. They no longer had to cut words and letters out of magazines and paste them onto sheets of paper to avoid detection. Even with the most sophisticated lab equipment, it was virtually impossible to identify a laser printout and trace it back to a specific computer.

She glanced at the other woman. ''Have you handled this a lot?''

Maribel shook her head. ''Just once. I opened it and read it, then put the thing away. I couldn't stand to look at it again.''

Jackie opened the envelope and eased the letter out. It was a single printed sheet, plain and featureless except for a neat little star that appeared to be hand-drawn in a lower corner. It read:

Dear Bitch,

You are a nasty and cruel person, and you think people don't know about your sins, but they do. You are being watched. That money you stole has not been forgotten, or the way you whored after another woman's husband. And you dare to judge others! The Divine One is not mocked. You will be the first to die. You will drown in your own tainted blood.

There was no closing or signature. Jackie folded the letter and slid it into the evidence folder along with the envelope. She looked up at Maribel, who was lighting another cigarette.

"What's this about stolen money?" Jackie said.

Maribel took a drag on the cigarette, avoiding Jackie's eyes. "It was years and years ago. I worked at a bank downtown, and I...took some money."

"Why?"

"Stanley was eighteen, just finished high school. He wanted to go to university. My husband had been dead for years, and I couldn't possibly afford the expense of college. I did it for Stanley."

"How much money?"

Maribel licked her lips nervously. "About twenty thousand dollars. I took it gradually over a year or so. When they found out, the manager said they wouldn't press charges if I paid it all back. But most of the money was already gone, so I had to mortgage the house. After a while I got another job, out at the nursing home, and I've been paying off that mortgage ever since."

"I see. How many people know about this?"

"I'm not sure. Nobody's even mentioned it for years. That's why this letter..."

She bit her lip and blinked back tears.

"And the part about somebody else's husband?"

Maribel's flush spread down onto her neck. "It happened about the same time as...as the problem with the money. He lived just down the street and worked at the same bank. They moved away more than fifteen years ago.''

''His name?''

''Tony Manari. I have no idea where he's living now. He patched things up with his wife and they moved away. I haven't seen or heard from him since, but somebody told me his wife died of breast cancer about five years later.''

Jackie nodded thoughtfully. ''So these two old secrets of yours…they wouldn't likely be known or remembered by anybody except family members?''

''I can't think who else would know.''

''Have there been any other things that've alarmed you?''

Maribel hesitated. ''Sometimes I have the feeling that somebody's watching me,'' she said at last. ''Peeking in the windows and so on. But whenever I go to check, there's nobody there.''

''When did all this start, Mrs. Lewis? You told me things were happening when the letter came, and that's why you hung on to it. Did you feel you were being watched back then?''

''Yes, yes. It's been going on for a long time. Ever since the divorce, when Stanley left and I sent Christine away.''

''And that was last year?''

Maribel nodded. ''In the summer. It's that woman,'' she said darkly, the cigarette trembling in her hands. ''I just know it is. She took my son away, and now she wants to humiliate me and scare me to death.''

Jackie rode in the passenger seat while Wardlow drove back to the substation. She looked down at the plastic evidence case, frowning. "This is really an ugly one. Did you get any information out of the kids, Brian?"

"Not much. But that Desirée is a piece of work, isn't she?"

"Pretty strange, all right. Did she tell you anything at all?"

He shook his head. "Just answered in monosyllables and stared out the window. It was like talking to a ghost or something. The girl's barely human."

"She looked human enough when she was watching Joel Morgan."

Wardlow nodded. "You noticed that, too?"

"It was pretty obvious. Naked breathless lust, and the guy didn't even notice her, poor thing."

"Why would any boy be interested in spooky Desirée when he's got a cute girlfriend like Cheryl?"

"You're right about that," Jackie said. "How about Gordie?"

"He certainly talked a lot more than Desirée, but he's got nothing to tell, really. He's just a scared little kid."

"What did he tell you about his mother?"

Wardlow shrugged. "He certainly seems to care about her a lot more than Desirée does. Christine Lewis trains horses for a living. She left early this morning to haul a couple of mares over to a ranch in Montana and won't get back until tomorrow night."

"And his father?"

"Gordie seems pretty neutral about his father. Apparently Stanley isn't in the picture much anymore. He promises sometimes to come over and take Gordie out on weekends, but he's either too late for them to do anything or else he doesn't show up at all. And the father and mother still fight a lot.''

"What do they fight about?''

"The kid didn't say.''

Jackie looked down at the picture again. Suddenly she held the plastic case up to the light and squinted at it.

"What?'' Wardlow glanced away from the traffic to look at her.

"There's a little star here in the corner. I didn't notice it because it's drawn right onto the picture, down in the shadows by the guy's foot.''

"A star?''

"Yes. Just like the one on the anonymous letter.''

"Aha!'' Wardlow declared. "The plot thickens.''

Jackie frowned. "You're not taking any of this very seriously, are you?''

"Not a bit. I think it's a bunch of childish pranks. Probably just our sweet little Desirée getting her kicks.''

"But there's blood on the picture. Where do *you* think it came from?''

Wardlow pulled up behind the northwest substation, a fully operational division of the Spokane Police Department located a few miles north of the main downtown station.

"My bet is that she pricked her thumb and squeezed some blood onto that picture just to make it look really scary.''

"But what's the motivation? Desirée's supposed to care about Maribel. Apparently it's her sister she hates.''

"That kid doesn't have feelings for anybody, as far as I can see,'' Wardlow said. "Except maybe some intense hots for the neighbor boy, who doesn't even know she's alive."

"Well, I'm not so sure. I don't believe this is just childish mischief."

"What do you think it is?"

"I don't know, but I've got a really bad feeling about all this, Brian. It seems so...twisted. Full of hatred."

He raised his eyebrows in surprise. "You really are concerned."

"I can feel it in my bones." Jackie stared down moodily at the pornographic image. "Somebody's going to get hurt."

For the past two weeks, Jackie and her partner had been investigating a gang of car thieves. It was believed the gang was stealing vehicles from Canada, stripping their registration numbers and sending them to the docks in Seattle for shipment to Africa, where they commanded top dollar on the black market.

Later that same day they were both on stakeout near the west-side service station that, according to police informants, served as a clearinghouse for the stolen automobiles. Wardlow was in a luridly painted van with mirrored windows, playing cribbage with a couple of uniformed patrolmen. Jackie was in an office across the street, where she'd been given a desk and computer at an insurance company on the second floor by the window. She was quite happy with her assignment once she discovered the computer was outfitted with word-processing software compatible with hers. It meant she could use her whole afternoon to catch up on her mountain of paperwork.

Nothing untoward was going on at the service station. Both detectives were relieved at nightfall by new personnel, and they made their way inconspicuously out of the area. They paused to confer in a parking lot a few blocks away.

"What time's your divorce hearing tomorrow?" Jackie asked.

"Two o'clock."

"Okay. While you're in court, I'll go out to the Valley to talk to Stanley Lewis, and you can see Christine after supper. She won't be back from Montana till evening."

Wardlow looked concerned. "Don't you think maybe you should come along when I talk with her?"

"I can't. I have a dinner date with the Calders tomorrow night, and I've already broken it twice. I haven't seen them for more than a month. Besides—" Jackie grinned "—you're the one who said there's nothing going on here. You think it's all a childish prank, so what's your worry? Just dazzle her with your boyish charm, get her to admit she's the one who's been harassing her ex-mother-in-law, and we can clear the file."

"Okay, okay." He opened his car door. "See you in the morning."

"I have the morning off. Did you forget?"

Wardlow laughed. "Oh, that's right, you're visiting the boyfriend tonight. Playing cowgirl again."

"Hey, I'm getting to be a pretty good cowgirl," Jackie said. "At least I can tell one end of a cow from the other."

"Wow, you really *have* learned a lot, haven't you?"

Jackie laughed and watched him drive away, then climbed into her unmarked car and headed across the city to the substation, where her own car was. She stopped by her apartment to change into jeans and pick up her overnight bag, already packed and waiting. At last she drove west into the sunset, her heart lifting with happiness as she left the city and her job behind.

More than half of Jackie's thirteen years of police service had been spent in Spokane, the past three years as a detective. It was, in fact, while she and Wardlow had been investigating a kidnapping case a year ago that she'd met Paul Arnussen.

She smiled now as she thought of the circumstances—she'd mistakenly arrested Paul as a suspect! When at last the case was solved, she and Paul realized their mutual attraction and began seeing each other; by their third date they were sharing a bed. Although they soon found themselves in love, they'd never actually moved in together. He was living in the run-down old ranch house he'd purchased and was now renovating and came into the city occasionally during the week for supplies. He spent at least part of each weekend with Jackie at her apartment.

A couple of antelope grazing on a gentle slope not far from the highway lifted their heads alertly at the sound of her car. She watched as they turned and loped away with easy grace, topping a hill and vanishing into a pastel swirl of clouds at the horizon. Jackie smiled at the sight, then frowned as her thoughts returned to Paul.

Despite the intensity of their feelings for each other, both of them, she knew, were frightened of the next step—moving their relationship to a greater level of commitment.

Sometimes she wondered if that next step was ever

going to happen. So many things stood between them, mostly growing out of their lonely troubled child- hoods. Their problems were real but still nebulous, almost invisible, which made them so much harder to deal with…

She pulled off the highway and drove through Reardan, heading south. Somewhere around here, she recalled, was the horse ranch where Maribel Lewis's ex-daughter-in-law worked.

Now, *there* was a family even more screwed up than her own, Jackie thought with a bleak smile.

She'd grown up in a slum in Los Angeles, aban- doned by her mother shortly after birth and raised by an alcoholic grandmother—who also had the care of a ragtag crowd of cousins. It had been a scrappy mis- erable childhood, and the family relationships still weren't much better.

Irene Kaminsky, Jackie's grandmother, had been sober now for almost six months, but that didn't make her any nicer to deal with. She was a bitter old woman, accustomed for years to venting her unhap- piness on Jackie. And Carmelo and Joey, the two youngest cousins who, though well into their twenties, still lived with Irene, were frequently in- volved in minor scrapes with the police. Jackie found their misbehavior both distressing and embarrassing.

But all thoughts of her troubled family disappeared as she pulled off the highway and turned onto the gravel road that led to Paul's newly acquired property.

He'd grown up on a ranch in Montana with a father whose parenting skills had been as lacking as Irene Kaminsky's. The family property was gambled away when Paul was still a boy, so Paul had been working as a carpenter when he and Jackie met.

His handiwork was clearly evident around the ranch. New fence lines, straight and taut, stood next to rotted stumps of posts and coils of barbed wire. A cord of lumber sat in the yard, gleaming yellow in the fading sunlight, and the old barn had been partially rebuilt since her last visit.

The man worked like a demon, Jackie thought, feeling a tug of worry. He spent his days out here all alone, dealing with machinery and power tools, and he didn't even have a telephone installed yet because it would cost a small fortune to string one in from the main line.

If anything happened to him, nobody would know for hours, even days.

The thought made her feel breathless with terror. She'd never known what it was like to love somebody this much, and she could hardly deal with her tumult of emotions.

She inhaled deeply, putting her fears firmly aside as she parked in front of the old house. Then she climbed out of the car and, overnight bag in hand, went up the veranda stairs and into the house. The place showed its years of neglect, but it was basically sound.

"A solid fieldstone foundation," Paul had told her in delight, showing her around before he closed the deal. "Nine-foot ceilings, solid oak moldings and wainscoting and a beautiful staircase. Look at this place, Jackie! Give me two years and I'll make it into a mansion."

She had to admit, looking around the silent hallway, that she couldn't share his vision yet. All she could see were rotting floorboards, tattered curls of ancient wallpaper and ugly brown stains where the moisture had come in through broken windows.

But if Paul said he could fix the house, she had no doubt he'd succeed. The man's determination was fierce and awesome, almost frightening. She'd never known him to take on a job and not finish it.

Jackie took her boots off and padded silently down the hallway to the kitchen where he'd already built new cabinets and installed some decent appliances. She paused in the doorway and her heart began to race.

Paul stood at the counter with his back to her. He wore jeans, work socks and a denim shirt. The overhead lights glistened on his straight blond hair.

Jackie smiled, weak with tenderness, treasuring this secret moment when she could look at him without his knowledge. He was slicing fresh mushrooms and tossing them into a big cast-iron skillet. The smell of baked potatoes drifted through the room, making her realize, suddenly, she was ravenous.

She tiptoed across the kitchen and put her arms around him from behind, resting her face against the warm denim.

"Hi, stranger," she murmured. "It feels like a year since I saw you last."

He reached back to touch her, then turned in her arms, gathered her close and began to kiss her hungrily. His lips moved over her eyelids, her cheeks and throat, down into the opening of her shirt.

"I love you," she whispered. "I love you so much…"

His hand reached to cup her breast, brushing against the gun at her waist. "Take that thing off," he said abruptly, drawing away. "I hate kissing a woman who's armed."

Jackie laughed and pulled away, drawing a lingering hand over his cheek and neck as she did so. Paul had the most intriguingly handsome face she'd ever seen, his blunt cheekbones and piercing brown eyes providing a stark contrast to his golden hair.

"Long long ago, a young Swedish homesteader kidnapped a beautiful Sioux princess," he'd once told Jackie. "She fell in love with him, they married and had kids. The gene pool was very interesting."

Jackie agreed completely.

Still smiling, she went down the hall to the old parlor he was using temporarily as a bedroom until he could make the upstairs rooms habitable. She took off her gun and locked it away in a small dresser next to his bed, then came back to the kitchen where the table was set neatly for two.

They lingered over their meal, happy to be together again, talking and laughing while the sky darkened beyond the window.

"How are the cows?" Jackie asked.

"Doing great. Twenty-two calves already, and no problems to speak of. More pie, sweetheart?"

"It's delicious," she said wistfully, "but if I eat another bite, I'll be too full and too sleepy to make love."

He cast her a glance and Jackie shivered with anticipation as she caught the expression on his face. When Paul looked at her like that, it usually meant they were going to explore some uncharted territory together, climb to new and dizzying heights of pleasure.

Paul got to his feet, removed the dishes from the

table and quickly stacked them in the sink. Then he crossed to her and lifted her in his arms. Jackie was anything but petite—rather, tall and statuesque—but he carried her as easily as a child.

"I'm taking you to bed right now," he murmured. "I've waited long enough."

In the darkened bedroom, he pulled back the covers with one hand, placed her full-length on the bed and began to undress her slowly, as if he were unwrapping a precious gift.

She smiled and stretched languorously, loving the feeling of being cherished and utterly desired. Nobody in her life had ever made her feel the way Paul did—so lovely, so womanly and irreplaceable.

Her shirt and jeans were gone now. He sat next to her on the bed, running his hands over her abdomen, across her thighs, around the edge of her panties. "Did you miss me, honey?" he whispered.

"All the time. Every single minute." She caught his hand and drew it up to her breasts. "Come on," she said, tugging at his shirt. "Get yourself undressed and hold me before I die from wanting you."

He pulled off his clothes and climbed into bed next to her, drawing the covers up over both of them.

She sighed with happiness and moved into his arms. This was always a moment of breathless excitement to her, the instant when their naked bodies first touched and her skin warmed with silken fire, all the way from her toes to the top of her head.

His hands began to move over her body, stroking and seeking, gently caressing. He knew her well and was deeply sensitive to her needs. Before long he had her strung out to a fine point of yearning, on fire for him, panting and clutching at him with incoherent whimpers.

All her loneliness disappeared, everything she'd ever suffered in her dismal childhood and troubled youth, lost in the golden sweetness of his love....

She floated back to earth, so utterly limp and satisfied that she could hardly find the strength to smile.

"There has to be some kind of law against you," she murmured against the warm pulsing column of his neck. "You can't possibly be legal. Nothing that wonderful is ever legal."

"Yeah, there's a law. There's also a penalty." He lowered his head to nuzzle her cheek. "You have to pay with your life, sweetheart. Forever. All the rest of your life."

She nodded silently.

Words like *forever* had never used to be in Jackie's vocabulary. She certainly hadn't grown up with the kind of trust that was required for a lifetime commitment.

But with Paul, these thoughts were filling her mind all the time. She found herself thinking about mortgages and babies and the kind of commitment they meant.

Scary things.

She turned away to stare at the window. It was so dark out here in the country. Stars dazzled against the blackness, and she could hear a distant scrap of coyote song.

"Jackie..."

"Hmm?" She reached out to kiss the mat of golden hair on his chest.

"Did something happen today?"

"To me?" She drew away and looked up at him in the darkness.

"This morning," he said slowly. "I was working on the new fence, and for a few minutes I had a feeling something was wrong."

"Jesus, Paul," she muttered. "You're not supposed to do that anymore."

"I can't help it." He gathered her in his arms and buried his face against her hair. "It hardly ever happens these days, sweetheart. Just little flashes of things sometimes, and I don't even know what they mean. But this morning I got the feeling you were in some kind of trouble. It scared me."

"Really?"

He nodded, looking somewhat sheepish. "I drove into Reardan and phoned the office to make sure you were okay."

Jackie stared at the ceiling, not knowing whether to laugh or be annoyed.

Paul Arnussen was a reluctant psychic, which was how he'd become involved in her kidnapping case a year earlier. At the time, his rare gift had helped Jackie recover a lost child and spare the little boy's mother terrible heartbreak.

Still, it was unnerving when her lover's psychic ability was applied to her own life. Paul was embarrassed by his gift and seldom spoke of it to anybody. Now, though, he was obviously concerned.

"I got shot this morning," she said at last.

He stiffened and drew away in alarm, staring down at her. *"What?"*

Jackie laughed. "Hey, don't look like that. It was just a training exercise. We have to do them a couple times a year. They set up a hypothetical situation with young recruits playing the bad guys. Everybody has guns loaded with blanks.''

She described the scene in the old apartment that morning, the way she'd misjudged the room and put herself and Wardlow both in danger.

''Brian says it's all your fault,'' she added, nuzzling his chest again. ''He says I'm too much in love to be on my toes anymore.''

Paul stared at the ceiling, his jaw tense. ''God, I wish you'd quit,'' he said.

''Because I screwed up a training exercise?'' She leaned up on one elbow and stared at him. ''You can't be serious.''

''It's too dangerous. When I think about you in a situation like that, being shot point-blank...'' His voice roughened and he turned away so she couldn't see his face.

''Oh, darling,'' she whispered. ''It was a phony setup, that's all. I'm an investigator *after* the fact. I don't get into those situations.''

''Then why do detectives have to do the training exercises?''

''Because you never know when a witness might get hostile. Or we could be in the car somewhere and hear a call from an officer in trouble...''

Her voice trailed away when she saw the strained, remote expression on his face.

''Sweetheart,'' she pleaded, ''don't shut me out. Let's talk about it.''

He rolled over and leaned above her, his face taut with emotion. ''I love you,'' he said hoarsely, staring down at her. ''Sometimes I can hardly stand it, Jackie.''

She wondered what to say, confused and a little

frightened by his intensity. But he was already turning away, drawing the blankets up around his shoulders.

"Let's go to sleep," he said over his shoulder. "Sleep tight, honey."

She got up to pull a nightgown from her overnight case and looked down at his bare shoulder, feeling chilled and unhappy. At last she climbed back into bed and put her arms around him, snuggled against the hard warmth of his back and willed him to turn over and talk with her again.

But he didn't. Long after his breathing had steadied into the rhythm of sleep, she lay awake watching the stars as they danced and glittered beyond the patched window.

4

She awakened the next morning to the pale glow of sunrise and a chorus of meadowlarks sounding crazy with happiness.

"Isn't it awfully early in the season for those birds to be around?" she muttered to Paul.

But he was clearly in no mood to discuss the local wildlife. He pulled her into his arms, all the tension of the night before apparently forgotten, and made love to her until she was limp with satisfaction. He smiled into her face, then got up and stepped into his jeans.

"Come on, sweetheart," he said as he moved to the doorway. "I'll put some coffee on and make breakfast, and then we've got a mile of fence line to string before you leave."

He was as good as his word. Within an hour they were out on the prairie, stretching and stapling barbed wire to the newly planted posts.

"I feel so used," Jackie complained, holding the wire stretcher while he pounded staples. "You don't love me at all. I'm only invited out here for sex and manual labor."

Paul chuckled, the morning sun glinting warmly on his tanned cheekbones. His big shoulders tensed as he drove a staple home with a few powerful strokes.

"Well, you're pretty good at sex," he said. "But I've still got a lot to teach you about manual labor."

She returned his smile, feeling weak with tenderness. He walked back to the truck for another coil of wire, and she looked around at the rolling sea of prairie, starred with little pools of melting snow.

Cattle grazed nearby, the new calves bounding and playing on unsteady legs. Pairs of waterfowl circled overhead as if looking for nesting places, and the meadowlarks still sang all around her, unseen in the tall grass.

I never heard birds singing when I was a little girl, Jackie thought absently. *There were no birds on those streets.*

Paul came back with the wire, handed her a can of staples and moved down the fence line. Jackie followed, her mind still wandering.

She was five years old, crouching in the hallway on a bit of carpet with a ragged doll in her arms. Cousins swarmed around her, fighting and yelling. Jackie was crying and she couldn't stop, even though Gram was angry with her.

Stop that bloody crying, the old lady shouted, *or I'll give you something to cry about! What's the matter with you, anyway?*

What she'd wanted, needed, was someone to hold her, someone to hold her tight and take away her loneliness and fear.

But she couldn't express that when she was five, and besides, Gram would never hold her, anyway. Gram was drinking again, and there was no food to eat in the crowded little apartment.

And Jackie had been so cold...

She shivered and Paul glanced at her over the fence post. "Something the matter, honey?"

Jackie shook her head.

"Are you cold? Want me to get your jacket from the truck?"

"I'm fine. I just wish I didn't have to leave at noon and go back to the real world."

He gripped the hammer and squinted at the cows on the horizon, looking wistful. "Wouldn't it be nice if you could stay here all the time?"

Yes, she thought, it would be nice to stay with Paul and never have to leave. Because he cared about her more than anybody ever had...

When she was eight or nine years old, Jackie had finally asked her grandmother the question that had burned in her for so long. Picking a day when Gram was feeling good and none of the cousins was making her angry, she leaned against the old lady's chair while Gram was knitting and watching television.

Where's my mother, Gram? What happened to her?

She died, Gram said, her mouth pursing. *Silly little bitch.* The metal knitting needles clicked angrily.

How did she die?

She shot some stuff into her arm with a needle and it killed her, the old lady said carelessly. *Now I got to look after you along with all these other kids. And I'm warning you, missy, you'd better stay away from that shit or it'll kill you, too.*

"One more strand," Paul said cheerfully, "and then I can start building the gate. Let's stop for coffee, okay?"

Jackie watched while he went to get their thermos from the truck, but her thoughts were still far away.

She was sixteen, already part of a gang, wearing a

black knitted cap and a black jacket with scarlet lettering. She had a knife in a leather sheath at her belt, and most of the time she wasn't afraid of anything.

She was the lookout, crouching in the alley and watching for cops. One of the gang members, an older boy, came running wildly out of the darkness and thrust a handful of bills at her.

Run, kid! he shouted. *Run like hell and don't look back!*

She stuffed the money into her pockets and took off, her heart beating wildly. But the policeman was young and wiry. He caught up with her after a few blocks, driving her to the pavement and thrusting a gun in her side. She could feel him panting as he rested his weight on her and snatched the cap from her head.

What the hell, he muttered. *It's just a girl! But you're still going away, sister,* he told her with angry satisfaction. *You'll be going away for a long long time....*

Jackie felt tears burning in her eyes and turned aside to brush at them furtively so Paul wouldn't see her crying for her lost childhood, her troubled lonely youth and those terrible years in juvenile detention.

She squared her shoulders and smiled at him as he came back with the coffee.

All that misery was over now. She had a good life and she had Paul. And nothing, Jackie thought with fierce determination, was going to take either of them away from her.

After lunch Jackie drove back to town, changed her clothes and headed for the section of the city generally referred to as the Valley, where Stanley Lewis lived and worked. She arrived at the feed mill around one and checked in at the front office, where she was given a yellow hard hat and a paper mask to cover her nose and mouth, then directed across the mill to an area at the rear.

She walked through the lofty building surrounded by clouds of sunlit dust, clanking machinery and the scent of milled grain, unmistakable even through her mask.

A loaded truck drove onto a weigh scale at one side of the walkway as she passed, then pulled slowly ahead, tilted its box and disgorged a shining flood of wheat into a floor-level chute. She could hear auger blades whirling as the grain disappeared.

Jackie stopped at a small glass-walled office near the front of the complex where a graying heavyset man in denim coveralls sat at a desk, making entries on a computer.

"Detective Kaminsky, Spokane P.D.'' she shouted over the roar of machinery, pulling down the face mask and displaying her badge. "I'd like to speak with Stanley Lewis, if I may."

The man looked up at her in alarm. "Is Stan in some kind of trouble?"

"Not at all. We just need his help with something."

"Okay." The man got to his feet and came out of the office, nodding courteously.

Jackie followed him down the narrow hallway to a small room with a pop machine, a sink and refrigerator, and a grouping of shabby vinyl chairs and couches. The room looked well-used but was empty at the moment.

"If you could just wait in here, ma'am, I'll get Stan for you."

"Thanks." Jackie removed her hard hat and sat on one of the couches, looking in distaste at the pile of girlie magazines littering the old coffee table.

She was tempted to leaf through them and see if any pages were missing, but resisted the urge. The doctored picture they'd recovered from Maribel's attic was a lot more hard core than this stuff. It had been torn from the kind of magazine that people kept hidden away and looked at when they were alone.

A man came down the hall and stood awkwardly in the doorway, removing his hard hat. He was tall and well-built, with light brown hair, blue eyes and a handsome yet somehow weak face. He wore dusty jeans and a denim work shirt. A paper face mask dangled around his neck on an elastic cord.

"Hi." Jackie got to her feet and extended a hand. "My name's Detective Kaminsky. You're Stanley Lewis?"

"Stan." He came into the room and sat in one of the vinyl chairs. "Only my mother calls me Stanley."

"Okay. I'll just keep you for a few minutes, Stan. I'm investigating a break-in at your mother's house yesterday."

"She told me about it." Stan Lewis glanced out the window at a covered shed where a forklift was moving around, transporting wooden flats piled with sacks of feed.

"Were you worried when she told you what happened?"

"Well, sure." He turned back to Jackie. "Of course I was."

But he didn't look particularly worried. He looked annoyed, uncomfortable and anxious to be gone.

The weakness in his face came from the mouth, Jackie decided. His features were good, but the set of his mouth was childlike, almost petulant.

Involuntarily she thought about the masculine hardness of Paul's face, the flinty strength that concealed such depths of tenderness. Suddenly she was overtaken by a flood of sexual warmth, and looked down at her notebook to compose herself while the man watched her warily.

"Your mother tells me you're a rodeo cowboy," she said, trying to set them both at ease. "That must be an interesting occupation."

He looked startled and uneasy. "I don't compete much anymore. Bronc riding and steer wrestling and such, that's a young man's sport."

"I suppose it would be. But you were a champion at one time, right?"

"I won quite a few rodeos, when I was in my twenties." He leaned back in the chair, smiling slightly, then shook his head. "These days it's pretty hard to get away from work."

"I see. When you were traveling the circuit, you didn't work full-time, did you?"

"I didn't have to. I was earning a lot of prize money, and Chris—"

He gripped his callused hands between his knees.

"Chris is your ex-wife?"

"Yeah," he said curtly.

"What were you going to say about her, Stan?"

"Just that she was working, so we always had *some* income. I didn't have to work steady because Chris was drawing a good paycheck."

"Training horses?" Jackie said.

"That's right. She's been working at the same ranch for at least ten years."

"Since Gordie was just a little boy," Jackie commented, watching his reaction carefully.

He shifted in the chair and his hands tensed again. "You've talked to my kid?"

"Yes, I have. He's pretty scared about what's been happening to his grandmother."

"What do you mean? Has something happened besides this break-in thing?"

"Well, your mother's been getting some threats. She hasn't said anything to you about them?"

He shook his head. "What kind of threats?"

"An anonymous letter, for one thing, saying some pretty nasty stuff about her." Jackie hesitated, then went on. "It contained a death threat, too."

He turned white beneath his tan and gripped the arms of the chair.

Jackie watched him with sudden interest. "You look upset."

"I got—" He stopped abruptly.

"What?"

"I got a letter like that," he said reluctantly. "But I never thought..." His mouth set and he looked away.

"You didn't tell anybody about it?" Jackie asked.

Stan Lewis shook his head. "I figured it was just a...some kind of prank."

"Did you keep the letter?"

"Hell, no. I threw it away as soon as I opened the damn thing."

"Can you remember when it arrived?" Jackie made an entry in her notebook.

"A couple of months ago, I guess. Sometime after Christmas."

"And what did it say?"

"Just a lot of stuff about...crazy things." He shifted uncomfortably in the chair.

"Like what?" Jackie said patiently.

"Things about...me and Chris." He took a breath. "Sex stuff."

"About you and your ex-wife?"

His face colored slightly, and he glanced out the window again. "We'd been...trying to work things out," he said in a low, choked voice. "Over Christmas, we spent a couple nights in bed together."

"But the reconciliation didn't work?"

He shook his head.

"You had a definite impression the letter was about you and your ex-wife?" Jackie asked.

"I know it was. It said I was a filthy sinner and that I'd be punished by God for fornicating with two women. The letter said I was going to die a thousand deaths."

"*Two* women?" Jackie asked.

"I have a girlfriend."

"Her name?"

"Laney Symons. That's short for Elaine. She has a place not far from here, works at an auto-body shop and sings with a country band at some of the local clubs."

"Did she know about these attempts to reconcile with your ex-wife?"

"No. Nobody knew. It didn't work out, so Chris and I just let it drop. We never told anybody."

"Didn't the kids know? Gordie and Desirée?"

"No way. They were up at my mom's house both

times Chris and I slept together. We had Chris's basement apartment all to ourselves. Nobody knew about
it."

"Well, *somebody* must have known," Jackie said.
"And it seems they were pretty upset by it."

She described the blood-smeared picture in his
mother's attic, with the photos of Stanley Lewis and
his ex-wife pasted over the two naked figures.

He shook his head in disgust. "Crazy," he muttered again. "Just crazy."

"Who do you think might have done it?"

"How would *I* know?"

"You must have *some* idea," Jackie said reasonably. "When you got that letter, for instance, who did
you suspect of sending it to you?"

He looked down at his hands, picking at a callus
on one of the hard palms. "Actually, I thought it was
my mother," he said at last.

Jackie glanced up, startled. "Why?"

"Because she's always hated Chris. I figured she
could tell somehow that we were thinking about getting back together and she didn't like the idea, so..."

"Would sending threatening letters be normal behavior for your mother?"

He took so long to answer the question Jackie had
to ask him again.

"I don't know," he said at last. "But she was a
real troublemaker during a lot of our marriage."

"Even though you were living in her house?"

"I think that made it worse," he said miserably.
"I didn't really want to live there, but it was practically rent-free and I wanted to save enough for a
down payment on a house."

Other couples managed to save for a house without

staying with their parents, Jackie thought. But she kept her face carefully expressionless.

"It was real hard on Chris." Stan continued to pick at his hands. "Living in my mother's house."

"I wouldn't doubt it," Jackie said dryly. "Living for ten years with a mother-in-law who hates you. That'd be pretty tough on anybody."

She spent another fifteen minutes asking him questions about his family background, his short-lived college education, marriage and rodeo career, about Desirée and Gordie and his own relationship with his mother.

Surprisingly he viewed the mysterious Desirée as "a nice shy kid, a quiet girl who wouldn't hurt a fly." And he seemed to feel guilty about his son, aware he was failing in his fatherly duties to Gordie. Also, his resentment of his mother's interference in his marriage became increasingly clear as he talked.

Finally Jackie got up to leave. She put on the hard hat, then paused in the doorway.

"By the way, that letter you got," she said casually. "Do you happen to recall if there was any kind of symbol on it?"

"Symbol?" He got to his feet, obviously relieved, and followed her into the hallway.

"Any kind of mark?" she asked, raising her voice over the roar of machinery. "Something drawn by hand on the paper?"

He frowned. "Yes, there was," he said at last. "It might have been a little star or something. I can't remember."

Brian Wardlow left the courtroom feeling utterly brutalized and headed back to his lonely apartment

through the snarl of late-day traffic. He let himself
into the dingy front room, looked around restlessly
and cursed under his breath, then wandered into the
kitchen to open the refrigerator.

It was six o'clock, time to eat something. Time to
choose between a stack of boxed meals in the freezer
or some kind of takeout.

Maybe the Chinese restaurant in the street below,
but he'd done that at least twice this week already....

While he was debating, his clothes started to feel
sticky and unpleasant, as if the day's proceedings had
soiled them. He pulled out one of the frozen dinners
and tossed it into the oven, then stripped off his jacket
and slacks, dropped them in an untidy pile on the
living-room couch and headed for the shower.

He stayed a long time under the hot jet of water,
trying to wash away all the pain of the afternoon. But
Sarah's image kept haunting him through the clouds
of steam.

How could a woman be so beautiful and then turn
so ugly?

One night she was your wife, holding you and
whispering that you were wonderful, you were the
best, she'd rather die than hurt you. Suddenly, without
any kind of warning, she was sitting across a courtroom with some asshole of a lawyer, calmly telling
the judge she'd suffered "intense mental anguish" at
your hands and needed three-quarters of your assets
to help her survive.

He stepped out of the shower and dried himself
harshly, thinking about women.

Maybe there were a few good ones left in the
world, but he didn't have much personal contact with
them.

Except for Kaminsky, of course.

Brian grinned when he pictured his partner's exotic face and warm luminous smile. She was a strange combination, Kaminsky was. Part hard-boiled cop and part sad little kid, not nearly as tough as she liked to pretend. She was good-looking, too, with a tall firm body and glossy black hair, and a pair of hazel eyes that could be shrewd or sexy by turns.

But Jackie wasn't really his type. She was far better suited to Paul Arnussen, that big prowling tiger of a man who loved her as much as she loved him. They were two of a kind, Kaminsky and Arnussen.

Two of a kind.

Thinking about their relationship made Brian feel even lonelier. He pulled on undershorts and a T-shirt and wandered across the room to look at his reflection in the mirror.

Not so bad, he thought, trying to comfort himself. Flat belly, good muscle development, still had all his hair.

But the loneliness wouldn't go away. He peeled the dry-cleaner plastic off a pair of brown wool dress slacks and a beige striped shirt, chose a tie carefully and laid it out next to his tan sports jacket, then went into the kitchen to eat his frozen dinner.

Afterward, feeling a little cheered, he tossed the foil tray in the garbage, got dressed, strapped his shoulder holster in position and put on his pager and handcuff pouch. Finally he pocketed his leather identification folder, shrugged into a topcoat and headed across town to interview Christine Lewis.

She lived in a basement suite in a modest home about three blocks away from her former mother-in-law's house. Brian parked the police car out front and studied the place, remembering the phone call in which Kaminsky had told him about her interview that afternoon with Stan Lewis.

You'd think the woman would want to get as far away as she could from an ex-mother-in-law like that, but people were strange. Maybe when Christine moved out, she'd simply chosen a place nearby so the kids could have regular contact with their grandmother. Or maybe she was a truly nasty bitch who wanted to stay close enough to torment poor Maribel with her continued presence.

He got out of the car, strolled up the walk in the gathering twilight and rang a bell labeled Basement with a piece of black sticker tape.

He heard footsteps, then the unlatching of at least two locks before the door was cracked open only to the length of a sturdy chain lock.

"Detective Wardlow," Brian said, displaying his badge. "Spokane P.D."

The chain lock was disengaged and the door swung open. The entryway was in shadow, and he couldn't get a good look at the face of the woman standing there.

"Please," she said in a husky voice. "Go right down. I have to make sure the door's latched."

Brian moved down the stairs and into the living room, where he stood waiting for her to appear. He looked around and was surprised at how pleasant the decor was.

The room was even smaller than his own, but obvious attempts had been made to brighten the place. A few handwoven saddle blankets hung on the walls, and there were pictures of horses everywhere. The chairs and sofa were covered with bright Navajopatterned afghans. Potted plants crowded the meager windowsills.

"Not much of a place," she said apologetically behind him. "We've only been here less than a year. It's hard to make something feel homey when you have to work all the time."

Brian turned and got his first good look at Christine Lewis. He stared at her, searching for words, and wondered why he was so taken aback.

Maybe he'd been expecting somebody horsey and tough, but this woman was dainty, almost tiny. Her face was fine-boned and rather childlike, and her voice was very soft. Her blond hair was cut short and parted neatly on one side, and her blue eyes looked direct and worried.

"Could I take your coat, Detective?"

"Thanks. Are the kids at home tonight?"

"No. They're spending the night with Gordie's grandmother."

Brian pulled off his topcoat and handed it to her. She moved away to hang the coat behind a flowered curtain in one corner of the room.

She wore faded blue jeans and a soft fleecy sweater of pale yellow, and looked like a small daffodil swaying in a springtime wind.

Startled by the poetic turn of his thoughts, Brian stepped away abruptly and picked up his briefcase, then seated himself on one of the afghan-covered chairs, while Christine sat on the sofa. He reached into the briefcase for his notebook.

"Your full name, please, ma'am?"

"Christine Anne Moreau Lewis."

"Moreau's your maiden name?"

"That's right."

"You and Desirée have the same father, right?"

"Yes. My mother died when I was six and Daddy remarried when I was ten. We were living in Wyoming then, working on a cattle ranch. Desirée was born a couple of years later, but her mother ran off with one of the wranglers when she was just a baby."

"So your father raised both of you?"

"Not so you'd notice," Christine said dryly. "He died in a rodeo accident when I was sixteen. I pretty much raised Desirée from then on. I just dragged her around with me while I went from job to job."

"And then you met Stan Lewis when you were eighteen, right?"

Christine sighed and gazed off into the distance. "Stan looked like a dream come true. He was so handsome, and he was actually offering me and Desirée a real home to live in."

"Even if it happened to be his mother's home?" Brian said.

"At the time, I didn't mind a bit. I was pregnant and naive. Besides, I really liked his mother. I thought we'd be one big happy family." Christine smiled sadly, then shook herself and sat straighter on the sofa. "Would you like a cup of coffee or maybe something to eat, Detective?"

"No thanks."

"You look tired."

"I do?" He glanced up to find her blue eyes resting on him with gentle sympathy.

"You have a real hard job," she said. "Working all day and having to make calls in the evening, too. It must be difficult for your family."

"I guess it used to be. But now I'm divorced, so nobody cares how much I work except me."

She sighed. "It's awfully lonely, isn't it, being divorced. I know exactly how you feel."

Brian was so distracted by this feminine gentleness that it was all he could do to pull himself together and continue with his questioning.

He cleared his throat and looked down at his notebook. "You and your husband have been divorced for about eight months, is that right?"

She nodded and curled up on the couch, tucking her feet under her.

"And you train horses for a living?"

"I work at Steve Lorimer's place, out by Reardan. I drive back and forth every day."

"You don't look like a horse trainer," Brian said.

She smiled, her eyes sparkling with shy amusement. "Really? What do I look like?"

A Barbie doll, he wanted to say. A delicate pretty Barbie doll. That's what you look like.

"I guess we all have lots of preconceived notions about people," he said brusquely, "and usually they turn out to be wrong. How has your relationship been with your former mother-in-law lately?"

The woman's face twisted with pain. "I've always tried to be nice to Maribel, but she blames me for... I don't know. For everything that's ever gone wrong in Stan's life, I guess."

"Is that why she has so much resentment toward you, Christine?"

"Call me Chris. Everyone does." She frowned thoughtfully. "I don't know. I guess we were so young when we got married, and maybe I pushed Stan too hard in those early years, because I wanted him to provide and make a real home for us, instead of living with his mother for the rest of our lives. But I don't think I…''

Her eyes glittered with tears. Brian remembered what Jackie had told him about her ex-husband, and the attempted reconciliation.

"What's your current relationship with your ex-husband?''

"Nothing, really. I'll always care about Stan, but I don't have any feelings for him anymore. There was too much unhappiness and fighting. All those loving feelings…they get sort of burned up in the fighting, you know? And then they don't come back.''

"Yeah, I know.'' He gripped the pen tightly. "Can you think of any specific reason Maribel might dislike you? Or fear you?''

"*Fear* me?'' Chris looked at him in astonishment.

"She seems to think you were responsible for the break-in at her house the other night, and an anonymous letter she got a while ago.''

Christine's eyes widened. "Letter?''

Brian's interest quickened. He and Jackie had already discussed the possibility of other poison-pen letters turning up in this case.

"Did you by any chance get one of those letters, Chris?''

She looked at the wall, hugging her knees, and refused to answer.

"Chris?'' he repeated.

"Yes,'' she said at last. "I got a letter.''

"Did you keep it by any chance?''

She nodded. "I'm a pack rat. I always keep everything. Once you've been really poor, you have a horror of throwing anything away for fear you might need it someday. But that letter…''

"Could you show it to me, please?"

Her face twisted unhappily. "I don't want to. It says such…awful things."

"It's important for me to see it," Brian said. "It might help us find out who the sender is."

She got up reluctantly, left the room and came back in a few minutes with an envelope and a folded sheet of white paper.

Brian had his evidence case ready. He showed Chris how to slip the paper and envelope between the heavy plastic sheets. Then he opened the case to read the printed words:

> Dear Bitch-Goddess,
>   You think you can whore with two men and your deeds will remain secret. Be sure you will be punished for your sins. The Divine One will take great pleasure in punishing you. You will scream with pain, but nobody will hear.

Again the little star hand-drawn in one corner of the page.

Kaminsky was right, Brian thought, suppressing a shudder. This wasn't the work of a prankster. There was something truly evil about the letter, something dark, chilling and dangerous.

He glanced over at Christine Lewis, who'd reseated herself on the sofa and was fingering the fringe on one of the blankets.

"Two men?" he asked gently.

"There's a stable hand who works out at the ranch with me," she said at last, her head lowered. "I was so lonely after my divorce, and Charlie's been my friend for a long time. He came here to visit a couple of times, and he..."

She paused awkwardly, her cheeks reddening.

"Spent the night with you?" Wardlow said without expression.

"Yes. But the kids were over at Maribel's both times when he was here. Nobody knew about it. I was just so lonely." She looked at Brian beseechingly, as if needing his understanding.

He softened under that gaze, but managed to keep his voice even. "Could I have his name and address, please?"

"Do you...do you have to talk with him?"

"I'm afraid we might. But it will all remain in a confidential file. You have my word on that."

"Okay." Reluctantly, she gave the information.

Brian steeled himself to ask the next question. "Your ex-husband told us that the two of you made some attempt at a reconciliation during the Christmas holidays. This other relationship of yours...was it before or after that?"

Again her delicate face turned crimson with embarrassment. "It was sort of...at the same time. I went kind of crazy during Christmas," she said in a low voice. "You just don't know how lonely it can be over the holidays in a place like this."

"Oh, I know," Wardlow said grimly. "Believe me, I know."

"And they were both calling, so I sort of...had them coming here on alternate nights for a while. They both parked way down the street and walked to the house, and the kids were over at Maribel's for most of the holidays. I had no idea that anybody knew about it until that letter came."

"And neither relationship has continued?"

"No, it was just craziness. Neither of them is the kind of man I want. I'm sleeping alone all the time now and feeling better about myself. At least I don't feel so...so ashamed."

"Do you have any idea who might have broken into your former mother-in-law's house?" Brian asked.

She hesitated almost imperceptibly, then shook her head. "Not a clue."

Brian looked down at the neat faceless type of the letter, contrasting so sharply with its vicious message.

"Do you really think it means something?" she asked. "It's not just some kind of sick joke?"

He slid the plastic folder into his briefcase. "I don't know. But I think the best thing is to have a look around outside the house. Somebody might have been peeking into your bedroom window, so I'll want to know where it is and if it's visible from the street."

She hurried to get a jacket from the makeshift closet and handed him his topcoat. Brian followed her up the stairs and into the moist darkness of the March evening.

For a moment she stood close beside him on the front steps. She was dainty and warm, and her hair smelled faintly of roses. The scent stayed with him as he drove away.

5

Adrienne Calder answered the front door wearing a strawberry-patterned apron over her slacks and holding a spatula. She took the bottle of wine Jackie offered, and the two women hugged briefly, then climbed back up the steps toward the kitchen.

"Puppies," Adrienne said cryptically as she paused on the upper landing.

Jackie reached the top of the stairs and looked at her hostess in confusion.

"Laska's having puppies," Adrienne explained. "Down in the laundry room. Harlan and Alex are both attending the birth."

"No kidding." Jackie glanced toward the lower floor. "Should I go down there?"

"Certainly not. You should stay in the kitchen and visit with me. Hey, listen up, you two!" Adrienne raised her voice suddenly as she leaned over the railing. "Jackie's here, and I'll be serving dinner in fifteen minutes."

A muted chorus of greetings came from the direction of the laundry room. The two women exchanged a smile and went into the kitchen, where Adrienne bent to peer inside the oven.

"Browning perfectly," she announced. "Would you like a drink?"

"Some wine would be nice." Jackie watched while her friend took a bottle of white wine from the fridge and poured two glasses. "You look terrific, Rennie," she said. "I really like that outfit."

Adrienne grinned. "See, Kaminsky? You're getting really good at small talk and flattery."

There'd been a time when Jackie had been incapable of either. "Oh, there's no doubt you and Harlan have had a very civilizing effect on me," she said. "What's in the microwave?"

"Stuffed potatoes." Adrienne took a thirsty gulp of wine. "How's Paul?"

"He's fine." Jackie held her goblet up to the light and squinted at the sparkles of gold. "He asked me to apologize again for not being able to be here, but he's too busy right now to come into town."

Adrienne stirred a pot of vegetables on the stove, then poured herself more wine and sat in the opposite chair.

She and Jackie were about the same age, and the two friends shared a number of tastes and attitudes, despite the fact that Adrienne had grown up in wealth and privilege during the same years Jackie suffered poverty and neglect.

The two women had first met a year earlier during the same child-kidnapping case in which Jackie had met Paul. The child's mother, Leigh Mellon, was Adrienne's sister. At the same time, Jackie had been instrumental in making Adrienne and her husband foster parents of fifteen-year-old Alexandra Gerard.

"So how's Alex doing?" Jackie asked.

"Okay, I guess." Adrienne frowned and took a sip of wine. "It's tough being a teenager, you know. She's not finding it easy to make friends. I think she's still a little nervous and self-conscious, even though none of the kids at her school know anything about her past."

Both women were silent for a moment.

Nine months ago Alexandra Gerard had been a runaway fleeing a sexually abusive stepfather. Jackie had plucked the girl off a downtown street corner and saved her from a life of prostitution, but despite the efforts of police and social workers, it hadn't been possible for Alex to return to her home in Seattle. Without the generosity of Adrienne and her husband, the girl's prospects would have been dim at best.

"It'll take time," Jackie said at last. "She's had some pretty terrible experiences."

"I know, and none of them her fault." Adrienne's eyes glittered with tears. "I just ache for her, Jackie. Sometimes she seems so lonely."

Jackie patted her friend's arm. "Do you want me to have a talk with her?"

"Would you, honey?" Adrienne brushed at her eyes and smiled gratefully. "That girl worships you."

"Of course I will. Maybe we can get together after dinner and I'll see if I can get her talking a bit. God knows," Jackie added, "I had my share of problems when I was a teenager. I wasn't exactly the homecoming queen."

Adrienne brightened a little. "You *weren't?* Why, sweetie, I can just see you up there on the stage, wearing your little crown and sash."

Jackie saluted her friend with her wineglass, then paused thoughtfully. "Alex goes to Wilcox High, doesn't she?"

Adrienne nodded. "It's clear across town, but Wilcox has a much better music program than Southwood. In fact, Alex plays third flute in the school orchestra. Why do you ask?''

"I met some kids from that school the other day, because of a case I'm working on. Maybe Alex can tell me a little more about them.''

"Terrific," Adrienne said cheerfully. "There's your excuse for having a talk with her. She'll be helping the police with their investigation. A very solemn civic responsibility, I might add.''

"You're always teasing me about my job,'' Jackie complained. "No respect at all.'' She looked down at the table, her smile fading.

"What is it, honey?''

"It's just…'' Jackie traced the stem of the glass with her fingertip. "Paul's not all that happy about what I do,'' she said at last.

"The cop thing, you mean?''

"He worries about it all the time. I think he'd probably like me to be a housewife or get a nice secure job in an office somewhere.''

Adrienne gave her a shrewd glance, then got up to check the oven. "And what do you think about that?''

"I like my job, and I worked damned hard to get where I am. It's not fair to ask me to give it up.''

"He just wants you to be safe.'' Adrienne lifted a saucepan lid and frowned at the contents. "And I can certainly understand the motivation. In fact, Paul's not the only one who worries about you. Every time I hear an item on the radio about a shooting or something terrible going on downtown, I find myself wondering if you're involved.''

"But you can't keep people safe by wrapping them in cotton wool,'' Jackie argued. "It's dangerous to cross the street or drive somewhere in your car. These days it's even dangerous to breathe, for God's sake."

"So have you talked to him about it? Does he know how you feel?"

"I can't talk to him about this. He shuts down and closes me out." Jackie took another sip of wine, still frowning. "Paul's actually a lot like you and me. He never learned to be close to anybody when he was growing up. He's able to say he loves me, but he's got all these other feelings locked up inside him, things he finds impossible to express."

"And?" Adrienne prompted.

"Sometimes...Rennie, I get so frustrated I could scream."

"You really love the guy, don't you?"

"I can't imagine living without him," Jackie said. "It scares me to love somebody that much. You know what I mean?"

Adrienne smiled sadly. "Oh, yes. I know, honey. But you really have to—"

"Hey, Jackie, guess what? Laska's got five new puppies!"

Alex beamed at them from the kitchen doorway, and Jackie turned to her, surprised all over again by how pretty the girl looked. She was turning into a real beauty with her classic features, her slim body and long braid of thick golden hair.

"Hi there," Jackie said. "You can take me down and show them to me after dinner, okay?"

"Okay." Alex hugged Adrienne and dropped an affectionate kiss on Jackie's cheek, then hurried into the dining room where she began to set the table, singing to herself as she worked.

Jackie and Adrienne exchanged another smile as Harlan Calder strolled into the kitchen.

"Hey, Jackie," he said, "did you hear about the new family members?"

"Pretty exciting news. What'll you do with all of them?"

"Oh, they're already spoken for. They have impeccable bloodlines." He bent closer to whisper in Jackie's ear. "We might let Alex pick one of them to keep, but no promises just yet."

She nodded, watching fondly as he removed Adrienne's strawberry-covered apron and tied it around his own waist. Harlan was at least fifteen years older than his wife, mild-mannered and balding. He was also one of Jackie's favorite people.

"Is this roast ready to carve?" he asked, peering into the oven.

"I think so." Adrienne handed him a couple of quilted pot holders.

"I feel guilty," Jackie said. "Everybody's working except me."

"You're our guest, so relax." Harlan lifted the roasting pan carefully from the oven. "I'm sorry Paul couldn't come."

"So are we, but he's working like a maniac these days."

While her friends prepared the meal, Jackie told them about Paul's ranch.

"There are birds all over the place, singing like crazy, and the little calves are so cute," she said. "I was thinking maybe some weekend I should take Michael out to see them." Michael was the little boy who was kidnapped last year. He was also Harlan and Adrienne's nephew.

Harlan smiled at the mention of the four-year-old and began to slice the roast with deft strokes. Meat fell away from his knife onto the plate, crisp and brown at the edges, pink in the center.

"You should give Leigh a call," he suggested. "I'm sure she'd love to have Michael go with you for the day."

"Okay, I'll do that," Jackie said. "Paul really likes little kids. You should see how he is with Tiffany whenever Carmen comes to visit."

Carmen and her little girl, Tiffany, used to live in the apartment next door to Jackie's. But Carmen had married the previous fall and moved with her new husband to a small town in Idaho where they ran a bakery. Jackie only saw her now every couple of months.

Alex came in from the dining room and leaned against Jackie's chair. Jackie put an arm around the girl and hugged her.

"I need your help, Alex," she said. "After dinner, maybe you can show me the puppies and I'll ask you a couple of questions, okay?"

"About what?"

"Just a break and enter I'm working on. Some kids from your school are witnesses."

"Sure." Alex headed back into the dining room to finish setting the table while Jackie's eyes followed her fondly. She was quite a kid.

"The father's a champion," Alex said proudly, holding up one of the squirming puppies. "And Laska's got a pedigree as long as your arm."

She and Jackie knelt by a padded basket next to the washing machine, where a big Irish setter was sprawled on the plaid cushions with her newborn brood.

"This one's my favorite." Alex cuddled the pup close to her cheek. "I'm calling him Rex. Hold him, Jackie. See how sweet he is."

Jackie reached out gingerly to take the blunt-nosed bundle of fur, surprised by his warmth and substance, the taut feeling of his fat little stomach. His eyes were squeezed shut and he moved blindly in her hands, squeaking in distress.

"They really are sweet, aren't they?" she murmured. She set the puppy back with the others, watching as he tumbled over his brothers and sisters to burrow close to his mother.

Jackie sat down on the carpet, her back resting against the washing machine. She looked at Alex who still leaned raptly over the basket. The girl seemed pale and a little thinner. Jackie remembered Adrienne's concerns and felt a tug of worry.

"So how's everything going?" she asked, reaching out to stroke one of the big setter's floppy ears.

Alex shrugged. "Okay, I guess."

"Is the schoolwork pretty hard?"

"Not really." Alex picked up another of the puppies and cradled it. "I was having some trouble with math, but Harlan's been helping me and I'm getting a lot better at it."

"They're really nice people, aren't they?"

"Harlan and Adrienne? They're wonderful. I think I'd have died without them."

Considering the circumstances in which Jackie had discovered the girl last summer, this statement was probably not an exaggeration. Both of them were silent for a moment while the puppies whimpered and squirmed in their basket.

Jackie cleared her throat. "How about the other kids at school? Have you made any friends?"

"Uh-uh." Alex's face clouded. "Most of those kids have known each other for years. They have these really tight little groups, and I feel like I'm—" She stopped abruptly, her cheeks turning scarlet with embarrassment.

Jackie reached out and patted the girl's knee. "Nothing that happened to you was your fault, sweetie," she said gently. "You're a good person and you deserve to have friends."

"But I don't know how to..."

"What?"

Alex shrugged. "It's just hard. I can't go up to other kids and say I want to be their friend, can I? And none of them seem all that anxious to have me around."

Her pain was so real that Jackie's eyes welled with tears of sympathy. She said gently, "They'll get to know you with time, sweetie. And when they do, they'll like you, I know it."

"Yeah, maybe. I just wish I wasn't the youngest person in the orchestra. I feel like such a baby."

Alex held the puppy to her face, kissing it and nuzzling her cheek against the wet little nose. Then she returned it to the basket and sat back on her heels to look at Jackie.

"So you want to ask me about those kids from my school who were witnesses?"

Jackie nodded. "A boy named Joel Morgan, for one. Do you know him?"

She was astonished by the reaction. Alex's face

flooded with color again, and her hand trembled as she turned away to stroke one of the puppies. Keeping her face hidden, she murmured something inaudible.

"What did you say, honey?" Jackie asked, leaning forward. "I didn't hear you."

"I said, Joel's in the orchestra. He plays the clarinet."

Jackie watched the girl with interest. "Is he any good?"

"Oh, yes. Way better than anybody else. He does two solos."

"No kidding," Jackie said, remembering the boy's pleasant face. "He seemed like a really nice boy."

Alex gave a brief jerky nod, still keeping her head turned away.

Jackie hid a smile. "Do you know him? Have you talked to him very much?"

"Not really. But the other day at practice he told the teacher my playing was really good," Alex said, her voice muffled. "He said I should have a solo, too, and he wouldn't mind giving up one of his."

"That was nice of him."

Alex suddenly looked anxious. "He's not in any trouble, is he?"

"Joel Morgan? Not at all. In fact, he was a big help to us. He just happened to be passing down the back alley one night when a neighbor's house was being broken into. He didn't know that, but he noticed some lights in the attic."

"What night was that?"

"Monday. Apparently he was coming home from a basketball game at the school."

Alex nodded, looking wistful. "A lot of the kids

were at that game. I wanted to go, but I didn't have anybody to..." Her voice trailed off.

"I know, sweetie, I know," Jackie said kindly, then repeated, "but you'll make friends soon." Once again she patted the girl's knee, then said casually, "This house, the one that was broken into, you know?"

"Yes?"

"It belongs to a lady who's sort of related to a girl at your school, and I wondered if you happen to know her. The girl, I mean."

"What's her name?"

"Desirée Moreau."

Alex's mouth twisted with distaste. "Yes," she said curtly. "I know her. She's in one of my classes."

"Really?" Jackie said. "Isn't she a few years older than you?"

"It's home economics. Anybody can take it. Kids from all different grades are in my class."

Jackie smiled. "It's hard for me to picture Desirée learning to cook and sew."

"She doesn't do anything in class," Alex said. "She just sits at the back and stares into space. The teacher keeps getting mad at her, but it doesn't do any good. Desirée's so *weird*."

"Have you talked to her much?"

Alex shook her head. "She never talks to anybody. Desirée has even less friends than I do, if that's possible. So maybe," she added bitterly, "we have something in common, after all."

"Honey, I've talked to Desirée. You're not a bit like her."

"I hope not. She's really..."

"What?" Jackie prompted when Alex turned away to play with the puppies again.

"Just weird," the girl repeated. "Kinda scary." She hesitated, then continued with obvious reluctance, "Sometimes in class I turn around and she's staring at me like she wants to kill me or something. It gives me the creeps."

"Do you think she might actually be capable of hurting anyone?"

Alex looked up quickly. "Why?"

"I can't give you any details of the case, honey. I'm just asking what you think."

Alex stared at the opposite wall. "I don't know if it's true, but I heard Desirée's mixed up in some ugly stuff. A few of the girls were talking about it one day in the bathroom."

"What kind of stuff?"

Alex looked down and began toying nervously with the denim fabric of her jeans.

"Come on, you can tell me," Jackie coaxed. "What kind of stuff is she involved in?"

"Satanism," Alex whispered.

Jackie looked at the girl in shock, thinking about the threatening letters with their talk of the "Divine One," which she and Wardlow had interpreted as some kind of religious fanaticism.

And that ugly pornographic image, the cutout heads...

She felt a chill of fear.

Joel Morgan had talked about a light "bouncing around" in the neighbor's attic and assumed it was a flashlight. But perhaps that light was actually a candle flame. Maybe the dusty attic had been the scene of some kind of satanic ritual, and the picture was left behind as a deliberate warning.

Maribel had been threatened by an anonymous letter, and so had her son. The letters and the pornographic picture contained a little hand-drawn star that might well be a satanic emblem. What was it called?

She frowned, trying to remember. A pentacle, pentagram? Something like that.

Jackie decided to visit the Lewis house in the morning and see if she could find any traces of candle wax on the attic floor.

She became aware of Alex watching her in alarm and tried to give the girl a reassuring smile. "Sorry. I was thinking about something."

"You won't tell anybody what I just said?" Alex asked nervously. "About Desirée, I mean?"

"I might have to tell somebody, but I won't breathe a word about where I heard it."

"Promise?"

"Absolutely. Is there much of that stuff going on with the kids at your school? Satanism, I mean?"

Alex shook her head. "I don't think so. There are some pretty weird types and sometimes you hear rumors, but I don't actually know of anybody else that's involved. I don't even know if *she's* doing it. I just heard those girls talking."

"What were they saying? Can you remember the exact words?"

Alex frowned. "Not really. Something about satanism and one of them was saying Desirée's name, but when they noticed I'd come in, they changed the subject right away."

"I see. So Desirée doesn't have anyone at school she hangs out with?"

The girl shook her head.

"How about a boyfriend who drives her to school or picks her up?"

"Boyfriends?" Alex asked in disbelief. *"Desirée?"*

Jackie thought about the strange, pale-eyed girl with her curtain of black hair and the avid lust on her face as she watched Joel Morgan and his friends.

Again she had the uneasy feeling that something was about to happen. But there was no hard evidence to support her premonition. Maybe all this was nothing more than the spiteful behavior of a troubled adolescent.

Still, Jackie decided it might not be a bad idea, when she visited Maribel Lewis in the morning, to warn her tactfully that she should be careful in her dealings with Desirée Moreau.

6

Paul came into Spokane unexpectedly on Thursday night. He said he'd come to town for building supplies, but Jackie suspected he still had some vague worries about her safety and mostly wanted an excuse to check up on her. Whatever the reason, she was delighted to spend the evening snuggling up to him on the sofa, eating popcorn and watching television, then making love.

But on Friday morning she awoke with a sense of foreboding, a dark cloud that drifted through her mind from the tatters of some dream she couldn't remember.

She rolled over drowsily and reached for Paul, but he was gone.

Startled, she opened her eyes and stared at the empty pillow, feeling a moment of desolation. It was only 6:00 a.m. Then she heard sounds from the kitchen, a clatter of plates and cutlery, a male voice raised pleasantly in song. The smell of coffee drifted down the hallway.

"I'm such an idiot," she muttered, swinging her legs out of bed and padding into the bathroom.

Jackie splashed water on her face, brushed her teeth, dragged a comb through her hair and pulled some jogging pants on under her plaid nightshirt, then went into the kitchen. Paul stood by the stove, bare-chested, in a pair of faded denim jeans, poaching eggs.

"What a view," she said, lingering in the doorway to gloat over the muscles rippling in his back. "Great backside."

He turned, set down the spatula and advanced on her purposefully, sweeping her into a lusty embrace over her laughing protests.

"That's for last night," he whispered, dropping a kiss on her cheek. "You are one sexy lady."

"That's 'cause you are one sexy guy," she said, then chuckled when he kissed her again. "So what was that kiss for? Payment in advance for tonight?"

"Nope. It's for taking the whole weekend off and coming to the ranch with me."

"I can't wait." She moved from his embrace and crossed the room to pour herself a cup of coffee. "Besides, I've been drawing way too much overtime lately. Even Sergeant Michelson thinks it's time I took a weekend off."

He returned to the eggs. "Nothing important going on at work right now?"

Jackie leaned against the counter, sipping coffee and brooding over her visit to Maribel Lewis's house the day before.

She'd found several globs of candle wax on the wooden floor in the attic, pretty much confirming her suspicions about those erratic lights reported by Joel Morgan. And poor Maribel had shown such obvious terror when Jackie hinted about the sort of things that might have been happening up there.

After she left the Lewis home, Jackie had spent part of the afternoon at the city library and a couple of

additional hours on the Internet, researching satanism.
She was still appalled by everything she'd learned.

No wonder her dreams weren't pleasant.

But they hadn't been able to find Desirée Moreau,
who apparently passed the time when she wasn't in
school hanging out at some mysterious downtown location.

On Monday, Jackie and Brian had agreed, the kids
would all be back in class. That was probably soon
enough to interview the girl and determine what she
was up to. Jackie had some strong twinges of worry,
especially after seeing the threatening letter Chris
Lewis had received.

The Divine One will take great pleasure in punish-
ing you, the letter said. *You will scream with pain,*
but nobody will hear.

Jackie frowned as she rummaged in the cupboard
for juice glasses. Maybe she *should* cancel her plans
with Paul, try to wrangle a bit more overtime out of
Michelson and get hold of Desirée on the weekend.

She kept having these feelings...

"No way," Paul said calmly.

She began to set the table. She found Paul's ability
to read her thoughts both unnerving and a little exhilarating. Unnerving to realize her thoughts weren't
private, and exhilarating to know that after a lifetime
of loneliness, somebody in the world was this close
to her.

Still, there were times when his prescience could
be downright annoying.

"What are you talking about?" She took a carafe
of orange juice from the refrigerator and filled their
glasses.

"No way you're going to plead some kind of police emergency and work through the weekend again. You gave me a solemn promise.''

"What a bully you are." She sat down and watched while he drained the eggs, then tipped them onto squares of buttered toast.

"That's right," he agreed placidly.

"Paul...I really love you," she said.

He grinned, raising an eyebrow. "Now what brought that on?"

"Just the way you..." She floundered, trying to explain. "You stand with your arm muscle tensed like that, and a bit of hair falls down over your forehead, and all of a sudden I feel weak as a kitten. Like I can hardly keep my hands off you. I don't know what to do with these feelings, Paul."

He bent to kiss her, his smile fading. "Neither of us knows how to deal with these feelings. It's scary, but we'll just have to learn together."

Jackie watched as he pulled on his shirt and buttoned it, then seated himself across the table and reached for the salt.

"Can we learn, Paul?" she asked. "Do you think we can really learn how to love each other without destroying what we've got?"

"We have to," he told her simply. "There's no alternative."

The substation was a new modern building equipped with an exercise room on the basement level next to the evidence lab, with tiled showers for male and female officers.

When Jackie arrived a few minutes after breakfast, still wearing her sweats and carrying her slacks and blazer on a hanger, the place appeared to be occupied though it was barely past seven o'clock.

She hung her street clothes in a locker and entered the exercise room to find Lew Michelson pedaling energetically on a stationary bike.

The balding sergeant wore shorts and a police-issue sweatshirt that bulged over his stomach. He looked up when she came in and gave her an embarrassed smile.

"Hi, Kaminsky. I heard you been using this place a couple mornings a week. Hope you don't mind having some company."

"You're always good company, Sarge." She grinned at his straining figure as he leaned over the handlebars. "But I had no idea you were a jock."

"Go ahead," he panted. "Make fun of the old man. No respect from the ranks anymore."

Jackie stripped off her sweats to reveal a pair of cotton track shorts and a yellow singlet. Her body was trim and shapely, her skin a warm olive color.

"You're lucky," Michelson complained, watching as she approached the weight machine. "You have a year-round tan."

"Just a little gift from some of my dark-skinned ancestors. Probably the Cherokee and African branches of the family."

Jackie positioned the weights and adjusted the machine to her height, wondering what kind of gorilla had been using it before her.

Michelson gestured at his own hairy white legs and freckled arms. "I could spend two months on the beach and not look like that."

"You could never spend two months on a beach anywhere," Jackie told him, settling on the padded seat and reaching for the overhead bar. "You're a complete workaholic."

"Yeah, right. Look who's talking. Like you haven't been drawing more unpaid overtime than anybody else in the squad."

"Hey, I'm turning over a new leaf." She lifted and stretched, trying to take it easy until her muscles warmed up. "In fact, I was thinking about doing some work this weekend, but Paul's convinced me to go away and spend a couple of days at the ranch, instead."

"Good for Paul. I like that guy." Michelson collapsed over the handlebars, breathing raggedly, then glanced at his watch. "Ten more minutes," he gasped. "This is torture, Jackie."

"So why are you doing it?"

"Promise you won't tell anyone?"

"Not a word," Jackie said solemnly.

"Well, I plan to lose thirty pounds. I'm getting rid of this lard belly."

Her eyes widened and she let the column of weights drop into place with a metallic thud. "Thirty pounds? That's a lot of weight, Sarge."

"I know, but an officer should look good in his uniform. And Beth's getting worried about my health. She nags me all the time."

"Beth keeps herself nice and trim."

"That woman's got a whole lot more willpower than I do," he said with rueful fondness.

Jackie wondered if the sergeant's appraisal of his wife was accurate. She remembered Beth Michelson as a shy little woman with big dark eyes and the edgy timidity of a woodland animal. There'd even been some rumors about a nervous breakdown. Jackie didn't know about that, but she did know that Beth tended to avoid police social functions, so none of the officers who worked with her husband had ever gotten to know her very well.

"Well," Jackie said at last, "losing weight's a good idea, and exercise is the way to go if you've got enough determination to stick with the program. I've been here three mornings a week all winter. Paul gets up really early and we like to have breakfast together, so I usually find myself with an extra hour in the morning."

"When are you going to marry that good-looking guy and make an honest man of him?"

"He's an honest man whether I marry him or not," Jackie said. "Anyhow, I decided I might as well make some productive use of the extra time, so I've started exercising in the morning. But I usually have the place all to myself."

"Maybe I could come at the same time," Michelson suggested almost shyly. "Then we'll have our own little club, sort of, and you can stay on my tail to make sure I do this. If you don't mind, that is."

"Sounds good to me," Jackie told him, moving the pin to increase her weights. "I'd enjoy the company. Besides, it'll be a nice change for me to be on *your* tail about something."

He sat erect, took a couple of deep breaths and began to pedal again. Soon sweat glistened on his broad face and dripped onto his collar.

"Speaking of which," he said, "if Paul wasn't dragging you away, what did you plan to work on this weekend? The car-theft operation?"

"Major Crimes has that pretty well under control.

They don't need us to cover until Monday. I was thinking about the Lewis case.''

"I thought we agreed it was low priority.''

"That was before I started learning so much about satanism.'' Jackie told him some of the details of ritual sacrifice, sexual excess and violence associated with satanic practices.

"We've dealt with this crap in the past,'' the sergeant said. "They're crazy, but it's usually confined to a pretty small group of consenting individuals. They don't threaten people outside the group.''

"So all this stuff I learned about killing pets and sacrificing human babies…you don't believe any of it?''

"I think it's public hysteria. We've never found any real proof of violence. The most we could ever pin on them was damaged property and nuisance charges. Disturbing the peace, things like that.''

He stopped pedaling and threw a towel around his neck, watching Jackie as she leaned back to strain at the weights.

"So what about all those letters?'' she asked. "Don't you think the threats should be taken seriously?''

"Anonymous letters are just like obscene telephone calls. The folks who do that stuff are satisfied by the act of making the threat. They hardly ever take it any further.''

"But lots of serial killers are also letter-writers,'' Jackie argued. "All the way back to Jack the Ripper. He wrote letters about his victims.''

"He sent letters to the press. That's the difference, Jackie. The real sickos have delusions of grandeur.

They like to taunt the media and the police, but they don't make personal contact with their victims."

She continued to strain thoughtfully at the weights.

"Why?" he asked. "Aren't you convinced it's the Moreau girl who's doing all this?"

"I'm fairly convinced."

"Then you have nothing to worry about." The sergeant rolled off the exercise bike and tramped gingerly around on the tiled floor. "Teenage girls just aren't serial killers."

"Maribel Lewis still seems to believe it's her ex-daughter-in-law who's been threatening her, but Brian met the woman and said he didn't think she could hurt a fly."

Michelson leaned against the wall. He was still breathing hard, but the blotches of scarlet were beginning to fade from his cheeks.

"If Chris Lewis is tough enough to train horses for a living, she's tough enough to hurt somebody if she wanted to," he said. "I think Wardlow was far too…impressed by the lady to have an objective opinion."

Jackie gave the sergeant a quick glance, then returned to her weights. "From what he told me about the interview, Brian seemed to like her, all right. A lot."

They were both silent a moment.

Michelson headed for the shower, then paused. "If we came up with enough evidence, would Maribel Lewis be willing to press charges against this girl?"

"I don't think so, but the hatred she has for Christine makes me think she might charge her." Jackie lowered the weights and took a few deep breaths. "Could *we* lay charges, do you think?"

"Of what?"

"Break and enter, uttering death threats?"

"I doubt it," the sergeant said. "We don't have any real evidence against her."

Jackie shivered with distaste. "There's just something so creepy about it. All that stuff I've been reading... God, it's ugly."

"So what's your plan?"

"I guess we'll have to let it ride for the weekend at least. If I can get away from the car stakeout for a few minutes, I'll head over to the school on Monday afternoon and see if I can get Desirée to tell me anything. Maybe I can convince her to cut out the nonsense and be a good little girl from now on."

"You'll have to be careful," the sergeant warned. "Interviewing kids, even with parental consent, is a touchy business. You'll probably need a teacher or counselor to sit in as a witness."

"I know." Jackie watched as he opened the door to the showers. "Sarge..." she said.

"Yeah?" He paused in the doorway.

"Did your..." She turned away, concentrating on an adjustment to the weights. "Did your wife ever object to the job? Did she worry when you were on duty?"

"Because of the danger, you mean?"

Jackie nodded.

"All the time." He stared at the row of barred windows above his head. "Beth couldn't stand the thought that somebody might want to shoot me just because I was a cop. She's had nightmares for years."

Jackie thought about the timid little woman. "Really? Is she getting over it?"

"She's learned to cope. But it hasn't been easy,

and in some ways my job's done her a lot of harm.''
Michelson looked down at the floor, kicking idly at a
loose tile. "If I had it to do over..."

"What?" Jackie prompted when he hesitated. "If
you had it to do over, what would you do?"

"I'd have found a different line of work," he said.

Jackie sat erect, shocked. "You're kidding," she
said at last.

"No, I'm not kidding. I'd never have entered the
police force if I'd known how much pain Beth would
suffer."

Jackie was left speechless. Michelson loved the
job, yet he'd have been willing to give it up for his
wife. Would she be able to do the same for Paul?

7

On Monday Maribel Lewis padded around her house in a pair of furry bedroom slippers, enjoying the luxury of having a whole morning to get ready for work. Afternoons were her favorite shift. She liked to sleep in and spend a long time over breakfast, reading the paper and doing the crossword puzzle. She could even watch her favorite talk show.

During the parade of television guests she lounged on the couch, thinking what a bitch the little blond actress was, taunting all the men with her looks and driving them crazy.

Just like Christine.

The memory of Stanley's ex-wife threatened to spoil her enjoyment of the morning, but so did the memory of the letter she'd received, the broken window in her back porch, those scattered photographs and the ugly horrible picture the detective had found up in the attic.

Candle wax, satanism, all kinds of dreadful things.

The woman detective who'd come to the house a couple of times had tried to hint that Desirée might be doing all these terrible things, but the idea was ridiculous.

Maribel had known Desirée since she was a little girl. When Christine and Stanley got married, she was the sweetest little button of a thing, always climbing into Maribel's lap and demanding to be read a story. Maribel had been the mother she'd never had, poor child.

Christine certainly wasn't capable of being anybody's mother. She was far too selfish.

Maribel lit a cigarette and inhaled thoughtfully.

Maybe Desirée was having a few problems adjusting to adolescence, but that was normal for all young people.

Even Stanley, who'd been such a wonderful boy, had had his share of troubles in those years. There'd been some fights and a brief run-in with the police, but Maribel didn't like to think about that, either.

She got up restlessly, carrying her cigarette, and went over to switch off the television.

The police had bullied Stanley. They'd forced him to admit he'd beaten a girl when he was nineteen, even though he hadn't done it. The wily little slut had teased him and chased him. When she couldn't get him, she tried to cause trouble by claiming he'd mistreated her. Maribel still got furious when she thought about it.

But she'd spent a lot of money on a lawyer to keep the girl's family from pressing charges against her son, and the whole problem blew over eventually. She hadn't thought about it in years.

Now the memory was enough to completely destroy the pleasure of her leisurely morning. Irrationally she blamed Christine. The woman continued to ruin Maribel's life even though she and Stanley were divorced.

Her lips pursed angrily as she trudged upstairs to the bathroom, nursing her resentment.

That bitch wasn't going to get her down. She'd have a nice long bubble bath and think about good things. The morning bath was part of her ritual, an indulgence that she'd always loved.

Maribel started the water running in the old claw-footed tub, then uncapped an expensive bottle of scented bath oil that Desirée and Gordie had given her for Christmas. She'd been saving it for special occasions, but today she felt like giving herself a little treat.

She splashed a liberal amount of oil into the tub and watched the bubbles begin to foam. Then she shrugged out of her dressing gown and hung it on the back of the door, kicked off the furry slippers and paused to examine herself in the mirror.

Under her dressing gown she wore an old blue flannel nightgown, and her brightly dyed hair was still tied up in a chiffon scarf. Maribel leaned toward her reflection, pursing her lips as she examined the network of deep lines etched around her mouth.

One of the supervisors at work had recently treated herself to collagen injections above her upper lip. Maribel envied the woman. She'd wanted to ask how much the procedure cost, but she was reluctant to broach the topic. She could never afford it, anyhow, not with all her debts.

The old resentments began to smolder again, along with a wave of self-pity.

It just wasn't fair, she thought, bending to turn off the faucet and test the fragrant bathwater with her hand. Everybody else had so much, while she was alone and had to work so hard. All her life she'd only tried to do the best for Stanley. Maybe she'd made a couple of mistakes, but it wasn't fair that she had to—

A sound at the bathroom door made her straighten and whirl around.

Her eyes widened in surprise. "What are *you* doing here?" she asked. "Aren't you supposed to be—"

But she didn't finish the question. A strong hand gripped her arm and pushed her toward the tub. "Get in the water."

"In the...?" Maribel looked up in confusion and tried to pull away.

"I said, get in the water!"

"You're joking," Maribel said. The situation was too bizarre to be frightening, though her heart began to pound crazily. "And let me tell you," she added with rising anger, "it's not very funny."

But the hands propelled her forward and she wasn't strong enough to resist. She stumbled against the tub and hurt her shins, then climbed in and clutched the nightgown around her hips, feeling ridiculous as water drenched the flannelette and turned it dark blue.

She looked up at the familiar face hovering close to hers. "This is some kind of joke," she whispered. "Isn't it?"

At that moment Maribel saw the knife, and realized it wasn't a joke at all.

Jackie was back at her desk on the second floor of the insurance office, munching a sandwich while she watched the grimy building across the street.

The ringleaders of the stolen-car operation, Carlos Vasquez and Remy Corda, were both inside the service station, having arrived a half hour ago in a black Mercedes. When a prearranged signal came from a van down at the curb, four detectives would move in to make their arrests and the tedious two-week stake-out would be over.

But the Major Crimes unit appeared to be waiting for something. It could be hours yet before she was able to leave her observation post and get busy with all the other things that needed to be done today.

She folded the square of wax paper on her desk and looked up dreamily at the sky beyond the windows, reliving the weekend.

On Saturday the clouds had drifted away, leaving the countryside fresh and bright with the promise of spring. All the fields at Paul's ranch glistened with silvery pools of melting snow. Waterfowl circled overhead in mating pairs, while calves played and tumbled around their mothers.

"My city girl," Paul kept teasing her fondly. "Anybody would think you'd never seen a cow before."

Jackie was a little surprised at how much she'd loved the bracing country air, the feeling of space and freedom, the sight of animals with their babies. At the ranch she felt close to the whole circle of life, some-how more real and vital.

Of course, a major factor was the way Paul looked in that setting, with the sun gleaming on his hair and his broad shoulders straining while he set fence posts and pried up rotted floorboards inside the barn.

She shivered and gripped her hands together, trying not to think about him. Instead, she thought about his ranch some more.

"Paul, it's going to be so much work!" she'd said to him one night. "Just the thought of it makes me tired."

He'd laughed and embraced her tightly. "Hell,

sweetheart, I've got enough energy for both of us. Come on, give me a kiss—''

The cell phone trilled at her elbow, startling her out of her reverie. "Hello?" she said.

"Jackie? Michelson here."

"Sarge, we've got them! Vasquez and Corda are both inside."

"You have to leave," he said curtly. "I need you right away."

She looked out the window in confusion. "But in just a few minutes we'll be—"

"They've already cleared you to leave. Wardlow will meet you at the car."

Jackie's hands began to sweat and her throat tightened. "What's going on?"

"I'm at the Lewis place in Corbin Park. I've spoken to Wardlow and I want both of you here as fast as you can get here."

He hung up. Jackie put the phone in her shoulder bag, gathered her notebook and left the building hastily, running down the street to find Wardlow standing by their car.

"Do you know what this is about?" she asked, unlocking the door.

He shook his head and climbed into the passenger seat while she shifted gears, heading for the freeway. "But it sure as hell can't be good," he said, "if Sarge is at the scene."

She nodded tightly. In a station as large as theirs, sergeants carried a heavy load of administrative duties and left the office only for very serious crimes.

"God, Brian," she muttered. "What do you think's happened?"

"We'll find out soon enough," he said.

When they arrived at Maribel Lewis's house, the place swarmed with activity. Several patrol cars were parked by the curb, along with a couple of unmarked vehicles. A television van circled the block slowly, looking for a place to park while a uniformed officer stood guard. Yellow police tape encircled the front steps and fluttered at the door.

Jackie and her partner stepped over the tape and went into the house. Michelson waited in the entry to the living room.

"It's a bad scene," he told them. "Really bad."

"Who is it?" Wardlow asked.

"Maribel Lewis. She's upstairs."

"Dead?" Jackie whispered.

He nodded grimly. "Homicide."

Fingerprint technicians and police photographers were already at work, moving through the lower rooms with quiet efficiency. A plump gray-haired woman sat on the couch in the living room, shaking and crying hysterically while a female officer tried to soothe her.

"Who's that?" Wardlow asked.

"A neighbor. She found the body."

Captain Alvarez strode in from the kitchen along with one of the lieutenants from the downtown office.

"Detective Kaminsky," he said gravely. "Detective Wardlow."

"Hello, Captain," Jackie said.

His shrewd dark eyes regarded her thoughtfully. Jackie only saw the man a couple times a month, but she was always impressed by his quiet professionalism and air of command.

"I understand you two have been working on something related to this," he said.

Jackie tensed. "We had a B. and E. here last week and there were some threatening letters, but we had no reason to—"

He interrupted calmly. "Detective, I'm not questioning your procedure. I'm telling you that you'll remain in charge of the investigation."

"A *homicide?*" she asked, stunned. "You're leaving us in charge of a homicide investigation?"

"You and your partner have been doing good work, Detective Kaminsky. And you already have some history with the case, so we feel you're the logical choice."

Jackie and Wardlow exchanged a glance and she felt a hot surge of triumph. This moment had been her goal for almost thirteen years as a police officer.

But she hadn't expected the murder victim to be a person she'd already met and spoken with.

She watched while Alvarez and the lieutenant left the house and hurried down the steps, ignoring the raucous demands of the television crew who were now busily setting up their equipment on the sidewalk.

"We'll have to put together some kind of statement for the press," Michelson said, moving closer to Jackie. "But they can wait until we've managed to contact Mrs. Lewis's son."

Jackie followed him up the stairs with Wardlow close behind. "Has the coroner been called?" she asked.

"The wagon's on its way, but the body hasn't been moved yet. She's in the bathtub." Michelson paused outside the open door of the bathroom where a police photographer snapped pictures with a brilliant flash. "It's pretty ugly," he warned Jackie.

The photographer stepped aside to let her into the room. She moved past him and caught her breath in horror.

"Jesus," she whispered, grateful for Wardlow's steadying hand on her elbow. She leaned against him for a moment.

The little bathroom had once been painfully tidy like every other room in Maribel's house. Now it was a slaughterhouse. Blood smeared the wall tiles, the floor and mirrors. Maribel's body was slumped forward, facedown in the crimson water. A yellow chiffon scarf around her hair was still tied into an incongruous bow. One arm hung over the side of the tub, the hand already bagged in paper by crime-scene technicians.

"She's wearing a nightgown," Wardlow muttered, peering over Jackie's shoulder. "The killer must have put her into the tub."

Numbly Jackie reached for her notebook and pen. "Has the floor been photographed?" she asked.

The technician nodded. "I'm all done now until the body's moved."

"Okay." She took a few cautious steps into the blood-smeared room, then paused.

For the first time she realized that the bloodstains on the wall and mirror weren't random at all. They were symbols scrawled in a deliberate pattern.

She glanced over her shoulder at Michelson, who nodded.

"The killer used her blood," he said. "We think somebody must have dipped into the gash on her throat and used the blood like finger paint."

Now that Jackie recognized the patterns, all the

walls seemed to be screaming at her. They were covered with scarlet pentagrams.

Two hours later, Jackie and Wardlow sat in Michelson's office with a hastily assembled task force of uniformed officers and a couple of senior officials from the downtown office.

"Has the autopsy been scheduled?" the sergeant asked.

"Tomorrow morning," Jackie said. "Brian and I will both attend. He's going to be looking after the chain of evidence."

"Good." Michelson shuffled papers, gazing at the group over the frames of his reading glasses. "What have we got so far?"

Jackie consulted her notes. "Body showed evidence of multiple stab wounds and incisions. Front door was unlocked, no sign of forced entry. No visible prints. No evidence of a weapon at this point. We'll need to do an immediate search of the area, including all the trash bins up and down the alley. Also a door-to-door to find out if any of the neighbors saw anything."

"Okay. Has anybody been able to interview the woman who found the body?"

Wardlow cleared his throat. "Name's Harriet Falls, aged sixty-eight. She talked to Mrs. Lewis this morning about nine o'clock and arranged to catch a ride downtown at eleven-fifteen. Apparently they do this quite often when Maribel works afternoons. Mrs. Falls waited at her own home for about fifteen or twenty minutes, then called and got no answer. She walked over to the Lewis house, found the front door unlocked, finally went upstairs and discovered the body. The poor woman,'' he added. ''She's in pretty rough shape.''

''I can imagine. She didn't see anything out of the ordinary before her discovery of the body?''

''No, nothing. And she was watching the street from eleven o'clock on, waiting for Maribel to come and get her.''

Michelson glanced at Jackie. ''Any word yet on time of death?''

''Nothing definitive. We're waiting for the medical examiner to make some kind of judgment. But the bathwater was lukewarm, not cold, when we first viewed the body around one o'clock.''

''We're still not sure of sequence,'' one of the patrol officers volunteered. ''The victim could have been killed and put into the bathtub and the water run in afterward, right?''

''I don't think so,'' Jackie said. ''The water was very greasy, as though scented with bath oil. That's not something a killer would be likely to do. I think she probably ran her own bath, then was surprised and got pushed into the tub by force before she could take off her nightgown.''

''So if we could determine when she ran her bath, we'd get a pretty good fix on the time of death?''

''The neighbor says Maribel had a standard routine when she worked afternoons,'' Wardlow said. ''She usually slept in, watched a talk show in the morning and had her bath afterward. The show ends at ten o'clock, and she never liked to be bothered until it was over.''

''Then we can estimate around ten-thirty?'' Michelson asked.

''It's a beginning, I guess. We know from Mrs.

Falls that the victim was still alive at nine o'clock.
I'll have to question the family and see if anybody
spoke to her later than that." Jackie frowned at her
notes. "I'm also going to run a tub at home tonight
and see how long it takes to cool to lukewarm."

A young patrol officer lifted her hand timidly.
"Couldn't the body have helped to keep the water
warm longer than normal? All that blood..."

Jackie repressed a shudder. "Good point," she
said. "I'll have to ask the pathologist for his opinion
on that."

"What about notifying the family and questioning
this girl?" Michelson asked.

"I'm heading over to Wilcox High in a few
minutes to see Desirée Moreau and find out if she
was in class this morning," Jackie told him.

"You won't let her know we suspect anything?"

"Not at this point. I intend to take the approach
that I'm breaking the news to her since her sister's at
work and couldn't be contacted."

"Okay. You'll be talking to the sister and her ex-
husband?"

"Brian's taking Officer Howe with him—" Jackie
indicated the female officer who'd spoken up earlier
"—and going to see both of them. Hopefully," she
added bitterly, "before they get the news on television."

"All right." Michelson glanced at the circle of officers. "We'll be setting up some assignments for the
search of the house and grounds, and interviews with
the neighbors. Detectives Kaminsky and Wardlow are
in charge of the investigation and will let you know
what else they need. Jackie, anything you want to
say?"

"Just one thing." Jackie clenched her hands, then forced herself to relax. "I went into my files and looked at a photograph of the anonymous letter that was sent to Maribel last month. It told her she was going to drown in her own blood."

There was a brief shocked silence.

She took a deep breath and looked around at the roomful of tense faces. "It also said she'd be the *first* to die."

8

Michelson began to organize the uniformed officers on a door-to-door campaign in the Lewis neighborhood and a concentrated search for the murder weapon. Wardlow and his young assistant went off to track down Maribel's son and his ex-wife while Jackie headed for Wilcox High.

As she drove, her mind whirled with thoughts and worries. The responsibility of supervising a homicide investigation was enormous, and everything moved so fast. She had to safeguard all the physical evidence and make sure it was properly collected and stored, keep the scene protected until it could safely be released, all the while attempting to interview people before witnesses forgot what they'd seen or suspects had time to get themselves organized and begin fabricating alibis.

In police work it was customary to wish that you could be three people, just to handle the workload. But during a murder investigation the pressure was even greater.

And there was a new worry, too, buried deep in her thoughts because she didn't want to face it yet—the concern over what Paul was going to think when he learned she'd been given this case. At least she didn't have to face him tonight, since he was staying at the ranch for a few days.

But she could hardly waste time brooding about her lover's reaction to her work assignment. A homicide investigation took precedence over the personal concerns of the investigator. Always.

She parked in the faculty lot and hurried up the walk to enter the school's front doors, then paused and looked around in surprise.

She hadn't been inside a high school for several years, and she found the setting a bit disconcerting, almost alien.

Wilcox High represented a solid middle-class neighborhood, nothing like the slum schools Jackie had attended in her youth, with metal detectors at every door and barred windows even in the library.

The students who wandered these halls wore sloppy baggy clothes and weird haircuts, but they still looked as if somebody packed their lunches and provided computers for them to do their homework when they went home at night.

What troubled her was the general sense of disorganization. Classes were apparently still in session but many students drifted idly through the halls and sat talking on benches in the foyer. When a bell rang, nobody seemed to pay attention. Behind lush banks of ferns at the entrance to the school office, a boy and girl were involved in petting so intense that Jackie wondered if it could be considered an act of public lewdness.

She paused to watch the two writhing young bodies for a moment, then shook her head and went into the office.

"I'd like to speak with the principal, if I may."

The secretary, who was chewing gum and making listless entries at a computer, shook her curly head without looking up.

"Sorry. The principal's very busy this afternoon. If you could just fill out one of those yellow request forms, we'll…"

Jackie leaned across the counter to display her badge. The secretary sighed and got up, cracking her gum loudly as she headed for the opposite door. She poked her head inside, conferring briefly with some unseen person.

"Go ahead." She tipped her head toward the door, then returned to her desk.

"Thanks for your help," Jackie said dryly. She strode around the counter and entered the inner sanctum where a thin dark-haired young man sat with his feet propped on the desk, studying a financial magazine.

"Sorry to interrupt while you're busy." Jackie showed her badge again and settled in the leather chair opposite his desk.

He grinned, looking abashed, and closed the magazine. "A whole lot of indignant parents have been calling on me to express their opinions about the condom machine we installed in the girls' washroom last week. I need a little break."

"Well, you won't catch me objecting. I think condoms in schools are a great idea. But then," Jackie added, "I probably see a lot of stuff those parents won't ever have to deal with. My name's Detective Kaminsky, by the way. Spokane P.D."

"Dave Leach." He extended his hand. "What have we done this time that's attracted the attention of the

She turned with a nervous gesture and led them into the stable. They walked on concrete floors dusted with straw, down a wide aisle between rows of box stalls. Horses watched their passage from both sides, nickering and stamping their hooves.

Jackie sniffed the mingled odors of hay, manure and warm horses, finding it unexpectedly pleasant. Again she felt a hot wave of yearning for Paul and had to force herself to concentrate on the business at hand.

They followed Chris Lewis past stacks of baled green alfalfa and equipment-storage areas, into a small office at the rear of the stable where a battered oak desk was flanked by a half-filled coffeemaker on a small table, and an old metal filing cabinet. Framed pictures of horses covered the walls. The little room felt uncomfortably warm, heavy with the scent of the barn.

Chris indicated a couple of plain wooden chairs, then went over to the table. "Would anybody like a cup of this awful coffee?" she asked, pulling off her cap and tossing it onto the desk.

Jackie and Wardlow both shook their heads. Christine poured a mug for herself and gripped it tensely as she sank into a chair behind the desk.

Jackie watched in thoughtful silence, wondering why both Maribel and Desirée seemed to hate the woman so much. At this point the violence of their feelings was a little hard to understand. Christine Lewis appeared sweet and diffident, almost childlike. She had a soft voice and a shy manner that probably made men, at least, feel big and protective.

It was certainly apparent that Wardlow felt protective. Jackie knew her partner well enough to be concerned by the intent expression on his face, the huskiness in his voice as he spoke.

"Chris," he began, "it's about your ex-husband's mother."

"Maribel?" She sat upright behind the desk, still gripping the coffee mug in both hands. Her eyes widened with surprise. "What about her?"

"She was found murdered this morning," Wardlow said.

"Murdered?" Chris echoed, looking dazed. "How...? What...?"

Either the woman was completely taken by surprise or she was a terrific actress, Jackie thought.

"She was murdered in her house," Wardlow told her.

"Oh my God." Chris put her hands over her mouth and stared at the two detectives. Her face drained of color, making her look more than ever like a frightened little girl. "Is Gordie all right? Has anybody—"

"He's fine, Chris," Wardlow said. "I went to the school to talk to him. We couldn't locate his father, so one of Gordie's teachers took him home for the evening. I'll give you the phone number and address where you can pick him up later."

"Thank you," she whispered, twisting her hands together on the desktop. "Thank you so much. Oh, God," she repeated, her voice quivering. "I just...I can't believe it. What happened? I mean, was she...?"

Jackie spoke up. "It was a stabbing. And an extremely brutal one. Maribel was stabbed to death in her own bathtub."

She kept her voice deliberately cold. Since Wardlow apparently intended to play "good cop" in this interview, she'd have to take the opposite role.

"Stabbed," Christine whispered. "But that's awful. Do you know who did it?"

"We're checking out a few leads," Jackie said. She glanced at Wardlow, who avoided her eyes. "And in conjunction with our investigation I have to ask what you were doing this morning."

"Me? I was...I drove to Idaho with a couple of mares. Steve Lorimer's brother has a registered quarter horse standing at stud. We're in the middle of our breeding season."

Jackie took out her notebook and pen. "Were you alone?"

"Yes. I drove there by myself in one of the ranch trucks, pulling a double horse trailer."

"Okay. What time did you leave here?"

Chris frowned. "Well, I got to work just before eight and had to exercise a couple of the three-year-olds on the track because the stable hand was late this morning. Then I loaded the mares and left. I guess it must have been about nine-thirty when I got on the road."

Jackie looked up quickly. "So you would have been passing through Spokane around ten?"

Jackie was conscious of Wardlow beside her, staring grimly at the opposite wall. She wondered what he was thinking.

"That's right," Christine said.

"And where exactly were you going with these two horses?"

"To Kellogg. That's in Idaho, twenty-five miles from the Montana border. It's interstate most of the way, but the trip to the other ranch still takes about an hour and a half with horses in the trailer.''

"So you were there by eleven?''

Again Christine frowned. "It would have been... probably closer to eleven-thirty when I got there. Maybe noon,'' she said at last.

"Why all that extra time if it's freeway right to Kellogg?''

Chris Lewis gave Wardlow an imploring glance. He looked away from her to a picture of a sorrel horse on the opposite wall, and Jackie could sense his growing uneasiness.

"Chris?'' she said in a neutral voice. "I was asking about this extra time.''

"I stopped for a while in Spokane,'' the woman murmured.

"Okay. Where?''

"At...at Maribel's house.''

Jackie's fingers tightened on the pen. "You were at your ex-mother-in-law's house this morning?''

"I wanted to talk to her. Things have been so awful lately. She won't...wouldn't have anything to do with me, and the tension between us was really hard on Gordie and Desirée. I felt sorry for her after her house was broken into last week. I hoped maybe I could talk with her and get her to... Oh, *God*.'' Her voice broke and she buried her face in her hands.

Jackie looked at the cropped boyish hair, the callused hands and slim body behind the desk.

"What time did you speak with Maribel?''

"I didn't actually speak with her. I parked for a while outside the house, trying to get up enough nerve to go inside. But I...I couldn't face her. I guess I was too scared. After a while I just drove away.''

"So it would have been around ten o'clock when you were parked there with the horse trailer?"

Chris nodded without looking up, her face still buried in her hands.

Jackie and her partner exchanged a glance. The story was very neat, she realized.

If Chris Lewis had really parked a ranch truck and double horse trailer on the street outside Maribel Lewis's house that morning, some of the neighbors would likely have noticed the vehicles. But in the shadows of all those big trees and shrubs, they probably wouldn't be able to say for sure whether she actually left the truck and went inside.

"Did you notice anything unusual about the house?" Jackie asked.

"Like what?"

"Were there any people around while you were there, for instance?"

Chris shook her head. "Not that I can remember. Everything was really quiet."

"Because," Jackie went on, "if you were parked outside the house this morning between ten and ten-thirty, the murder could well have been happening right while you were sitting there. That's what we've fixed as the approximate time."

"While I was... Oh my God!"

The woman's voice trailed away. She swayed on the chair and closed her eyes briefly.

"You and your family lived with Maribel Lewis for more than ten years," Jackie said after a moment. "Do you know of anybody who might have hated her enough to want her dead?"

Chris stared into her coffee mug, gripping it tightly

between her hands. "Maribel wasn't...she wasn't a very nice person," she said at last.

"Can you elaborate on that a bit?"

The woman shook her head, showing a brief flash of stubbornness. "I don't want to start saying mean things about her when she's dead."

"Then could you just list some of her enemies for me?" Jackie said.

"I don't know if you'd call them enemies. Maribel fought with everybody at one time or another." Chris held up a hand and touched the callused fingers one by one. "Me, Stan, the people she worked with, most of the neighbors, Laney..."

"Laney?"

"That's Stan's new girlfriend. Her name's Laney Symons." Chris's mouth twisted into a humorless smile. "Maribel never did approve of any woman who dated Stan. Nobody was good enough, I guess."

Jackie made a note in her book, then flipped back through the pages, waiting for Wardlow to speak.

He cleared his throat and shifted awkwardly in his chair. "Chris," he said, "you remember that letter you showed me when I was at your place?"

"Yes," she said, looking helpless and frightened again. "What about it?"

"Well, Maribel got one of those letters, too."

She stared at him. "And you think..."

"It's a very serious situation. Anonymous letter-writers are seldom violent people, but your former mother-in-law has certainly died a pretty gruesome death. So now we have to consider the safety of everybody who received a similar letter."

"Everybody?" she whispered. "Other people got them besides Maribel and me?"

"Yes, they did," Wardlow told her. "Including your ex-husband and your half sister."

"*Desirée?* She got a letter like mine?"

"She told me she did," Jackie said. "But she didn't keep it."

Chris's mouth began to tremble. "This is all so horrible. A nightmare."

"Chris," Wardlow said carefully, "in that letter you got, there was mention of a...relationship you had with a man other than your husband."

When the woman didn't answer, Wardlow leaned forward a little, watching her intently. "I think you told me he works here at the ranch? Charlie, I believe you said?"

Chris looked up, her delicate face scarlet with embarrassment. "Do you really have to talk to him? Can't we just...forget all that?"

"I'm afraid not," Wardlow said. "If the letter-writer is also the killer, and we have pretty good reason to believe he is, then your relationship is already known to him. For the safety of everybody involved, I think we have to learn more about what's going on."

"It's...his full name's Charlie Roarke," Chris said, looking increasingly miserable. She jerked her thumb in the direction of the rear door. "I think he's out there loading bales."

Jackie and Wardlow exchanged another glance. "I'll go talk to him," she said. "You can leave Chris the address where Gordie is, then come outside, okay?"

"Sure."

By the time Jackie left the office he'd walked around the desk to write something on a pad of yellow notepaper. Christine was crying, and Wardlow's hand rested on her shoulder. Jackie moved away from the door, feeling uncomfortable and worried.

Outside the barn she saw a brown truck parked near a stack of hay bales. A man stood high on the stack, silhouetted against the sky as he tossed bales down into the truck box.

Jackie picked her way carefully through the dampness and manure of the stable yard and called up to him, holding out the leather folder containing her badge.

"Could you come down and talk to me, please?" she called. "I'm Detective Kaminsky from the Spokane Police Department."

He jumped down lightly into the box of the truck, balancing on the ragged pile of bales, then vaulted to the ground and came toward her, removing his cap as he approached.

She studied the man, a little taken aback by his appearance. He was quite young, probably in his mid-twenties, and almost too handsome to be real. His hair was black and straight, his eyes vividly blue, with dark curling lashes.

Charlie Roarke's face had such fine planes and flawless skin that if he were a woman, he'd probably be described as beautiful. He was a little taller than Jackie, rangy and muscular, dressed in faded jeans and a blue denim jacket lined with sheepskin.

"You're Charles Roarke?" she asked.

"Yes. What's this about? What's happened?"

"In a minute. Could you describe your relationship with Christine Lewis?"

He looked startled and increasingly edgy. "We're friends." He glanced toward the stable, then back at

Jackie. "I've been working here almost four years. Chris was here when I came."

"Nothing more than friends?"

He showed a flash of anger. "What the hell is this about?"

"Chris got a threatening letter a while ago, and you got a mention in it. I'd just like to hear your side of the story."

"A mention?" he asked warily. "What do you mean?"

"The letter-writer implied that you and Chris were lovers."

Charlie's handsome face turned a dull red. "Oh, for God's sake, that was just a dumb…" He stopped, then looked at Jackie aggressively. "So why are you asking me about it? I never knew it was a crime for two unattached adults to spend time together. Don't the police have better things to do?"

"What you do in your free time is no concern of mine," Jackie told him calmly. "Except that we're in the middle of a murder investigation and every bit of information is important."

"Murder?"

"Chris's former mother-in-law was stabbed to death in her home this morning."

The reaction was extraordinary. Charlie Roarke's face registered blank disbelief, then a look of amazement.

"Maribel?" he whispered. "She's *dead?*"

Jackie watched him with interest. "You don't exactly seem broken up over it. I gather you were acquainted with Maribel Lewis?"

"I lived there for a while." He masked his expression and turned away to study a herd of cows grazing in a nearby field.

"You lived at Maribel's house? When?"

"About three years ago, just after I came to work at the ranch. I was traveling with Stan on the rodeo circuit."

"That's Stan Lewis?" Jackie interrupted. "Maribel's son?"

"Yeah. I'm a bull rider in the summertime. Stan and me, we knew each other for a while before he quit rodeo. Matter of fact, that's how I got the job here at the ranch—through Stan."

"Okay." Jackie wrote busily in her notebook. "So how did you happen to be living in Maribel's house?"

"My apartment went condo and I couldn't afford to buy it. I had no money and no place to live. Stan said I could stay at their house for a while until I got things back under control."

"Where did you sleep?"

"Maribel had a little room in the basement with a bathroom right next door."

"I've seen the room," Jackie said. "You lived there…how long?"

"Not very long. A few months, maybe." He began to look uncomfortable. "Me and Maribel, we didn't get along. She's…she was a real bitch. Excuse me, ma'am," he added automatically.

"What did you argue about?"

"Nothing important," he said. "She just didn't like me. Maybe she thought I was a bad influence on Stan, going to rodeos all the time."

"So you moved out?"

"As soon as I could scrape the money together."

Jackie looked at his fine-boned face, struck by a sudden thought. "Chris said you were late getting to work this morning. As I recall, she even had to exercise some horses for you."

"That's right," he said cautiously.

"So where were you?"

"I was hungover. I drank most of a bottle of rum last night."

"At a party?"

"No, I was all alone in my apartment. I passed out on the couch, woke up feeling like hell and went to bed for the rest of the morning. It was noon before I could drag myself to work."

She gave him another thoughtful measuring glance. "Did anybody see you this morning?"

"How could they?" he asked. "I just told you, I was home in bed."

Jackie remembered the strange expression on his face when he heard about Maribel's death. She could hardly wait to get back to the office and do a bit of serious checking into Charlie Roarke's background.

She turned away to glance at Wardlow, who was approaching them across the barnyard. "So you only slept with Christine a couple of times?" she asked the ranch hand.

"What the hell business is it of yours?"

"I already told you, in a murder investigation everything's my business," she said calmly. "Could you answer the question, please?"

"Yeah," he said with obvious reluctance. "It was during the Christmas holidays."

Wardlow reached them and gave the younger man a level glance. Jackie made brief introductions, conscious of her partner's tension.

"And nothing came of your relationship?" she went on.

Again the man's handsome face colored a little. "It just didn't…work out," he said, evading their eyes. "But we're still good friends. Chris is a really terrific person."

"Okay. I guess that's all for now." Jackie closed her notebook. "But we'll probably want to talk to you again. Oh, and by the way, Charlie…"

"Yeah?" He hesitated, on the point of heading back to the haystack.

"I told you about Christine's letter. A lot of people close to Maribel seem to have received threatening letters. Did you by any chance get one of them, too?"

Jackie was watching him intently and noticed the brief hesitation, the flash of startled uneasiness on his face.

"Did you?" she repeated.

"It was stupid," he muttered. "Just a lot of junk. I ripped it up and flushed it down the toilet. That's all it deserved."

"You got a letter?" Wardlow asked, moving closer. "What was it about?"

"Mostly me and Chris," he said reluctantly. "And some other stuff."

He seemed so uncomfortable that Jackie was intrigued. "What kind of stuff, Charlie?"

"I can't remember all of it." He looked evasive again. "But the letter said I was going to die. I was going to be…" He didn't finish.

"What?" Wardlow asked. "What was going to happen to you, Charlie?"

"It said I was going to be castrated." He licked

his lips and gave them a miserable frightened glance. "Castrated like a dog and then cut to pieces."

"So how many letters have we got so far?" Wardlow asked as they drove back to the city.

Jackie leaned back wearily in the passenger seat and counted on her fingers. "Let's see. Maribel, Chris, Desirée, Stan Lewis, Charlie Roarke. Five that we know of." She gave him a humorless smile. "I told you this was an ugly one, Brian."

"I know. You felt that way right from the beginning. And I can tell you," he added, "I wish we could've pulled something nice and easy like a bar-knifing or a gangland execution for our first murder investigation. This goddamn thing gets more baffling all the time."

Jackie sighed and ran a hand through her hair, wondering absently when she could ever find time to get it cut. "I think the key is probably in those letters, but only Chris and Maribel saved them. With the others we just have to go on what they tell us, and we know for sure they're probably leaving something out."

"How do we know that for sure?"

"Think about it, Brian." Jackie stared at the dark prairie, spangled with lights from farmyards along the highway. "Every letter seems to talk about some kind of shameful secret, mostly nasty sexual stuff. And all of them threaten death."

"Among other nasty things. Castration...my God." Wardlow shuddered.

"Like you told Chris, we have to start taking those threats seriously. After all, Maribel died pretty much the same way her letter said she would—drowning in her own blood.''

"She didn't really drown," Wardlow argued. "The unofficial report says her throat was slashed and she bled to death in the bathwater."

"Well, it sure *looked* like a drowning. If I were Charlie Roarke, I might be feeling just a little nervous. Maybe I'd even be wearing a suit of armor."

"Jesus, Kaminsky! Would you please stop talking about that?"

"I think," Jackie said, "I'm going to get the guys in Ident to make up a chart showing all the anonymous letters and as much information as we can scratch together on each one. When they arrived, what was said, what was threatened."

"Maybe we just need to interview the whole crowd and find somebody who didn't get a letter, and we'll have our man."

She smiled and punched his shoulder lightly. "That's what I love most about you. All that childlike optimism."

"So what's wrong with my theory?"

"For one thing, if our letter-writer is smart—and I suspect he probably is—he'll send himself a letter just to avoid the very thing you're talking about."

"But in that case," Wardlow argued, "if that letter was his proof of innocence, he'd hang on to it, right? He'd keep it and show it to us."

"I agree. So then we'd have to look at the people who saved their letters. Only one of them is still alive."

There was a brief strained silence. "Yes. Chris," Wardlow said at last.

"I wondered about that before," Jackie said.

"Why hang on to a letter that says such awful things?"

They exchanged a quick glance. Wardlow turned away to concentrate on his driving.

"It doesn't look good, Brian," Jackie said quietly. "Chris Lewis has already admitted being at the scene during the time of the murder. The patrols have been out interviewing neighbors all afternoon. If they come up with a witness who also places her there, we'll definitely have enough to bring her in for questioning."

"Bullshit!" he exploded. "We'd need a hell of a lot more before we could lay charges."

"We need means, motive and opportunity. With Chris, I think we've probably got all three."

"What's the motive?"

"Her former mother-in-law was nasty to her and interfered in their marriage. Maribel tried to turn the kids against Chris, and apparently succeeded with Desirée. You've been a cop long enough to know how these family squabbles can lead to murder."

"So if Chris is the killer, and we agree that the killer is also the letter-writer, then why would she send a nasty threatening letter to the little sister she's supposed to love and a harmless cowboy who's also her good friend?"

"I don't know."

"Come on, Kaminsky, think about it," he went on. "Can you really see Chris Lewis up in Maribel's attic with a bunch of candles, pasting cutout photos of herself and her ex-husband on top of that filthy picture? Personally I think Desirée is a far more likely candidate for that kind of stuff, despite her alibi."

"Which I'm checking out more carefully."

"Good thing," Wardlow said. "Maybe we should go over to the high school together and do an intense sweep, talk to her teachers and classmates and anybody else we can find. And we'll have to sift through all the witness statements from the neighborhood, too. Somebody might even have seen something this morning outside Maribel's house."

"Besides Christine's truck and horse trailer," Jackie said, giving him a sidelong glance.

Wardlow was silent for a moment. "I like her, Jackie," he said at last. "She's a really nice person."

"Brian, she's a—"

"I know. She's a suspect in a murder case. But my gut instinct tells me she's innocent."

Jackie nodded thoughtfully. "Fair enough." She turned to look at him. "Tell me, how did you have enough time to get to know her so well? You've only interviewed her once, right?"

"We talked for a long time that night. We feel the same way about a lot of things. And we've both been burned in relationships before, so we know what it's about. She is a nice person, Kaminsky. She's shy, but very warmhearted, and really funny when she relaxes a bit. She's just…nice," he concluded awkwardly.

As they approached from the west, Jackie gazed at the sprawl of city lights, thinking how fervently she'd hoped Brian would meet a woman he could care about.

God. Why did she have to be a murder suspect?

Life could be such a mess sometimes.

"So what about tomorrow?" he asked. "What's top priority?"

"Well, Michelson says a couple of the uniformed guys finally managed to locate Stan Lewis late this afternoon and passed on the bad news. So we'll want to get to Stan pretty quick and interview him before he's had a chance to recover his equilibrium.''

"Jesus, do you think this guy could have stabbed his own *mother?*"

"In this case," Jackie said wearily, "I don't know what to think. We also have to talk to Stan's girl-friend, this Laney Symons. According to Chris, Laney may have had a motive to do away with Maribel, too."

"But first we have to attend the goddamn autopsy." Wardlow pulled into the substation and parked next to her car.

Jackie got out, gathered up her briefcase and shoulder bag and headed for the back door of the station.

"Kaminsky, aren't you going home?"

She shook her head. "It always feels so lonely at my place when Paul's not around. I think I'll just go inside and type up a few notes."

He stopped next to his car and rummaged for the keys. "Okay, have fun, kiddo. See you at the morgue."

11

Birds sang in the trees overhead and new green leaves shimmered in the slanting light of early morning. The world seemed fresh and beautiful, washed clean after a rain shower that had come just before dawn.

Jackie parked her car in a private lot at the hospital and leaned against the rear fender, gazing up at the trees while she waited for Wardlow to join her.

"Nice day," he said, strolling across the damp pavement toward her. "Makes you feel glad to be alive, doesn't it?"

"Is that supposed to be a joke?"

He sobered at the tension in her voice. "No," he said quietly. "I hear this new pathologist is really thorough."

"I've heard that, too."

They walked in silence to a side door at the hospital where they displayed their identification, were admitted by a uniformed security guard and asked to sign a ledger before being directed to one of the autopsy rooms near the morgue.

"I'm thinking about Paul's ranch," Jackie said as they walked, "and the little calf we delivered on the weekend. It was so great, Brian. I almost cried. The calf was all wet and shivering, completely helpless.

Paul and I dried him off with some burlap sacks and put a heat lamp on him, and within an hour he was up and nursing.''

Wardlow shook his head in disbelief. "The last woman on earth I would have expected to become a cowgirl,'' he said. ''Next you'll be milking eggs and candling Holsteins.''

''Very funny.''

But their chatter stopped abruptly when they entered the autopsy room. Although she was familiar with the procedure, Jackie always found the autopsy room a surreal unnerving place.

The new pathologist was already giving instructions to his assistant, a pretty young black woman dressed in a jumpsuit and rubber boots. A police photographer sat on a metal chair nearby, sorting through his cameras and equipment.

''Good morning. I'm Dr. Klein. Don't believe I've encountered you folks before.'' The pathologist came forward briskly to shake their hands.

''This is Detective Wardlow,'' Jackie murmured, gesturing at her partner. ''And I'm Detective Kaminsky.''

''My assistant, Raelynn Hayes.'' The doctor rubbed his hands together and smiled at his assistant, who ducked her head shyly. ''And,'' he added, ''I suppose you both know this fellow.''

''Hi, Ken,'' Jackie said to the police photographer. ''How's the new baby?''

''She pretty much cries all night long,'' the photographer said with a haggard grin. ''Otherwise she's great.''

Dr. Klein rubbed his hands together again, clearly

a mannerism of his. He was a small stocky man with a fringe of reddish hair around a bald pate.

"Well now, I guess we're all present and accounted for," he said, pulling on a pair of rubber gloves. "Raelynn, would you fetch the body, please?"

The woman vanished through a metal side door, her boots squeaking on the cold tile floor. She returned a few minutes later wheeling a stainless-steel table containing a white plastic body bag. The bag was closed by a long zipper down the middle, covered with paper seals.

"Which of you is in charge of the exhibits in this case?" Dr. Klein asked.

Wardlow cleared his throat. "I am."

"All right. Detective, if you could just verify these as the seals you signed and attached when the body was collected?"

Wardlow stepped forward to examine the seals, then nodded. He and Jackie both opened their books and began to make notes while the photographer snapped a few pictures of the unbroken seals.

The pathologist unzipped the bag and tugged it off with Raelynn's help. She took the white plastic and carried it to a bin near the door while Jackie and Wardlow looked down at the body.

Maribel Lewis had been sealed into the bag exactly as she'd been discovered at the scene, still wearing the blue nightgown and yellow chiffon headscarf. Her body was stained and caked with dried blood, and her thin legs looked sad and vulnerable sprawled on the steel table.

But most dreadful of all was the wound at her throat, gaping from ear to ear like a second mouth and wide enough to expose severed arteries and trachea.

"A nasty blow," the doctor commented when he saw Jackie examining the wound with horrified fascination. "But also merciful. I doubt she felt very much after the initial attack. Her body likely emptied of blood in very short order."

The assistant moved around to the other side of the table and gripped the lower edge of the nightgown.

"Careful now, Raelynn," the doctor instructed her. "I'm sure Detective Wardlow will be planning to preserve this garment along with the rest of his evidence."

Skillfully they stripped off the nightgown. The girl deposited it in an evidence box. Maribel's head was propped on a small platform built into the table, while her body lay naked on the metal surface, waxy pale except for some heavy discoloration in her legs and feet, and deposits of dark bluish tissue around her buttocks that looked like bruising.

"Lividity," the doctor explained, touching the discolored areas. He lifted the woman's naked hip to show an irregular whitish area on each buttock. "And these are impact marks. Their presence at this stage makes it reasonable to assume the victim was seated throughout the attack, and the body wasn't moved after death until rigor mortis set in."

Jackie and Wardlow continued to jot down notes while the doctor and his assistant weighed and examined the body, speaking together in low tones. Raelynn wrote their findings on a blackboard near the examining table for formal recording after the autopsy was completed.

They shone lights into the mouth and ears, took

scrapings from under the fingernails and checked the vaginal area.

"No visible signs of intercourse, forced or otherwise," the doctor told Jackie. "We'll take a tissue sample just to be safe, but I really doubt it's going to show anything untoward. Raelynn—" he turned to his assistant "—could you clean this lady up for us, please?"

She nodded and moved silently around the table, using a small flexible hose with a powerful spray nozzle to clean the accumulation of dried blood from the body.

While the technician worked, Jackie stole a glance at Maribel's face, which still seemed surprisingly human.

Her brilliant red hair was the only flare of color in the sterile room, giving her the same air of rather pathetic defiance that Jackie recalled from their first interview. Her withered mouth hung slackly and her eyes were wide and dull, staring at the ceiling.

Jackie shivered, realizing the killer's face was probably the last thing those eyes had seen.

If only human eyes could work like little cameras and store their final images on a bit of film somewhere at the back of the head, Jackie mused. It would certainly make life a whole lot easier for homicide investigators.

The pathologist was displaying various knife wounds on Maribel's body, now cleared of most of the dried blood.

"Twenty-one altogether," he said as the photographer moved around the table, bending and crouching to get accurate pictures of each wound. "All inflicted on the arms and torso except for this single broad incision at the throat.''

Suddenly he moved closer to probe the neck wound with the blunt end of his scalpel, then looked up, eyes bright with interest. Dr. Klein was a man who truly loved his job, Jackie realized.

"This is unusual," he told her. "Come and have a look, Detective Kaminsky. Can you see the end of the wound here where I've positioned the scalpel?"

She bent to peer at the V-shaped mark in Maribel's neck. "What about it?"

"This is the entry point. The knife was jabbed in deeply at this point, then dragged across the throat to exit here at the shallower portion of the wound." He indicated the other side of the throat, then gave Jackie a significant glance. "Nothing registers?"

Jackie shook her head. "I'm afraid not. It just looks like a cut to me."

"All right." He smiled happily, like a child with a secret. "Then we'll try some of the other wounds."

The photographer continued to snap pictures while the young assistant worked stoically, cleaning and exposing areas of the body for their view.

"See this one?" The doctor indicated a vertical gash above the left breast. The cut was an inch or so long, its sides gaping to show tissue beneath.

Wardlow leaned closer to look at the body along with Jackie.

"These injuries on the torso are classified as stab wounds," the pathologist said. "That means they're deeper than their width, whereas the wound to the throat is the only incised injury."

"That's a cut wider than its depth, right?" Wardlow said.

"Good!" The pathologist beamed at Wardlow like a teacher rewarding a bright student. "Now, it should be fairly straightforward for us to determine the angles and trajectories on all those nice clean wounds. Raelynn, if you would?"

The girl went to a cupboard and returned with a set of shining metal probes resembling long needles. Like a conjurer, the pathologist whipped them out of the case and inserted them one by one into the stab wounds on Maribel's chest.

He stood back for the photographer to film the angle of the probes and the numbers on their sides indicating the depth of each wound.

"Clearly the blows were struck by someone standing upright while the deceased was in a sitting position," he said.

"Can you tell if the attacker was right- or left-handed?" Jackie asked, fascinated.

"Definitely right-handed. Look at the angle of entry. And considerable force must have been involved because the wounds are extremely deep. It would probably have been difficult on a few of these, at least, to extract the knife afterward."

Jackie looked at the gleaming probes. "So does that indicate the killer was a very strong person?"

The doctor shook his head. "Not necessarily. Because of the positioning, you see? It's much easier to strike downward with great force, especially against a helpless victim already rendered immobile by a mortal blow to the throat. But the sheer number of stab wounds seems to suggest a killing frenzy—not unusual in cases where the attacker knows his victim."

"So, for instance, a small woman could have done all this damage?"

"Oh my, yes. A child could probably have done it, if he was old enough to hold and use a knife."

There was a brief silence while the pathologist continued to point out wounds for the photographer. Dr. Klein turned back to the two detectives.

"So, have either of you noticed anything interesting about these stab wounds and the long incision at the throat?"

Jackie and Wardlow shook their heads.

The doctor led them across the room to a chart on the wall displaying various colored photographs of knife wounds in flesh. He rapped one of the pictures with his scalpel.

"This is the lip of the cut," he said. "In our autopsy report we always refer to it as the 'margin' for evidence purposes, since 'edge' can be a confusing term. And this—" he moved his scalpel to the outer portion of the wound "—is the corner. A blunted or squared-off corner at the entry point indicates a single-bladed weapon."

"I see," Jackie murmured. "So on a stab wound, you'd be more likely to have a blunted corner at the top and a clean corner at the bottom where the sharpened part of the blade was inserted?"

"That's right, Detective."

Wardlow returned to study the body on the metal table. "But here we've got no blunted corners at all. Look at this, Kaminsky." Excited, he checked the gaping throat and the stab wounds on the torso. "Every one of these corners is sharp."

"Excellent!" The pathologist rubbed his gloved hands together and moved back to stand beside Wardlow. "Which means we're looking at something quite rare. This killer appears to have used a double-edged blade."

"Sharpened on both sides, you mean?" Jackie asked.

"Something like that. A stiletto, perhaps, though not quite as slender. I'd suspect some unusual type of ceremonial knife or dagger. We rarely see wounds like this."

"So recovering the weapon is going to be even more important than in most murder cases," Wardlow said.

Jackie made a note to ask Michelson if they could scratch up enough additional manpower to expand and intensify their search of the neighborhood.

"That pretty much concludes our external examination." Dr. Klein took a scalpel from a steel tray on the counter. "Do you have everything you need so far?" he asked the police photographer.

The young man nodded. Jackie and her partner watched while the pathologist made a branched incision across Maribel's upper chest and down her abdomen. His assistant held back the flaps of skin while Dr. Klein took a pair of shears and began to cut away the breastbone and ribs.

Jackie flinched at the sound of crunching bone. Conscious of Wardlow's eyes resting on her in concern, she set her jaw and willed herself to stand upright.

The pathologist continued with his task, exposing the internal organs packaged neatly together within the body cavity.

"Specimen jar, please," he murmured to his assistant, lifting something with bloody hands. The heart, Jackie realized.

A window was open at the side of the room, and the scent of damp earth and new growth mingled with the smells from the examining table. Birds sang in a noisy chorus as they flitted among the shrubbery.

Dr. Klein weighed and measured the organ, displaying a clean stab wound through its lower portion. "Inflicted after the heart had virtually stopped beating," he commented. "Clearly not the cause of death."

Wistfully Jackie remembered the trill of larks at Paul's ranch, the smell of damp earth, the shining pools of melting snow....

She forced her attention back to Dr. Klein.

"The liver appears healthy. Gallbladder has been previously removed. Raelynn, could you get me another jar, please?"

The pathologist cut open the stomach and dumped its contents into another specimen jar. "Appears to have been a light meal," he murmured to his assistant. "And only partially digested."

Soon the doctor was stitching up the empty body with long blanket stitches. Jackie looked at the sack of skin and bone that had once been Maribel Lewis, then at her face. Again she marveled at how the corpse stubbornly retained an aura of humanity in spite of all the indignities done to it.

Yesterday morning this was a living person with dreams and plans, a woman who feared and hated and loved.

Jackie felt a rising tide of sadness so intense she found herself on the verge of tears.

The police photographer was packing away his

equipment. Dr. Klein's assistant cleaned the room and prepared for the next autopsy. Wardlow moved over to examine the seals on the evidence boxes, which he would now transport directly to the police lab.

Jackie walked out of the hospital beside him, carrying one of the boxes, and sighed with relief when she felt the spring breeze on her face.

She paused by Wardlow's car and watched while he stashed the boxes in the trunk.

"Going to the office?" he asked.

Jackie checked her watch. "I think I'll stop by my place and grab a bite of early lunch," she said, avoiding his eyes. "I need to pick something up."

"Okay. You'll be seeing Stan Lewis this afternoon, right?"

"At three o'clock at his apartment. He's on compassionate leave until after the funeral. And I've got an appointment with his girlfriend right after that."

Wardlow headed for the door of the car. "I'll catch you later, then. We have to check on what the neighborhood search is turning up and find out what Sarge wants to do next."

"There's a meeting right after lunch. I'll see you there."

Jackie could hardly wait for her partner to leave. She wanted nothing more than to get in her car, drive as fast as she could to Paul's ranch and fling herself into his arms. After Wardlow drove out of the parking lot, she checked her watch again and frowned, wondering if she could manage the trip.

Twenty minutes out to the ranch, half an hour with Paul, twenty minutes back to town. It was going to take more than an hour out of a crowded day, and she wouldn't have time to eat anything.

Still, she yearned for Paul so desperately it was hard not to head west and keep driving into that springtime horizon until she reached him.

Sighing, Jackie settled behind the wheel of her car and started toward her own apartment. She needed some kind of human contact, somebody to touch and hold. If Carmen and her daughter had still lived next door, Jackie could have gone over and taken Tiffany onto her knee, held her and hugged her warm little body until her loneliness eased a bit.

Carmen and Tiffany had been like a family to her when they lived next door, and there were times when Jackie missed the two of them desperately.

She parked in front of her building and trudged upstairs, letting herself into the silent apartment. At least there'd be some comfort in the familiarity. She didn't feel like eating anything, although she had a long day ahead of her.

Maybe she'd just curl up on the couch for a while, cover herself with one of Gram's ugly knitted afghans and pretend the warmth was Paul, holding her.

12

In the foyer Jackie paused to put her keys away, then went into the living room. She stopped abruptly in shock.

A man with long denim-clad legs and booted feet lay sprawled on the floor under her coffee table.

At her gasp Paul slid out from under the table, almost bumping his head, and clambered to his feet.

"Jesus," she whispered, staring at him, her heart pounding. "You scared the hell out of me."

"Hi, sweetheart. I didn't expect you home. I was about to call the office and see if I could take you out for lunch."

"What were you doing under the coffee table?"

"Checking the construction." Grinning fondly, he put his arms around her. "I can't believe you built those tables. What a woman."

"I like making things," she muttered against his chest. "If I had the time, I'd take another carpentry course."

He kissed her hair. Jackie shifted nervously in his arms, wondering if any of the smells from the morgue still clung to her.

"Why...why are you here in the middle of the day?" she asked. To her dismay, tears filled her eyes.

"I need another roll of barbed wire." He stepped

back to hold her at arm's length. "Hey, what's the matter?"

"N-nothing." She began to sob and pulled him close to nestle against his shirtfront.

"Like hell." His arms tightened around her. "I don't think I've ever seen you cry before. Jackie, what's going on?"

She reached up and drew his head down, her mouth seeking blindly, hungrily. "Paul," she whispered, her voice breaking. "Paul…"

He led her down the hall to the bedroom. She stumbled along next to him, frantic with need, and helped while he pulled her clothes off, tossed them onto the chair and threw his own on top of them.

Then they were in bed and he was holding her, yet despite the warmth her body still trembled.

Gently, tenderly, he made love to her, his big body covering and enclosing hers until the whole world was bounded by him and there was nothing, anywhere, to make her afraid.

"I love you," she whispered, her face streaming with fresh tears. "I love you so much.…"

He hushed her and held her close, stroking her hair while she cried. At last the storm of tears subsided and she rested in his arms. The thatch of hair on his chest tickled her face, and she could feel the steady thump of his heart beneath her cheek.

She thought of Maribel's heart, a bloody lump in the pathologist's cupped hands, and realized how fragile human life really was. One blow, a single moment of carelessness, and Paul's heart could stop beating, too.

And then her world would end.

She moved restlessly in his embrace. "I went to an autopsy this morning," she whispered.

His arms tightened in sympathy. "Was it awful?"

"Pretty bad. I've been to them before, but this time it was somebody I *knew*. I didn't realize how much difference that would make."

"I wish you'd quit that damned job," he muttered against her hair. "Wouldn't you rather come out to the ranch with me this afternoon and help me string barbed wire?"

Wistfully Jackie thought about the sunshine, the fields of bleached waving grass and spring flowers, the healthy work that tired her body and left her mind free to roam.

She shook her head. "I've got so much to do this afternoon, I probably won't even be home till after nine o'clock."

"Then I'm lucky you decided to stop by for lunch." He pulled away to look down at her. "Are you feeling better, honey?"

"Much better."

He traced her mouth with a callused fingertip. "So what's this all about? Was it just the autopsy that upset you?"

She bit her lip and looked at the ceiling. "Not really. A lot of things, I guess. I've been thinking about my childhood, and how unhappy I was most of the time."

"I wonder if we can ever really escape our childhoods. Any of us."

Jackie turned to him in surprise. "But you always say that stuff is all a crock. You've told me lots of times that people who keep dwelling on their troubled childhoods are just looking for an excuse to keep from getting on with life."

"In a way that's true. I have no patience for people who go around pointing at something in their past and blaming it for all their problems."

"Why not?" Jackie asked.

"I think knowledge equals responsibility. Once you're able to recognize the source of the problem, I believe that obligates you to deal with it."

She glanced at him curiously, then nestled in his arms again, toying idly with the curling hair on his chest. "So what did you mean just now, about never being able to escape our childhoods?"

"I guess," he said, "I'm talking about the difference between intellect and emotion. Even though we can recognize these things objectively, it's hard to change the way we feel."

"And how do you feel?"

"Sometimes I'm scared as hell."

His voice was husky with emotion. Jackie looked at him in surprise. "What are you afraid of?"

"I don't know." He moved his long body restlessly in the bed. "Losing you, I guess."

"Me? You're afraid of losing *me?*"

"You sound so surprised. Don't you know how much I love you?"

She kissed him and nuzzled the hollow of his throat where the tanned skin was soft and silky.

"My mother died when I was a little kid," he went on, stroking her hair. "And my father wasn't very good at being a parent, so I grew up pretty much on my own. I suppose a psychologist would tell me I have a fear of being deserted by another woman I love."

"Why would I desert you? I can't even imagine living without you."

"You might not leave me by choice. You could die like my mother did, and then I'd be alone again."

"But that's crazy, Paul. I'm young and healthy. There's no reason to think—"

"Yes, there is," he interrupted her softly. "Your job. It involves a lot of risk."

Of course. She'd known he felt that way. She tensed in his arms, trying not to think about Maribel's lifeless body on the metal table.

"So does yours," she argued. "Your job is just as dangerous as mine. Probably more."

"How?"

"I was thinking about it a few days ago. You're out at that place alone all the time, miles from anybody. You could be…gored by a bull or caught in machinery or something, and nobody would even find you for a long time."

When she spoke the words aloud her irrational fears about losing him came rushing back, almost suffocating her.

"Come on, Jackie," he said. "There's nobody shooting at me. I'm not a target for every lowlife who's got some kind of a grudge against authority."

She stared at the ceiling.

"Sometimes I can hardly stand it," he went on tightly, his hand gripping her shoulder. "The woman I love more than anything, the center of my life, is out where some little creep can blow her away just because he doesn't like the job she's doing."

Jackie thought about Michelson down in the police exercise room, telling her that given another chance, he'd find a different line of work rather than subject his wife to a lifetime of fear.

She pushed the memory aside. "Paul, you know I love you, but you can't ask me to give up my job. It's not fair. I've worked so hard."

"So what's the deal?" He looked at her directly. "Is being a cop what defines you? Is the job the most important thing in your life? Because I have to tell you, Jackie, I'm not sure I can deal with that."

"You can't deal with my job?"

"I didn't say that. I'm asking if it's more important to you than anything else."

Jackie felt a rising panic. She pulled away from him and sat up, reaching for her clothes.

"Love shouldn't be like this," she said. "Nobody should have to give up everything for another person. I'm not asking you to sell the ranch and go back to your nice safe job in the city, even though it scares me to think of you working out there all alone."

"And I'm not asking you to do anything, either. I'm just trying to establish what your priorities are."

"For God's sake, Paul!" Anxiety made her lash out at him. "I've been working at this job for thirteen years, and I'm good at it. Right now I'm in charge of a homicide investigation. Do you know how few women ever get to this level in the police force?"

"Probably not many." He watched her with a calm level gaze. "But one of them just happens to be the woman I love."

"So because you love me, I'm trapped? I have to spend my life wrapped up and stored in some box where I'll be safe?"

He got up and strode across the room, his naked body gleaming in the sunlight filtering through the curtains. "Let's not talk about this anymore," he said, pulling on his undershorts and jeans.

Jackie stepped angrily into her slacks and buttoned her shirt. "No way," she said. "This thing's been hanging in the air between us for months. Now that it's finally come into the open, you're not shutting me out again, damn you!"

He turned to face her, holding a shirt in his hands. "Why are you yelling at me? I'm not the one who came home in tears after seeing a goddamn autopsy."

"So I'm having a bad day!" she snapped. "Does that mean I should quit my job? Can't you just comfort me and let me live my life?"

"I can do anything you want me to. I'm prepared to give you all the comfort you need for the rest of your life. But I can't live with knowing you're a target for every creep and weirdo with a gun looking for a cop to kill."

The pain in his voice made her hesitate. She knew exactly how he felt, but she realized it wouldn't do either of them any good to yield to his fear.

"Paul," she said quietly, moving closer to him, reaching up to touch his rigid jaw. "Look at me."

He stared down at her in silence, his dark eyes blazing with emotion.

"Paul, that woman at the autopsy was stabbed by somebody in her own house. Yesterday morning she was alive, and today I watched a pathologist putting pieces of her into jars."

He waited while she groped for words.

"Somebody's got to catch the people who take the lives of other people," she said. "Somebody's got to stop them."

He stared over her head at the window curtains for

a moment, then looked down at her again. "Why does it have to be you?"

"Because sometimes we have to step forward and take responsibility. We can't always leave things up to other people. This is my job," she went on passionately, "and I'm good at it. I know it sounds corny, and I'd probably never say it to anybody else, but I really believe I can make a difference in the world by doing this. I've always felt that way."

She put her arms around him, conscious of the tension in his body.

"I love you, Paul," she whispered. "And I need you so much. Please don't let this fear of yours come between us."

"Would you at least start wearing a bullet-proof vest when you're on duty?"

She drew away and bent to retrieve her loafers from under the chair. "Hardly anybody wears a vest with street clothes. Besides, people aren't shooting at me, except during training exercises. This is just a fear of yours that has no basis in reality."

"And in the real world police officers are never killed in the line of duty." He sat on the bed to pull his socks on. "Nobody ever draws a gun on a cop. It's all good cheer and sunshine out there, right?"

"Of course it isn't. But I'm not on patrol anymore, and I investigate crimes *after* the fact. I take reasonable precautions for my own safety. I want you to trust me and love me, not cripple both of us by being afraid of life."

"I've never been afraid of life," he said. "But now I'm afraid of life without you."

"Then don't drive me away." She stood erect and

looked at him steadily. "Because you will, Paul, if you start forcing me to be something I'm not."

He met her eyes, and the challenge hung between them for a long moment. He was the first to turn aside.

"Come on," he said abruptly. "You're probably hungry. I'll make you a sandwich before you have to go back to work."

She followed him down the hall to the kitchen, watching his broad shoulders and gleaming blond hair, wondering if anything had been resolved at all.

Her body had been comforted by their lovemaking, but Jackie still felt troubled as she left the apartment after lunch and drove over to the office.

She sat through the meeting of the homicide task force, thinking about Paul. He was gone now, back to the ranch until the weekend, and despite their conflict, she missed him already.

The loneliness was even worse because of the strain between them. Jackie could hardly endure the feeling of unresolved tension. Their love was so important to her that she needed a free flow of trust and happiness. Anything less made it difficult for her to function properly.

When the meeting broke up, she went back to her desk and updated the file, though there was really nothing new to report, aside from the findings at the autopsy. She and Wardlow spent a few minutes discussing strategy and coordinating their schedules. Then she gathered up her jacket, notebook and briefcase, shouldered her bag and left, heading for the unmarked car in the parking lot.

She drove east, on her way to the Valley. Stan

Lewis's apartment building looked old and unkempt, fronted by some ragged shrubs and a weedy brown lawn. A chair was propped at the front door to hold it open and the intercom panel hung loose, sporting a couple of frayed wires.

Out of Order, a hand-lettered sign read, already fading in the spring sunlight. Apparently the intercom had not been functional for some time.

Jackie studied the names under the panel. Many of the slots were empty, though all the apartment windows were curtained and she didn't see any Vacancy signs posted. Probably a lot of the tenants were the sort of people who didn't like to advertise their presence.

Stan Lewis, though, had his name printed neatly on a slip of paper next to his apartment number. Jackie edged past the chair to enter the grimy foyer and climbed a flight of stairs to the third floor.

There was no elevator. The halls were wide and high-ceilinged and perhaps had once been elegant. Now the wallpaper was peeling, the paint was chipped and the wooden floors sagged and creaked noisily.

She paused for a moment outside Stan's apartment, collecting her thoughts. Then she knocked and waited while approaching footsteps echoed hollowly from the other side of the door.

"Hi," he said, stepping aside to let her enter. "I've been waiting for you."

Jackie followed him into the apartment, looking at him closely.

Stan Lewis seemed surprisingly composed for a man who'd just suffered a serious bereavement the day before. He wore jeans, moccasins and a white shirt. His belt was made of tooled leather with a big silver trophy buckle. Again she had the dual impression of good looks and weakness in his face.

"How are you, Stan?" she asked, sitting in a worn velour armchair and glancing around.

The apartment was sparsely furnished with thrift-store goods and showed little personality of any kind, except for some colorful rodeo posters and a big stereo set flanked by a bookcase full of compact disks.

He sprawled on an old sectional couch, extended his legs and rested his arms along the back. "I guess I'm okay," he said. "It's been quite a shock. I still can't believe it."

Jackie thought about the thin body on the metal table. "I'm really sorry," she said with genuine sympathy.

"That's okay. I'm not blaming the police." He picked at a bit of torn upholstery on the couch while Jackie looked at him in surprise.

"Why would you blame the police?"

"Because she got that letter, had the break-in at her house and everything, but you didn't protect her. I could probably make an issue of it, but I'm not that kind of person."

She gripped her notebook and took a deep breath. "We can hardly put a twenty-four-hour watch on everyone who receives a threat. We don't have the manpower."

"Yeah, I know. Makes me wonder what happens to all the taxes I pay."

Jackie watched him with interest, wondering what had suddenly caused Stan Lewis to make this transition from itinerant millworker and rodeo rider to fiscally responsible citizen.

"Do you pay a lot of taxes, Stan?"

He shrugged. "Seems like most of my paycheck goes to the government. Sometimes I get really pissed off about it."

No kidding, Stanley. And do you care at all that your mother was brutally stabbed to death yesterday in her own bathroom?

"I guess you would," Jackie said aloud, cringing a little at the sympathy she'd forced into her voice. "It must be a pretty hard job, working in that mill with all the dust and machinery."

"Damn right it is." His handsome face looked indignant. Or maybe it was petulant.

"You do get out of the mill sometimes, though, don't you?" she said casually. "I understand that yesterday you were over at Richland, hauling feed or something. We had a hard time getting hold of you."

"Yeah, I took a load of bagged feed down there. It's a special blend for ostrich ranchers. Really expensive."

"And the trip takes…what? Must be a couple of hours, right?" Jackie glanced up as she opened her notebook.

"That's right."

"What time did you leave?"

He glanced at a rodeo poster on the wall next to him, showing a Brahma bull whirling in clouds of dust while a man clung to its back.

"I don't know for sure. I loaded the truck on Sunday and brought it home so I could get an early start. Must have been on the road about nine o'clock, I guess."

"Then you got to Richland at eleven?"

He looked uncomfortable. "No, I think it was probably after twelve. I had some sandwiches and a thermos of coffee, and I stopped along the way to eat and look at some horses in a field."

His story sounded eerily similar to Christine's. The loaded truck, the purpose of the trip, even their off-kilter times of leaving and arriving were alike, though the destinations lay in opposite directions.

"So you had a little picnic?" Jackie said, trying to sound casual.

"Yeah, sort of."

"Could you give me an idea how far you'd traveled by, say, ten o'clock?"

He leaned forward and cast her a sharp glance. "Why are you asking me all these questions? You don't think I killed my own *mother,* for God's sake?"

"It's just routine, Stan," Jackie told him with a soothing smile. "We have to ask everybody where they were yesterday morning."

He settled back, but still looked annoyed. "At ten o'clock I was probably down at Ritzville, heading off the freeway. Yeah," he added, frowning. "Matter of fact, I remember stopping at a service station around that time to use the washroom."

"Did anybody see you? Can you recall talking to any of the staff?"

"No. I just parked around back and went in the washroom, didn't fill up with gas or anything. But I called Laney from a pay phone outside the station."

Jackie looked at him alertly. "Your girlfriend, Elaine Symons?"

"Yeah."

"So you called her in Spokane?"

"That's right."

"Why?" Jackie asked.

He shrugged. "Just to say hello."

"At ten o'clock Monday morning?"

Stan looked even more annoyed. "We had a fight the day before. I wanted to see if she was still pissed off."

"Was she?"

"Sort of. Laney can be real moody." He grinned suddenly. "You women, you're all the same. Sweethearts or bitches, depending on the time of month."

Jackie controlled herself with an effort. "Must be really hard on you poor men."

"That's for damn sure," Stan said, oblivious to her sarcasm.

"So you called Laney from Ritzville at ten o'clock?" Jackie asked.

"That's what I just said."

"Collect call, or did you use a card?"

"No, I used quarters. We only talked for a few minutes. Then I got in the truck, drove down the road and stopped by a field where some horses were grazing. I got out and looked at the yearlings for a while, ate my lunch and took a little nap."

Jackie remained silent as he went on, "Probably I was looking at those colts just about the same time my mother..."

He, too, fell silent. His face contorted and he brushed a hand across his eyes. Jackie was fairly certain the emotion was faked.

"So then what?" she said briskly, flipping to a clean page in her notebook.

"Then I drove to Richland. Got there around noon."

Which still leaves a whole hour unaccounted for,

Jackie thought. *Unless there's some way we can have that call traced...*

She followed Stan's glance and saw him looking through an open door at another room, apparently a bedroom. Jackie saw the edge of a cardboard box and a messy pile of clothes on the floor.

"Are you packing, Stan?" she asked.

He shifted uneasily. "Sort of. Just putting some things in boxes."

"Where are you going?"

"Over to my mother's house."

Jackie paused, startled. "Your mother's house?"

His edginess changed to sort of a sulky defensiveness. "Look, what else can I do? Everybody knew she lived there alone. I can't very well leave the house empty, can I? Punks are going to knock out the windows and climb inside. They'll trash the place and steal everything in sight. Somebody has to be there."

"The house is still a protected crime scene. We haven't released it yet."

"I know, but I called the police station a little while ago and they said I could probably have the place in a day or two, so I'm getting ready. As soon as your people say the word, I'll be in there."

Jackie just looked at him.

"It's my house," he said with growing anger. "You can't stop me from living there. She left it to me in her will. The place belongs to me."

"How do you know? Have you seen a copy of your mother's will already?"

"I don't need to see it. She showed me her will just a month or two ago. She got the mortgage paid off last year, so she had clear title to the house. She left everything to me."

"I see." Jackie looked down at her notebook. "Isn't that a pretty big place for one man to be living in all alone?"

"I'm thinking probably I'll rent out the upstairs. Maybe the basement room, too."

"That should be a nice little source of extra income," Jackie said.

"With that house I can finally start getting somewhere. I might even be able to quit my job and travel the rodeo circuit a bit, once I've got some paying tenants. And I can get out of this dump." He looked around with a grimace of distaste.

"So this death wasn't a complete tragedy for you," Jackie said.

"What the hell does that mean?" His eyes glittered with an anger Jackie found unsettling, almost frightening. "Look, you're trying to imply something, lady. And let me tell you, I don't appreciate it."

"Take it easy, Stan. I'm not implying anything. I'm just making a comment."

"Well, it's out of line."

He got to his feet and moved across the room to stand uncomfortably close to her. His face was flushed with emotion, his hands curled into fists.

"Listen to me, Detective. You'd better catch the scumbag who did this to my mother. If you don't, I'll find him and kill him myself."

Jackie got up and stood facing him, her eyes cold and level. There was a long tense moment, so quiet she could hear a clock ticking somewhere in the kitchen, before he took a couple of steps backward.

"Don't kill anybody, Stan," she said quietly. "Because we get really, really upset when that happens."

13

Clem's Autobody and Salvage was a small business clinging to life on the outskirts of Spokane. A rusty iron fence encircled the lot, where burned-out corpses of trucks and cars lay scattered in the weeds. Rusted engines sat on blocks and hung from chains inside the murky depths of the shop.

It looked like a place made to order for Jackie's younger cousins, Joey and Carmelo, who ran various scams related to auto salvage. Fortunately, though, the pair operated *their* business in L.A., not Spokane. They weren't generally an embarrassment to Jackie except for occasions when she had to go down there and bail them out of trouble or intervene in some noisy dispute between the cousins and her grandmother.

While she studied the mess of old cars, a boy in jeans and a sweatshirt came around the corner, rolling an oil drum with a sneakered foot. His cap was on backward, revealing a freckled face and a sexy grin. He leered at Jackie.

"Well, hi there," he drawled. "Are you lookin' for me, gorgeous?"

Jackie dug into her coat pocket and showed him her badge.

"Hey, that's okay," he said with a look of cherubic innocence. "I dig women with power."

"Let's go around back," she suggested. "I'll handcuff you to a radiator."

"Yeah?" His eyes brightened. "And then what?"

"And then I'll go away."

The grin faded. "You're no fun."

"You got that right, kiddo. Look, I need to have a talk with a woman named Elaine Symons, and I understand she works here."

He jerked a thumb toward a corner of the building where the word Office was written on the window in peeling letters. "Laney works in there."

"Thanks."

The boy fell into step beside her, rolling his drum ahead of them. "Now Laney, there's a woman with power," he said. "She's awesome."

"Really?" Jackie looked at her young admirer with interest. "You mean physical power, or a really strong personality?"

"Both. She used to be a biker. Now she's the lead singer in a country band and practically runs the whole nightclub besides. And that's in addition to handling this business for Clem and keeping poor ol' Stanley under complete control. That's her so-called boyfriend," he added scornfully.

"So her boyfriend's under her control?"

"Hell yes. Stan's so whipped, he can't even pee unless Laney holds his hand." The boy shook his head. "It's a sad, sad thing."

"Well, maybe you'd better think about it." Jackie paused at the door to the office and smiled sweetly. "That's what happens to guys who are attracted to powerful women."

The boy grinned back at her, gave her a mock bow and started around the building, still rolling his barrel.

"Hey," he called, pausing at the corner.

"Yes?"

"Ask Laney to show you her tattoos. She's got some totally wicked tattoos."

"Thanks. Maybe I'll do that." Jackie watched him go, then at last she pushed the office door open and went inside.

The office was empty at the moment and so neat it seemed at odds with the rest of the salvage operation. From the scrubbed linoleum tiles to the tall metal file cabinets set at precise angles, the room bespoke order and efficiency.

The desktop was bare except for a couple of letters and invoices held down by a metal paperweight in the shape of a cowboy boot. On a battered metal console, a branch of pussy willows stood in a preserving jar.

Jackie looked at the pussy willows, then reached out to touch their velvety smoothness.

Another thing I never got to play with when I was a kid, she thought. *It must be fun to gather these in the spring, take them home and stick them in a water glass and pretend each bud is a little gray kitty sleeping on a branch.*

The door to the shop opened. A man poked his head inside.

"Lookin' for somebody?"

"Elaine Symons."

The man came a few steps into the room, wiping his hands on a grease-stained rag. He paused, looking sheepish and apologetic. "Laney don't allow none of us in this room unless we're clean," he said. "I'm the owner, Clem Walstadt."

"Hello." Jackie showed him her badge. "Detective Kaminsky, Spokane P.D."

Walstadt was about fifty, bald and bullet-headed, with a stocky torso and heavy abdomen sagging under his overalls. His jowly face was pleasant, though clearly nervous at the moment.

"Laney, she ain't in no kind of trouble, is she?"

"Not at all. Her boyfriend's mother was found murdered yesterday, and I'm questioning anybody who might have information about the family."

"Oh, yeah, I seen that on TV at lunchtime. Terrible thing when folks ain't safe inside their own house anymore."

"Murder's still not all that common here in Spokane, Mr. Walstadt. But I agree, it's really a terrible thing when it invades somebody's house."

He was silent, looking down at the plastic under his feet. Apparently Laney didn't allow him to venture beyond the mat.

"Is this a one-woman office?" Jackie asked. "Laney looks after it all by herself?"

"She's a great gal, Laney is. Been here almost twelve years. Couldn't manage without her. She knows where all the stuff is."

Jackie glanced at a door opening from the office into a shadowy little bathroom. The wall above the sink was fitted with an ornate gold-framed mirror, and a pink fluffy rug lay on the floor. Both touches looked incongruous in the midst of this gritty place.

She turned back to the manager. "Do you happen to know where Laney is right now?"

"I told her to take the rest of the day off. She's been real tense lately, and this murder thing, it don't

help. She had all the invoices done for month-end, so
I told her to take off.''

"That was kind of you. What time did she leave?''

He shrugged. "Must've been around two, I guess.''

"Did she go home?'' Jackie flipped through her
notebook to check on Elaine Symons's home address.

"No, she wouldn't go home in the middle of the
day. She hates the place.''

"It's a basement suite, isn't it? Over in Mill-
wood?''

"Yeah, and it's a real dump. Laney, she don't like
it one bit, but she can't afford nothin' better. Lucky
she's a night person,'' Clem added.

"Why?''

"Because she don't spend much time at home. She
works all day, goes out in the evening to sing a couple
of sets at the club, then catches a few hours' sleep
and comes back here. I think she went over to the
club to practice, if you're looking for her right now.''

"Where's the club?''

"It's the Bum Steer, down on East Sprague. Kind
of a cowboy hangout. Line-dancing, lots of whiskey
and loud music, some girls, usually a poker game in
the back—'' He stopped abruptly and flushed.

Jackie smiled at him and put the notebook away in
her shoulder bag. "Thanks for your help.''

"You won't mention nothin' about me sayin'...''
he floundered wretchedly. "That poker game, I doubt
they even have it anymore. I think that was a long
time ago, back when the—''

Jackie looked for a place on his overalls not stained
with grease and patted his shoulder. "Forget it, Clem.
I'm not interested in poker, at least not at the moment.
I'm investigating a homicide.''

He exhaled a huge sigh of relief.

Jackie paused in the other doorway. "By the way, was Elaine here yesterday morning?" she said casually. "Somebody told me she hasn't been feeling well lately, and she's missing quite a lot of work."

This was a deliberate lie, but it accomplished the intended purpose. Clem looked at her indignantly and shook his head.

"I sure don't know who's been telling you stuff like that," he said. "Laney, she's the most reliable gal you could ever find."

"So she was here all morning?"

"Well…she usually is. But not yesterday, come to think of it."

"Do you know where she was?"

"She got here early, just after eight, looking like hell. Said she had the flu and didn't sleep well, but I think she was fighting with that creep she's been going out with."

"Stan Lewis, you mean?"

Clem's heavy face twisted with dislike. He shook his head. "Guess I shouldn't be saying mean things about him when his mother's just died, should I? But I never did like the guy."

"We were talking about how Laney felt yesterday morning," Jackie reminded him.

"Yeah. By nine-thirty she could barely drag herself around. I told her to go to the doctor."

"And she did?"

"I was a little surprised," Clem admitted. "Usually Laney don't pay no attention to anybody. Shows how sick she was feeling that she'd leave work and go see the doctor just because I told her to."

"So what time did she get back to the office?"

"She didn't. Called in around noon to say she had a sack full of medicine and she was going to bed for the rest of the day. Looked a whole lot better this morning, too. 'Course," Clem added fondly, "Laney, she always looks pretty good."

"Would you happen to know if Stan Lewis called here after Elaine left this afternoon?"

Clem's smile faded. "He might've. I heard the phone ringing a while ago in her office, but I didn't bother to answer it."

Jackie thanked him and left, walking slowly back to her car.

Apparently Elaine Symons and Stan Lewis hadn't gotten together yet to coordinate their stories. If his ten o'clock phone call to her yesterday morning was supposed to provide his alibi for the time of the murder, Stan's girlfriend was letting him down badly. She hadn't even been there to receive the call.

Jackie got behind the wheel of her car and stared at the windshield, thinking.

Elaine's boss had sent her away unexpectedly this afternoon, and she'd seized the few hours off to go over to the club and practice her songs. Stan couldn't have known that was going to happen. Apparently he didn't even know she'd been out of the office yesterday morning, as well, or he wouldn't have told Jackie the elaborate story about the phone call.

Today he'd probably called Laney right after she, Jackie, had left his place, anxious to give her instructions on how to back up his story.

But Elaine had already been gone by then, and Stan was getting deeper in trouble all the time.

Unless, Jackie thought, Laney carried a cell phone, which would clear everything up. Still, in that case, the records would probably be traceable and she could learn the truth about all these alibis.

The first order of business was to get over to the Bum Steer as soon as she could and have a talk with Laney Symons before Stanley managed to get hold of her.

In the course of her job, Jackie tended to visit a lot of nightclubs during daylight hours. Still, she was always surprised and a little disconcerted by the contrast between how a club looked at night and how it looked at high noon. At night there was glitter and a certain glamour; in the day the glitter was more like grit, and glamour was nonexistent.

The Bum Steer was no exception. She paused on the street outside to examine the wall fronting the "saloon," as the place billed itself. It was covered by a huge mural painted with women wearing leather chaps and not much else. Their body proportions were ludicrous—huge breasts, impossibly slender waists and pink curved buttocks that evidently gave the place its name.

Jackie pushed the door open and went into a small room dominated by a chipped wooden bar and a mass of tables topped with upside-down chairs. She wrinkled her nose in distaste at the smell of stale cigarette smoke and spilled beer.

A wiry little black-haired man worked in the center of the room among the tables and stacked chairs, mopping the floor.

"Hi," Jackie said. "Anybody else here?"

He looked up at her blankly, then wrung out the mop, wiped his hands on his apron and sloshed more water onto the floor.

Jackie moved closer. "Excuse me," she said. "I wanted to know if there's anybody else around."

The janitor muttered something in Spanish and looked down at the pail of dirty water. His thin body trembled with fear.

Jackie studied him thoughtfully. The people who worked at such jobs were mostly illegal immigrants. They seemed to have an infallible instinct for police officers, even ones in street clothes.

While she hesitated, a few strains of music came drifting out through a partially closed door at the opposite side of the room, followed by an angry murmur of voices.

"Sorry," she told the man in her street-level Spanish. "I guess you'd better get back to work."

He flashed her a glance that was both startled and grateful, and resumed mopping the floor with renewed energy.

Jackie crossed the room, pushed the door open a little farther and peered inside, finding herself in a larger, wood-floored room, empty except for a raised platform at the front, a few chairs and a bank of audio equipment.

A man sat on a three-legged stool in front of a sound mixer, fiddling with knobs and levers. He was small and whip-thin, probably in his early thirties, with a full beard and thinning hair pulled back into a greasy ponytail. He wore faded jeans and a black leather vest that showed off a mass of tattoos on his bare forearms and skinny biceps.

On the small raised platform, a tall blond woman was tapping her foot impatiently as she watched the man. Neither of the people in the room had yet noticed Jackie, so she had time to observe them closely.

The woman, who must be Laney Symons, was a little surprising, even though Jackie hadn't known what to expect. She was tall and a little overweight. Her pink T-shirt and tight jeans displayed ample breasts and hips. Her long hair, too blond to be natural, was puffed and curled to frame a face like a pouting kitten's, and she wore long pink earrings in the shape of feathers.

Laney's wide-lipped mouth was turned up slightly at the corners, her eyes were slanted and accented heavily with makeup and her cheekbones were skillfully highlighted to create hollows where they didn't exist. Overall she gave an impression of smoldering sexuality, a little garish but probably irresistible to some men.

She certainly didn't look like a woman who'd worked for twelve years in that dismal autobody shop and who kept the office so painfully neat her boss was afraid to venture more than a couple of steps inside.

But Jackie's job had taught her not to be surprised at the many facets of personalities she encountered. People were endlessly varied and unpredictable. It was what made the work so interesting.

While she watched, the man in the ponytail flipped some more levers, music began to pound and Laney stepped close to a microphone, raising her voice in a moody rendition of "Walkin' After Midnight."

The woman was really good. In fact, she was terrific, with a full-bodied, soaring voice that sent shivers up and down Jackie's spine.

She stood in the doorway, listening with openmouthed respect while Laney ran through a couple of verses and a chorus, then stopped abruptly.

"Shit," the woman muttered, glaring at her skinny companion. "Come on, Archie! Can't you get the goddamn thing *right* for a change?"

"Now what's wrong?" he asked in a long-suffering tone. "Sounds good to me."

"Like hell. There's still way too much bass. I can feel it pounding right through the soles of my feet. What's the point in singing if I can't even—" She stopped, noticing Jackie at the door.

"Hi," Jackie said, walking into the room and holding up her identification. "Detective Kaminsky, Spokane P.D. Are you Elaine Symons?"

Archie glanced over at Jackie, his pitted face tightening, then he busied himself switching off the audio equipment. "I'll just slip out for a bit," he muttered, apparently speaking to Laney though he was concentrating on his levers and knobs. "Got to pick up a few groceries."

Before either woman could respond, he was gone, snatching a battered leather jacket from a chair nearby and sprinting out the door.

Laney stood at ease on the platform, hands on hips. She watched him go with an amused smile, then turned to Jackie. "Archie's not all that fond of cops."

"So I gathered," Jackie said. "But that's okay. I'm not here to talk to Archie. Not yet, anyway," she added.

Laney gave her a quick wary glance, then stepped down from the platform and waved her hand languidly at one of the wooden chairs pushed back along the wall.

"Sit down," she said. "Take a load off."

Jackie seated herself and took out her notebook, conscious of the other woman's frank appraisal.

"I never expected a lady cop to be coming over here," Laney said. "You must be the same one who talked to Stan last week, right?"

"That's right."

"And you investigate murders, too?"

"Sometimes," Jackie said.

After all, there was no need to tell Elaine Symons this was her first homicide.

"Well, I'll be damned." Laney seated herself in another of the chairs and leaned back. She stroked her thighs under the faded denim, then reached absently to knead the flesh of her left upper arm with her right hand.

The woman reminded Jackie of a cat stroking itself with its tongue. The feel of her own flesh seemed to give her intense satisfaction. More than ever, Jackie had the impression of femaleness and a hard-edged sensuality.

She recalled the boy at the salvage shop saying how firmly Stan Lewis was under Laney's thumb. She found that she wasn't all that surprised. Laney appeared to be a lot of woman for a man like Stan.

"I loved your singing," Jackie said. "You have a terrific voice."

"Hey, thanks." Laney looked startled and pleased.

"You're as good as anyone I hear on the radio," Jackie went on, realizing that praise was probably the best way to soften the woman. "Have you ever been recorded?"

"You mean why am I singing in a dump like this, right?"

"You have a terrific voice," Jackie repeated. "I'd pay to listen to you, and I'm not even a big fan of country music."

Laney stroked her other arm, then touched her mouth and picked thoughtfully at a small blemish on her neck. "Things have just never come together for me. I've had a few chances but they didn't work out, and in this business, so many people have talent that, if you blow your chances, you miss the boat. Still, I might—"

She stopped abruptly. Jackie looked at her. "Might what?"

"I might have a shot at something in the next couple of months. It's under discussion." The blonde turned away to look at the platform. "I don't want to talk about it right now."

Jackie digested this in thoughtful silence. "How are you feeling?" she asked.

"What do you mean?" Laney gave her a sharp glance.

"I stopped by the office and your boss told me you haven't been feeling well. But you look okay now."

Laney snorted with laughter. "That poor old fart," she said callously. "Clem's been dying to get into my pants for years. He'd do anything for me. Ugly old bugger, isn't he?" she added. "But his heart's in the right place."

"So you weren't sick today?"

"Sick of that place, maybe. And I had the work all done up, so what's the point in hanging around? I'd rather come over here and practice."

"How about yesterday morning? Clem says you went to the doctor."

"I wasn't feeling good at all yesterday," Laney said, sobering immediately. "Felt like I was coming down with something."

"What doctor did you see?" Jackie flipped open her notebook.

For the first time, Laney began to look uneasy. "I didn't actually go to a doctor. It's tough to see anybody on short notice. I tried to get in at the clinic, but it looked like there was going to be a long wait. So I just picked up some medicine, went home to dope myself and slept for the rest of the day. Did me a world of good."

"What time did you get home?"

"I don't know. Probably around eleven, by the time I hung around the clinic for a while, then bought the medicine and stuff."

"Do you have a cell phone by any chance?"

Again Laney hooted with laughter. "Me? A *cell* phone? I can barely pay my phone bill as it is."

"That's odd." Jackie looked at the woman directly. "Because Stan Lewis says he called you yesterday morning just after ten o'clock and talked to you for a few minutes."

Laney met Jackie's gaze without flinching. Her eyes were deep blue, almost turquoise, such an improbable color that Jackie suspected tinted contacts. No matter how broke she was, Laney Symons probably wasn't the kind of woman who'd be comfortable wearing glasses.

Jackie could almost see the other woman's thought processes moving swiftly, weighing and assessing, deciding on her next move. Elaine Symons was no dummy. In fact, she would probably be a formidable adversary.

"God, look how mixed up I'm getting," Laney said with an easy laugh. "Must be all those drugs I'm taking for my cold. I lost a whole hour somewhere."

"So you were home at ten o'clock, after all."

"I must have been if Stan says he called me then. I guess I didn't hang around the clinic as long as I thought, and I must have slept a whole hour more than I thought. That's real scary, isn't it, when you're sick enough to sleep like a log in the middle of the day?"

"So you do remember talking to Stan Lewis yesterday morning?"

"Of course I do." Laney gave her a scornful glance. "I wasn't *that* sick."

"Do you remember where he was calling from?" Jackie asked, watching her closely.

"Somewhere down toward Ritzville. He was hauling a load of ostrich feed."

At least they agreed on that much, Jackie thought as she jotted notes in her book. They just weren't clear on the times.

She decided to leave the topic of alibis for a moment, sensing that Stan was going to be easier to crack than his girlfriend.

"How was your relationship with Maribel Lewis?" she asked.

Laney shrugged. "Okay, I guess. The old lady hated my guts, but I didn't like her much, either, so you might say we had an understanding."

"Why did she hate you?"

"Because I was going out with Stan. Maribel never cared for anybody who got involved with her precious baby boy."

"I've heard she wasn't too thrilled about his ex-wife."

"Christine?" Laney's lip curled. "You can't blame Maribel for that. Nobody likes a snake."

"You think Chris Lewis is a snake?"

"I think they both are. Chris and that spooky kid sister of hers. They'd just as soon kill you as look at you, either of them. Those are the people you should be talking to."

"We'll get around to them, don't worry." Jackie glanced at her notes, trying to think of something that would catch the woman off guard. "I talked a bit to the boy who works at the salvage place," she said on a sudden inspiration.

"Jimmy? He's a horny little brat. Always hanging around the office trying to feel me up."

"He tells me you have some great tattoos."

Laney smiled placidly. "Yeah, I got a couple. Used to ride with a biker gang in my wild younger days."

"Could I see?"

"Sure." The woman pulled up her sleeve to reveal a colored illustration of a dog performing a lewd act.

"Very interesting," Jackie said. "I don't know if I've ever seen one quite like that." Her voice was calm, but her heart pounded madly.

The dog tattoo wasn't the only one on Laney's rounded arm under the sleeve of her T-shirt. Higher up on her shoulder, nestled between a dagger and a snake, was a small blue pentagram.

14

On Wednesday morning Sergeant Lew Michelson hosted the daily briefing of the homicide task force in a corner of the squad room, seated at the desk next to Jackie's. In addition to Wardlow and Jackie, two other detectives from the squad sat in to hear the case summary, along with patrol officers Howe, Klementz and Pringle from the task force, and Lieutenant Travers who was visiting from the downtown office.

"Okay, Jackie." Michelson looked around at the group. "I guess we're all here. So let's hear what you've got so far."

The sergeant looked tired and haggard. Jackie recalled his determination to lose thirty pounds and wondered if he was starving himself. Their early-morning conversation in the exercise room seemed to have taken place at least a month ago, though it was probably less than a week.

Everything was like that in police work. So much detail got compressed into such a brief space of time, along with occasional moments of high emotion and long spells of boredom, as well as the ever-growing mountains of paperwork that accompanied every case. Sometimes she had trouble recalling what season she was in, let alone what day of the week.

"Detective Kaminsky?" Michelson said. "Are you with us?"

Jackie shook herself and got to her feet, lifting a pile of charts mounted on hardboard, each about three feet square.

"This case is really a convoluted sucker," she told the group. "To help clarify things in my own mind, I asked Officer Howe to come in last night and help me put the elements in some kind of order. I think we can all agree she did a great job."

Brenda Howe was an attractive blonde, neat and trim in her blue uniform. She smiled, clearly gratified by the murmur of praise from her fellow officers. Brenda had been a commercial-art major at the local college, but switched to police work after realistically assessing the chances of getting a job in her own field.

The charts were clear and neatly labeled, with suspects, alibis and motives listed and joined by intersecting lines.

Jackie set one of them on an easel and turned to face the group.

"This is the anonymous-letter chart," she said. "We've listed all the people who got threatening letters and what we know of their contents. Two of the letters are actually reproduced here, the ones sent to Maribel and to Chris Lewis."

She lifted another chart and set it above the first one. "This is the suspect chart. Here we've listed everybody who warrants investigation and their possible motives for killing Maribel Lewis."

Lieutenant Travers took a pair of reading glasses from his shirt pocket and bent forward to squint at the charts. "So I assume we're completely ruling out a random act of violence? An intruder startled during a housebreaking, for instance?''

"There was no sign of a struggle," Wardlow said, "even though she was in the bathtub with her nightgown on. Nothing stolen. Less disturbance, in fact, than during a break-in at the same house last week."

"And the nature of the attack indicates a rage killing," Jackie added. "The pathologist believes the gash to her throat was the lethal blow, but the victim was stabbed another twenty times after that. He called it a killing frenzy, which usually happens in cases where the victim is known to the attacker."

"What's that other chart?" Michelson asked.

Wardlow handed it to Jackie. "Alibis," he said. "And let me tell you, folks, most of them are pretty damned shaky."

"Okay." Michelson leaned back in his chair. His stomach rumbled and he colored with embarrassment, glancing furtively around at the group. "Let's deal with the letters first."

Jackie brought out the first chart and set it on top of the others. "All the chief suspects got a letter except Elaine Symons."

"Is that significant?" Travers asked.

"I don't know." Jackie frowned. "She seemed genuinely blank when I talked about the letters. I don't think Stan showed her his letter, or she would have mentioned it. Laney really likes being in charge of things."

"So why wouldn't he show her the letter?" Wardlow asked.

"Because it said explicitly sexual things about him and Christine. I'm sure he wouldn't want Laney to know he was sleeping with his ex-wife over the

Christmas holidays. Poor Stan, he seems terrified of the woman.''

"How about the picture up in Maribel's attic, the one with blood on it?" Bill Klementz offered. ''That also looked pretty sexual, and it involved Chris Lewis and her husband.''

"So you're thinking maybe Laney Symons was motivated by jealousy?'' Travers asked.

"She seems like the type, from what Jackie says about her,'' Klementz said.

"I wouldn't be surprised, Bill.'' Jackie nodded at the young patrolman. ''Trouble is, the wrong person got killed. If Laney was jealous, why not kill Stan or Chris? Why Maribel?''

"Okay then, who had a motive to kill Maribel Lewis?'' the sergeant asked.

Jackie propped up another chart. "Quite a lot of people. First of all, she was really nasty to Christine. Both her son and his girlfriend apparently weren't too crazy about her. Charlie Roarke, the stable hand, seems to have hated Maribel for some reason. And there are also some pretty shady events in her past that might have come home to roost, like an affair she had years ago with a neighbor's husband.''

"But we've already checked out that angle,'' Wardlow said. "The boyfriend's wife died ten years ago and he's happily remarried, living in Dallas and selling vinyl siding.''

"That's right. So far, Stan and Laney seem to have the strongest motive,'' Jackie said. ''Stan didn't hesitate to tell me he's going to inherit the house. In fact, he's apparently planning to move over there and rent out some of the rooms before he even gets his mother buried. And Laney's hinting about a big opportunity coming up in her music career. I'd guess it might involve spending some cash.''

''So they slap a new mortgage on the house,'' Wardlow suggested, ''and Laney records a demo and heads for Nashville.''

''If she wants to, she'll certainly do it,'' Jackie told the group. ''Stan will have no say at all in the matter. You know, I'm still really interested in these letters,'' she added. ''So is our police psychologist. We even tried to get an FBI profiling team to have a look at the letters and tell us what they could figure out about the person who wrote them.''

''No luck?''

Jackie shook her head. ''They're so backlogged, they can't possibly respond to all requests.'' She consulted a note on her desk. ''They do about eight hundred psychological profiles a year on murder cases, and have to turn away hundreds more. And right now they're in the middle of a round of budget cuts that will mean even further cutbacks in the profiling service.''

''God, I hate budget cuts,'' the lieutenant said bitterly.

''But one of the profilers works out of the Portland field office,'' Jackie went on. ''He's agreed to come over one day next week if we haven't cracked the case by then. He'll at least be able to sit in on a meeting with us and see what he can give us.''

''Well, that's something,'' Michelson said. ''Not goddamn much, but something.''

Wardlow looked at the charts, frowning and rubbing a forefinger thoughtfully across his chin. ''Do we all agree that the letter-writer is also the killer?''

There was a brief silence.

"Well, Brian, it's likely, isn't it?" Michelson said at last. "Because of the explicit nature of the threats plus the fact that Maribel died the way the letter suggested she would."

"Then there's a couple of problems with the Stan-and-Laney theory, don't you think?" Wardlow said. He leaned back in his chair and looked at the others.

When no one said anything, he continued. "First, if Stan Lewis and Laney Symons decided they wanted to off his mother and get their hands on the house, why all the complication? Maribel lived there all alone. They could have just pushed her down the stairs and made it look like an accident. Why would they send a bunch of silly letters to other people or break into the house and leave a nude picture of Stanley and a mess of candle wax on the floor?"

"I've thought about that," Jackie said. "They could have been trying to pin it on Desirée in case any suspicion came their way. Everybody knows what the girl's like, and the kind of satanist stuff she's into. I'd suspect Laney knows quite a lot about what that involves. So the mumbo jumbo immediately makes everybody suspect Desirée as the killer. I certainly did."

"But you don't anymore?" Michelson asked.

"I don't know what to think. Most of the teachers I've questioned believe she was in class all morning, but they can't swear to it. People seem to disagree a lot about Desirée in general. Maybe," Jackie said wryly, "she really *can* make herself invisible."

"But she has no motive." Brenda Howe stared at the chart. "Jackie and I couldn't think of a single motive for her to kill Maribel."

"Unless she just likes the idea of killing people," Klementz suggested. "Maybe the kid's made some kind of pact with the devil to kill all those people she sent letters to, and she chose Maribel as the easiest one to start with."

Everybody in the room stared at the young officer while the silence lengthened uncomfortably.

"My God, Bill," Jackie said at last, turning away with a nervous shudder. "Quit saying things like that! We don't want to come up with any more bodies in this case."

"But there's another problem with the Stan-and-Laney scenario," Wardlow went on, doggedly pursuing his own line of thought. "If the killer is also the letter-writer, then the two of them were the ones who sent all the letters. That means Laney would have to know the contents of Stan's letter, right? But Kaminsky thinks he'd move heaven and earth to keep her from knowing he was in bed with Chris a few months ago."

"And if they were using the letters to deflect suspicion from themselves," Brenda said, "wouldn't they have sent one to Laney?"

"This is making my head ache," Michelson complained. "What do we have in the way of physical evidence?"

"Almost nothing. Certainly not enough to get a warrant for any kind of search." Jackie told them about the autopsy findings. "We have a right-handed killer using an unusual type of double-edged blade, possibly a ceremonial dagger. Again, this ties in neatly with Desirée's pagan religion. But Laney Symons had some ties to satanism in her past, as well. She laughed it off and called it 'kid stuff' when I asked about the pentagram tattooed on her arm, but who knows what's really going on there?''

"Anything else?" Travers asked.

Wardlow shook his head. "No prints from the first break-in, at least nothing that hasn't been cleared to family members. In fact, prints wouldn't mean anything in this case since we're assuming the assailant was known to the victim so his prints might reasonably be found around the house, anyway."

"Nothing tracked away? No bloody shoe prints?"

"Not a thing."

"Any blood left at the scene not belonging to the victim?"

"No evidence of defense wounds on the body," Jackie said. "And Maribel was already in the water when her throat was cut, so she bled quite neatly into the water. It was a tidy little crime scene," she added grimly, "if you don't count a poor lady drowning in her own blood, and pentagrams all over the walls."

"So the killer might even have got away without a lot of blood on his clothes?"

"Dr. Klein figures he could have, depending on where he was standing relative to the bathtub and how quickly he shoved her underwater after slashing her throat."

Another silence fell. People glanced at each other, then looked away quickly.

"We've pulled records on three of the suspects so far." Brenda consulted a sheaf of papers on her desk. "Elaine Symons served probation eleven years ago on drug charges and prostitution, and did thirty days for assault in 1990."

"What kind of assault?" Michelson asked.

"A fight in a bar. She beat up another woman, sent her to the hospital."

"Any weapons involved?"

Brenda shook her head. "Apparently Laney's a gal who uses her fists."

"Who else has a record?" Travers asked.

"Stan Lewis has a nice little sheet. Two petty thefts, two assaults and one possession of cocaine but no proof of intent. And Charlie Roarke went down for two years on a burglary rap."

"Charming bunch," Michelson commented. "Anybody else showing anything?"

Brenda shook her head. "Not that we could find out. Jackie's searching the FBI computer files for anything out of state."

"Okay. Let's look at alibis. Who's got an ironclad one?"

"Nobody," Wardlow said. "I drove to Richland last night and couldn't find anybody who saw Stan Lewis along the way, though he did get there around one o'clock. That would have been lots of time to kill his mother, get in the truck and haul his load of ostrich feed."

"And Elaine Symons wasn't seen at the clinic at all on Monday morning," Jackie added, "although the nurse on duty admitted it was a real zoo in there and she could easily have missed somebody who didn't come up to the desk and check in."

"How about this phone call they're talking about?" Michelson asked.

"I'm not sure what I think of that." Jackie frowned at one of the charts. "Brian says there's a phone booth outside the service station at Ritzville. Stan Lewis could have made his call from there like he says he did. But Laney's not clear on the time, so it doesn't mean anything as an alibi. Especially when they could be covering for each other.''

"Charlie Roarke didn't show up for work at all on Monday morning," Wardlow said. "He claims he was in bed with a hangover, but there's no proof of that."

"What else do we know about this Roarke guy?" Michelson asked.

Jackie nodded at Bill Klementz, who sat up straighter in his chair and opened a file. "He's twenty-six. Knocked around a lot, been a rodeo rider and worked at a few restaurant jobs, busboy and such. In 1991 he was convicted of burglary for breaking into the hardware store he was working at and cleaning out the safe. Served sixteen months in a medium-security prison over in Oregon."

"Family or friends? Anybody who knows anything about him?"

Klementz shook his head. "Seems to be pretty much of a loner. The landlady calls him a nice boy, but says she doesn't see much of him."

"Does he pay his rent on time?"

"No problem with that. He's got a steady job at the horse ranch now, been working there for almost four years."

"And he sleeps with Christine Lewis."

"Just a couple of times," Wardlow put in quickly. "It happened over the Christmas holidays, but it never went any further than a two-night stand. Nobody else even knew about it."

"Somebody did," Jackie said grimly. "Whoever sent those letters knew about it."

Again the officers exchanged nervous glances.

"We've talked about the Moreau girl and her alibi." Michelson cleared his throat and continued, "She was in school during the time of the murder, right?"

"I'm still not convinced of that," Jackie said. "I want to have another chat with her, but Desirée's a pretty tough case. Talking to her is like trying to hold water in your hands. She just keeps slipping away."

"And finally we have Chris Lewis," Michelson went on with a glance at Wardlow.

"Chris is a strange one, too," Jackie said. "Everybody seems to have a different opinion about her, and nobody's neutral. Either she's a monster or an angel, depending on your point of view."

"Who thinks she's a monster?"

"All the women in the case seem to have that opinion. Maribel hated her, Laney's certainly not thrilled about her, and even her sister has lots of hostility toward her." She avoided Wardlow's eyes. "On the other hand, all the men I've talked to think Chris Lewis is a great person."

"So, Detective, what do you think?" Travers asked her. "You're a woman."

Jackie grinned. "Thank you for pointing that out, Lieutenant."

Her comment made everyone chuckle and helped to ease the tension. The other two detectives on the squad, neither of whom had contributed to the discussion, got up and nodded to the rest of the group, then left quietly.

"I don't know what to think," Jackie said in answer to the lieutenant's question. "Chris seemed like a pretty straight shooter to me, and really concerned about her kid. I liked her. But," she added, "we only talked for a few minutes. I plan to have another interview with her as soon as I can arrange it.''

At the side of the room, Officer Pringle cleared his throat and shuffled some papers on his desk. Everybody looked at him in surprise. David Pringle was a competent policeman, but notoriously reserved. He worked by the book, paid little attention to the gibes and teasing of other officers and spoke only when necessary.

"Yes, Dave?" Michelson said with an encouraging smile. "You got something for us?''

"I talked to one of the neighbors yesterday just before I went off shift," Pringle said. "She told me Chris Lewis committed the murder.''

The others sat up a little straighter and looked at the young patrolman.

"So who's the neighbor?" Wardlow asked.

"Her name's Morgan," Pringle said, consulting his notes. "Fiona Morgan.''

"You're kidding." Travers stared at the junior officer. "*Fiona Morgan* is a witness in this case?''

"Who's Fiona Morgan?" Brenda asked.

"City councillor," Michelson told her. "Very powerful woman. Routinely votes against increasing the policing budget for the city. Fiona Morgan is one of the main reasons your salary's so low and you don't have enough manpower in your squad.''

"So why does she think Chris Lewis is guilty?" Wardlow asked.

Pringle consulted his notes again. "She witnessed a serious altercation between Chris Lewis and the victim during the summer. And she saw the truck and horse trailer parked outside the house on Monday morning at the time of the murder. I told her a detective would probably be coming around to talk to her sometime today.''

''Well, thanks a bunch for mentioning this so early, Dave,'' Wardlow muttered grimly. ''You've been a really big help.''

''Leave him alone, Brian,'' Jackie said. ''Thanks, Dave.'' She cast a smile at the solemn young officer. ''I'll go see her as soon as I can. What's the address?''

She wrote it down, then looked up in surprise.

''Wait a minute. That's the big house on the corner, right? Just down the street from Maribel's place?''

The patrolman nodded.

''Morgan,'' Jackie said thoughtfully. ''I think I've met her son. In fact, he's the neighbor kid who saw the lights in Maribel's attic during the break-in last week. Remember, Brian?''

''She's a single mother.'' Pringle consulted his notes again. ''Divorced for twelve years. One son named Joel, aged seventeen.''

''That's the one. Is she a reliable witness, Dave, would you say?''

The officer nodded. ''She seems like a pretty bright lady. Very sure of herself.''

Jackie looked around at the group and began to clear her desk. ''This could be just the break we've been looking for. I'll talk to Fiona Morgan right away and let you know what I find out.''

15

Jackie had never actually met Fiona Morgan, though now that she'd been told the connection she could recall the woman's picture appearing frequently in the local newspapers.

She rang the doorbell and stood restlessly on the front porch of the big house, hoping the councillor was going to live up to Officer Pringle's estimation of her as a witness. In any sticky case, especially a homicide, investigating officers prayed for an eyewitness. A firsthand account of a crime was worth a mountain of painstakingly gathered circumstantial evidence, but only if the witness was believable.

While she waited, Jackie looked around at the exterior of the house. It was old but well-kept, with the appearance of having been recently renovated. A lot of the wooden trim seemed new. Idly she wondered if Paul had done some work on the house during the years he'd labored in this city as a skilled carpenter, doing restoration projects on many of the heritage homes.

The thought of him made her remember their quarrel the day before, and the frantic passionate lovemaking that preceded it. She felt a fresh tug of unhappiness, accompanied by a hot wave of yearning that almost made her forget her errand.

Abruptly the carved oak door opened and a woman appeared. "Yes?"

Jackie held up her badge. "Detective Kaminsky, Spokane P.D."

Fiona Morgan smiled and held the door wider. "Do come in, Detective. They told me you'd be dropping by. You're very prompt."

"I try to be." Jackie stepped past Fiona into a hardwood entry foyer covered with an Axminster rug. An old brass-bound chest stood along one wall, topped by a huge blue glass bowl filled with daisies.

Jackie followed the other woman into the living room and sat in a wing chair near the fireplace. She looked around. The house was gracious without pretension, comfortable and cozy without any cloying elements.

"I really like this place," she said. "It seems so warm."

Fiona Morgan beamed with pleasure. A tall big-boned woman, she wore a green tweed skirt with a matching pullover and cardigan of moss green cashmere, flat shoes and a single string of pearls. Her dark hair was worn straight and chin length, held back with a tortoiseshell barrette.

The woman appeared to be in her late forties, a few years younger than Maribel Lewis. She had a hearty country look, as if she might be most happy striding through the heather on a Scottish hillside. She had, in fact, a voice that retained a touch of a Scottish brogue, and her green eyes were direct and alert.

"What a nice thing to say, Detective. Would you like a cup of coffee or tea?"

"I'd love some coffee," Jackie said.

Her hostess smiled and vanished, leaving Jackie to examine her surroundings.

The living room seemed luxurious but well-used. Jackie had the feeling that family members actually sat in the big leather chairs, made fires on the hearth and rested their feet on the comfy ottomans while they read. Plaid-blanketed pet baskets flanked both sides of the hearth, one large and one small, though the animals themselves were not in evidence.

A drum table near Jackie's chair, inlaid with ivory and ebony, was covered with pictures of Joel Morgan as a winsome golden-haired baby, a leggy child, a skinny teenager and the handsome, square-jawed young man he was now. He looked happy, and Jackie found herself returning his smiles. She glanced up when Fiona came back with a laden tray.

"My goodness!" Jackie got to her feet and cleared a space on the coffee table. "Look at all this. I should have come and helped you."

Fiona waved a hand dismissively and picked up the coffeepot. "Nonsense, my dear. Elsa's in the kitchen, and we had everything ready in advance. Now, would you prefer milk with your coffee?"

"Just black, thank you."

Fiona poured the coffee, handed it over and filled her own cup, then settled into the other chair. "I saw you smiling at my son's picture just now. Do you know Joel, by any chance?"

"Yes, I've met him a couple of times in conjunction with this case we're working on. In fact," Jackie added, "I think Joel and I may have a friend in common."

"And who might that be?"

Jackie felt uncomfortable. If Joel hadn't yet mentioned Alex to his mother, she didn't want to betray any confidences.

But the woman laughed heartily. "Don't look so frightened, Detective. I know all about this wee lass. Alexandra, isn't it? She seems to have thrown my poor lad into quite a spin."

"Really?" Jackie said, pleased. "Things must be really progressing."

Fiona smiled. "Well, if two-hour phone calls are any indication, I'd say so. Here, Detective, have one of Elsa's oatcakes. It's taken me fifteen years to teach the dear woman how to make them properly."

"Oh my." Jackie bit into one of the warm oatcakes and sighed in bliss. "This is delicious, Mrs. Morgan."

"Call me Fiona."

"Thank you. And my name's Jackie."

By now she was so seduced by the warmth and charm of her surroundings, she'd almost forgotten the reason for her interview.

"I understand you're a city councillor, Fiona," she said, flipping open her notebook.

"I am indeed. Have another oatcake. You're just skin and bones, my dear."

Jackie chuckled. "Hardly, but I can see how you'd be a success in politics."

"Ah, but there are many who think I'm no success. The chief of police among them," Fiona said with a wry smile.

"I understand you regularly vote against increasing the budget appropriation for city policing. It causes some tension in the department."

"I do indeed, but not from nastiness," Fiona said firmly. "There was such terrible waste in the previous

civic administration, you see, a level of fiscal irre-
sponsibility that was practically criminal. We need to
restore balance and get our financial house in order
before we can start looking at any frills."

Jackie set her cup on one of the leather coasters
protecting the carved wood of the table. "Proper policing for a major urban area should hardly be considered a frill, Fiona."

Her hostess laughed, clearly unruffled. "Of course
it shouldn't. And I didn't mean to imply that it was.
I only meant that we have to repair our system and
look to the infrastructure. We need more schools, better roads and hospitals, along with some of the other
essential services, before we can start mucking about
with extra spending."

"So a larger allocation to the police force won't be
ruled out forever? We're really short-staffed and over-
worked, you know."

"I know you are." Fiona leaned across the table
to pat her visitor's arm. "And city council appreciates
your efforts, Jackie, more than you'll ever know. If
we can all be patient, these hard years will pass soon
enough. Here, try a shortbread cookie. They're my
mother's recipe, straight from Edinburgh. Joel loves
them, so it's hard to keep them in the house."

Jackie felt herself beguiled again by the woman's
charm, though she suspected there was quite a lot of
the professional politician beneath that winsome
brogue. And a bit of steel, as well, she thought.

For all her coziness and humor, Fiona Morgan
probably wasn't a woman you'd want for an enemy.

"I'd better get down to business," Jackie said with
an apologetic smile as she reached for her notebook

again. "Much as I'd like to, I can't just relax here all day, gobbling cookies and oatcakes."

Fiona settled back in the chair with her hands folded, waiting calmly while Jackie uncapped her pen and turned to a fresh page.

"I guess we'll start with your full name," Jackie said.

"Fiona Elspeth Blaylogh Morgan."

"Age?" Jackie felt a flash of embarrassment. "I'm sorry. You don't really have to be specific if it's—"

"Forty-seven," her hostess interrupted firmly. "I've no patience with all this coy nonsense about concealing one's age. I'm proud of every year I've spent on this earth."

"Me, too," Jackie said, liking the woman again. "And how long have you lived at this address, Fiona?"

"For twenty-one years. My husband and I came here when we were newlyweds. He'd finished a course in engineering at the university in Edinburgh, and there were job opportunities in America, so we screwed up our courage and decided to emigrate."

"Was there any particular reason you came to Spokane?"

"My older sister lived here." Fiona's strong face softened. "Margaret, her name was, but we called her Molly. She and Tony lived just down the street in that big green house you pass when you come from downtown."

"That must have been nice for you, to have a family member so close when you'd just moved to a strange country."

"It was wonderful," Fiona said with a faraway smile. "Like being little girls again, playing house,

only now we had real houses. I could run over to
Molly's place for tea, and she could come over to
mine and bring her embroidery while our husbands
were working. And then we had the babies..."

"Babies?" Jackie asked when Fiona paused, looking dreamily out the window.

"Molly had two little ones, and I had Joel a few
years after James and I came here. We'd dress them
up and take them out in their prams to walk in the
park, or stay indoors to play on rainy days. It really
was heaven."

But there was a deep sadness in the woman's voice
as she talked. Also a peculiar edge of anger.

"I take it your sister doesn't live there any
longer?"

Fiona Morgan gripped her hands tightly in her lap.
"My sister is dead. She moved away from here a few
years after Joel was born, and she died ten years ago
in southern Texas."

"I'm sorry," Jackie murmured.

"Breast cancer," Fiona said. "Molly died of breast
cancer. At least," she added, her voice hardening,
"that's what it said on the death certificate."

"But you think it was something different?"

Fiona turned to look at Jackie directly. Her face
was a mask of hatred and pain. "I think," she said,
her brogue more pronounced, "that Molly died of a
broken heart."

"Why?" Jackie asked.

"Because she'd lost faith in her man. He betrayed
her and she never got over the pain."

Scattered impressions began to come together in
Jackie's mind. She felt a growing tension and a surge

of excitement. "Could you give me your sister's married name?"

"It was Manari. Margaret Joyce Manari."

So her husband was Tony Manari.

Jackie wrote down the information without expression, but her mind was racing. Tony Manari was the name of the neighbor who'd been involved with Maribel Lewis in that long-ago affair, about the same time she'd been embezzling twenty thousand dollars from the bank where she worked.

But did that mean...?

"I assume you've already heard about this unpleasant bit of family history?" Fiona said dryly, watching her face.

"Some of it, yes."

"Well, then, you can be sure I had no reason to love Maribel Lewis. But that doesn't mean I can't be a reliable witness to recent events."

As if suiting action to words, Fiona cleared the emotion from her face and voice. Once again she was all business.

"All right," Jackie said. "Then I guess we'd better talk about those recent events, all right?"

Fiona leaned back in her chair. "Very well, and I'll try to be as accurate as possible. Now, I told the young policeman about their altercation last spring, did I not? That dreadful scene in the back alley?"

"I think you mentioned something about it to Officer Pringle," Jackie said. "But if you don't mind, I'd like you to tell it again so I can hear the whole story in your own words."

"It was late in June," Fiona began without hesitation. "I recall the date clearly because I was hosting the annual summer garden party for my literary group."

"Literary group?"

"There are about a dozen of us. We get together to talk about books we're reading and discuss the classics. Also, a few of us who do some writing on our own try to encourage one another."

"That sounds nice," Jackie ventured.

"You're being diplomatic, I presume. You probably think it sounds dreadfully boring. Actually the group is very nice. We've been meeting for years, but I must say, we've never had a party like the one Maribel Lewis and her daughter-in-law treated us to last year."

"What happened?"

"It was twilight," Fiona began. "You know that lovely misty time of day when the petunias smell so wonderful? Well, I'd served the cheese and fruit and we were all settling in for a nice cozy chat when we heard the most awful noise."

Fiona shook her head and shuddered dramatically, but her eyes were bright. Jackie could see she relished telling the story.

"We could hear this dreadful screaming, crying, filthy swearwords," her hostess continued. "The noise seemed to be coming closer to us down the back alley. Naturally we all drifted over to the fence to see what was going on."

"Naturally," Jackie agreed. Fiona gave her a quick glance, then continued.

"Maribel Lewis was chasing her daughter-in-law down the alley with a broom. I swear, it looked like something from an old movie. The whole thing would have been comical if it weren't so tragic. Christine was almost naked, wearing nothing but panties and a bra. Maribel kept shrieking at her like a madwoman, beating her with the broom until she actually raised welts on the poor girl's body.''

"My God," Jackie said. "In full view of all the neighbors?"

"Maribel was like a woman possessed. I don't think she knew what she was doing, or whether anybody was watching her. She seemed insane with rage."

"Do you have any idea what she was upset about?"

Fiona shrugged. "Something involving Stanley, I expect. Maribel was always so protective of that loutish young man, and he and Christine were in the middle of their breakup at the time. The next day Chris had a friend come over to remove her belongings. As far as I know she left Maribel's house for good immediately after that scene in the alley."

"I can certainly understand why," Jackie said. "What happened that evening? Did Christine go back to Maribel's house to get her clothes?"

Fiona's handsome face twisted with distress. "It was dreadful. Maribel finally stopped beating the girl and tramped off down the alley with her broom, still screaming abuse. Christine sat down on the gravel in the alley and curled up, sobbing. I still recall the way she tried to hide her body because she'd begun to realize, of course, that all the neighbors were watching over their back fences. We had no idea what to do."

Jackie looked down at her notebook for a moment. "It surprises me that nobody offered to take her inside their house."

"Why don't you say what you mean, Jackie?" Fiona asked sharply. "I presume you're wondering why I didn't help?"

Jackie looked up and met the woman's eyes. "She was half-naked, hurt and crying. It would be the neighborly thing to do, wouldn't it?"

Fiona's face hardened again. "I've tried not to get involved with that family and their troubles. Over the years they've been so..." She paused. "I didn't even like having Joel work over there, but he's been mowing lawns and shoveling sidewalks for most of the neighbors since he was twelve, and I don't like to interfere in his business."

There was a brief silence while Jackie wrote notes in her book.

"In fact," Fiona went on, "it was Joel who finally came to Christine's rescue."

"What did he do?"

"He'd been trimming a hedge down the street when the uproar began. After he realized what was happening, he came running down the alley and gave Christine his shirt to cover herself, then went back and asked Maribel for the girl's handbag so she could get her keys. I assume she drove to a friend's house and borrowed some clothes, but I never heard the details."

Jackie thought about the handsome boy she'd met, the only one with enough courage and decency to do the right thing for poor Chris Lewis. While the rest of the neighbors were gawking and enjoying the spectacle, he'd given comfort to the woman, even braved Maribel's outrage.

"It must have taken a lot of courage," she said,

"for him to go over to Maribel's house when she was so angry."

"I suppose it did," Fiona said idly. "But Joel's that kind of boy. Besides, he's always been a special pet of Maribel's. She never liked any of the other neighborhood children, but she's been fond of Joel since she began giving him cookies when he was just a little tyke."

"I recall him telling me that. So you think," Jackie went on, "that a humiliating scene like that would be a motive for murder?"

"Don't you agree? Think about it." Fiona leaned back in her chair with an expansive gesture. "That was an episode witnessed by others. There must have been a dreadful amount of tension and abuse in that household for such a scene to spill out into the open. Normally people try to keep such things hidden."

"But why would Chris Lewis be motivated to kill the woman after all these months? She'd moved away from the house and from all accounts has been living successfully on her own."

"Ah, but feelings of hatred and revenge can fester." Fiona poured more coffee in each of their cups and offered the cookie tray again. "Besides, neighborhood gossip maintains that Maribel wasn't done with her mischief."

"What do you mean?"

"She was trying to turn the children against Chris. Word has it she wanted to get custody of Gordie and take him away from his mother. I expect she was doing it mostly to hurt Christine. That was Maribel's style, after all."

"I see." Jackie looked thoughtfully at her notes. "I take it you really disliked Maribel Lewis."

"I've known the woman ever since I moved here," Fiona said coldly. "And as I've said, I had no reason to be fond of her. She was a perfectly dreadful person. No doubt there were lots of people who wanted her dead, but I should think Chris wanted it more than anyone."

"And you saw Christine's truck parked outside the house on Monday morning?"

"As clear as I see you sitting there," Fiona said promptly. "I had the day off and I was working with my houseplants, taking them outside one by one to spray them and bring them in again."

"If I could interrupt," Jackie said, "you mentioned having the day off. Where do you work?"

"I have a part-time job at a local veterinarian clinic. I usually work there in the afternoons, helping out in the large-animal surgery."

Jackie looked at the woman's strong square hands, folded calmly in her lap. "That must be an interesting job. Were you trained in veterinary work?"

"Not really, though I liked to help out in the stables at my father's estate when I was a girl. I've always been fond of animals."

"I never asked about your husband," Jackie said. "I understand you're divorced?"

"Is that relevant at all?" Fiona's tone was cold.

"It's just routine. If you should happen to be called as a key witness at a murder trial, the prosecutor will certainly want to establish all these background details for the jury."

"James and I divorced twelve years ago, just before Joel started school. My ex-husband moved to Oregon shortly afterward."

"Could you give me his name and address?"

"I'm afraid not." Fiona fingered the edge of a woolen afghan thrown over the back of the sofa. "James died two years after our divorce. He was shot to death late at night on a street in downtown Portland. The police never charged anybody with the shooting. Apparently they assumed it was a purely random killing."

"I see." Jackie paused. "Getting back to this past Monday morning," she said after a moment, "can you tell me exactly what you saw?"

"I saw a truck and horse trailer pull up in front of Maribel's house," Fiona said. "I was on the front porch dusting my impatiens and I remember being surprised to recognize Christine behind the wheel. I knew she worked with horses, but I'd never actually seen her driving around with a trailer like that."

"You're sure it was her?"

"Absolutely. She drove by just a few feet away from me."

"Okay. Anything else you noticed?"

Fiona frowned. "I think there were horses in the trailer," she said at last. "I could see how it kept shifting and rocking after she'd parked."

"And what time was this?"

"Probably around ten-fifteen."

"Are you sure of the time?" Jackie asked.

"Quite sure. I'd been watching 'Good Morning America,' which ends at ten. As soon as it was over, I started working on my plants. I always do them in the same order, taking the begonias outside first for a rinse and a dusting of insecticide powder. Next I do the impatiens."

Jackie gave the woman an encouraging smile. "You're an excellent witness, Fiona. My job would be a whole lot easier if everybody was so observant. Did you happen to notice anything else?''

"Not that I can recall."

"Nobody coming or going? Nothing unusual around the Lewis house or the rest of the neighborhood?''

"It was a quiet Monday morning. The children had gone back to school and the entire street was deserted."

"All right. Did you see Chris Lewis get out of the truck and go into the house?''

"I wouldn't have been able to see her if she had. The tree branches hang close to the street and there's a big lilac hedge along the sidewalk that was just beginning to leaf out.''

"So what time did the truck and horse trailer leave?''

"I didn't see them leave. I finished with the last of the impatiens, took them inside and had a cup of tea. When I came out with the Boston ferns, the street was empty again.''

"What time was that?''

"About ten forty-five. I remember looking at my watch and thinking Chris hadn't stayed more than half an hour, so if she came to hash things out with Maribel they probably hadn't resolved very much.''

The two women exchanged a glance while Jackie thought about what had actually happened inside that house on Monday morning.

There was an awkward silence. Finally she got to her feet and gathered up her briefcase and shoulder bag. "Thanks for the coffee and cookies, Fiona. And thank you very much for all your information. You've been a big help. I'm sure we'll be in touch with you again.''

Fiona followed Jackie to the door and stood watching as she descended the steps. "I hope you get to the bottom of this. It's a terrible thing to have happen right in one's own neighborhood.''

Jackie looked up at the woman as she stood framed in the doorway of her house. "We're doing the best we can,'' she said.

Back at the police car she hesitated for a moment, then dropped the keys into her pocket and walked down the street to the Lewis house, looking at its dark silent bulk against the blue arch of springtime sky.

16

While she stood with one hand resting on the front gate, brooding over the Lewis house and all its mysteries, a couple of teenagers ambled down the walk toward her.

"Hey, Jackie!" one of them called.

She turned, startled from her reverie, and saw Alex approaching with Joel Morgan. Both of them wore faded jeans and dark green sweatshirts with some kind of insignia on the front.

"Band clothes," Joel said when he saw her looking at the shirts. "We performed at the pep rally this morning." He put one arm around the girl beside him. "Alex played her first solo."

"I was terrible," Alex said. "I made a ton of mistakes, Jackie. I could just *die*."

Joel hugged her cheerfully and grinned at Jackie over the girl's head. "Don't listen to her, Detective Kaminsky. She was great. The whole school applauded."

Jackie smiled, warmed by their youth and exuberance and their obvious happiness with each other. "So where are you two going?" she asked.

"We have to drop by my place to pick up some stuff. And I want Alex to meet my mother. She's at home this morning."

"But…" Jackie looked at the two young faces in confusion. "How are you allowed to be out wandering around at ten o'clock in the morning? Is this legal?"

"We both have a spare in the third period," Alex said.

"So if you have a spare period, you don't have to stay on school grounds?"

"Not if you have a legitimate errand and you get a pass slip from the study-hall supervisor," Joel said.

Jackie smiled. "And taking a girl across town to meet your mother—that's considered a legitimate errand nowadays?"

"Actually," Joel said, "I'm collecting some research materials that I need for biology class. I've been doing a conditioning experiment with white mice in a maze."

"And Alex?"

"She's helping me carry the mice," he said placidly. "They're in a really big cage. Besides," he added, hugging the girl again, "she did such a great job on that flute solo, the teachers would probably let her get away with anything right now."

The change in Alex was certainly astonishing. She was radiant, so unlike the shy teenager of only a week or two ago. "You look beautiful, sweetie," Jackie murmured, reaching out to lift a strand of the girl's shining golden hair.

"She sure does," Joel agreed proudly.

Jackie let the strand of hair fall onto Alex's collar, her mind returning to what Joel had told her. "If you didn't have a spare period," she asked, "would there be any way you could still get off school grounds without being in trouble?"

"All kinds of ways," Joel said. "You could get a friend to log in for you, or forge a teacher's initials on a hallway pass, or—"

He stopped abruptly when Alex stared at him in surprise.

"Not that I'd ever do any of that stuff," he told Jackie quickly, looking a little abashed. "But everybody knows how to beat the system if they want to."

"I see."

Alex squeezed the boy's arm and leaned close to him. "Joel is going to show me his room," she told Jackie. "He's got all kinds of neat stuff. He collects Native American artifacts."

Joel grinned. "My room's such a mess right now I wouldn't even want any of the guys to see it, let alone you."

"I won't care. My room's always a big mess, too," Alex said. "Isn't it, Jackie?"

"As I recall," Jackie said thoughtfully, "the place did look like a bit of a war zone last time I visited, all right. And I don't suppose it helps to have a herd of puppies trampling around in there."

Joel rolled his eyes and groaned. "Not the *puppies!* Don't get her started on the puppies or we'll never get back to school in time for class. Come on, Alex, let's hurry up so you'll have a few minutes to spend with my mother."

Both young people began to move away, smiling over their shoulders.

"Bye, Jackie," Alex called.

"See you, honey. Congratulations on your first solo. And tell Adrienne I said hi, and I'll call this weekend, okay?"

"Goodbye, Detective," Joel said, his blue eyes crinkling with warmth. "Have a nice day."

He paused a moment, then murmured something to his companion and came back toward Jackie while the girl waited on the sidewalk.

"Thank you for introducing me to Alex," he said with boyish sincerity. "I really appreciate it. She's a terrific girl."

"She certainly is. I'm glad you're getting along so well."

Jackie watched as they hurried away, laughing and talking, their heads close together. She smiled, feeling cheered and a little more optimistic.

Those two teenagers didn't really care what had happened a few days ago in that dark house beyond the lilac hedge. They were wrapped up in each other and the excitement of their young lives.

The world moved on, Jackie thought. Life kept rolling forward, and misery eventually turned back to happiness. The only problem was that her job didn't tend to move on. No matter what happened in other people's lives, she was stuck with all the misery of the world, and the dreadful things human beings kept doing to each other....

She shook herself a little, opened the gate latch and went inside, starting up the walk toward the place where Maribel Lewis had lived her quarrelsome life and died a grisly death.

Desirée crouched in the dank leafy cavern between the two old buildings watching the policewoman talk with Joel and the blond girl.

She saw the young people walk away, arm in arm. When Joel's head bent toward the girl, Desirée felt bile rising in her throat and wondered if she was going to throw up.

You don't know anything about him, she told the girl with silent fury. I've lived here since he was a little boy. I could tell you all kinds of things about Joel Morgan that you'll never even know, you bitch.

They were gone now, out of sight around the corner of the Morgan house. He'd told the policewoman he was taking that girl home to meet his mother.

She sank onto the moldy leaves and, hugging her knees, curled in a ball of misery as she stared at the opposite wall.

Fiona would probably love Alexandra Gerard, who was such a little golden princess. They'd sip tea by the hearth and chat about music while Joel sat in one of the big plaid armchairs looking proud and happy.

Desirée wanted to kill all of them. Some slow torturous death that would make them really suffer, and all the time they'd know who was killing them.

Fingering her golden nose ring, she gave serious thought to the matter.

A fire would be good, she decided. Burning was a terrible way to die. She could set fires around the perimeter of the house and light them all at once, then throw a brick through the window with a letter attached telling them why they were dying. That old place would go up like kindling, and by the time the firemen came, there wouldn't be a soul left alive.

The thought of their agonized screams entertained her briefly, but Desirée knew she couldn't bear to kill Joel. He was the center of her existence, the reason for almost everything she did. Without Joel, not even the goddesses would be enough to fill the void in her life. Maybe she could just kill the girl and his bossy mother, but run bravely through the flames in time to rescue Joel.

He'd realize she was the one who'd saved his life, and he'd be so grateful. Joel would tell her how wonderful she was and hug her the same way he hugged Alex Gerard....

Again her stomach began to churn. She tried to distract herself by thinking about other things, like Maribel's death and the ongoing murder investigation.

Apparently the police suspected Chris of killing Maribel. Desirée was both astonished and pleased by this development.

She'd overheard Chris talking to Stan Lewis about the investigation one night after they thought the kids were asleep. Their voices had been so low that Desirée was forced to crouch in the hallway with her ear pressed onto a water glass against the wall before she could hear what they were saying about the police.

In fact, this was another surprising thing that seemed to be happening lately, though it wasn't nearly as appealing as Chris's being hounded by the police. Stan Lewis was spending more time at their place again, coming by secretly to talk with Chris late at night.

Desirée didn't know what the visits meant, but she didn't like them at all. She couldn't stand the thought of Chris and Stan moving back together, maybe even living in Maribel's house where Chris would rule like a queen in her own palace.

She tried to imagine what Maribel would have thought about everything that was going on, but whenever she pictured the woman, she saw a river of blood that made her feel sick again.

Maybe Chris would go to jail, instead of living with Stan in his mother's house.

Serve her right to be convicted of murder, Desirée thought bitterly. And in jail she'd be stuck with other women all the time. Chris would really hate that. No men to tempt or flirt with, to have at her beck and call whenever she crooked her finger and gave one of those phony little shy smiles of hers.

But if Chris went to jail, Gordie would have to live with his father.

Desirée didn't know what to think about that prospect. Though he was her nephew, he was more like a little brother and she felt very protective of him. Still, Gordie was sort of a creepy kid. Most of the time he acted like a fat whining baby. But he was almost twelve and in some ways he was starting to change.

For instance, he was getting interested in sex. He even kept smutty magazines under his mattress. Desirée knew this because she'd found them more than once and been both fascinated and disgusted by the crude images of bondage and sadism.

Gordie, though, was probably just excited by the naked women. Boys were so gross.

Desirée grimaced, peeking out through the screen of branches to see what the policewoman was doing.

Kaminsky was standing on the front walk, staring up at the house as if her thoughts were a thousand miles away. She wore charcoal gray pants and a navy blazer over a cream-colored woolen turtleneck, and looked both beautiful and businesslike. Her dark hair lifted and stirred in the morning breeze, and her cheeks were pink with cold.

She's so strong, Desirée thought, watching the woman. She even carries a loaded gun at her belt. I'll bet she could probably draw it and shoot me right now, and not even blink.

The thought gave Desirée a delicious shiver of terror. She had an irrational desire to attract the policewoman's attention, make her realize somebody was hiding between the two old buildings. It would be fun to have Kaminsky chase her, try to catch her. Desirée knew she could get away. She was familiar with every inch of this neighborhood.

But it would be too risky.

She pulled a slip of creased yellow paper from her pocket. "Desirée Moreau is excused from physical education," it said in Miss Cooper's childish handwriting. "The nurse confirms that she's suffering from menstrual cramps."

Cramps, Desirée thought scornfully. As if you ever had cramps when you drank tea-tree tonic.

But the note also said she needed to be back in class by ten-thirty, and that didn't give her much time. She watched Detective Kaminsky move up the walk, hesitate by the front door of Maribel's house then head around toward the back.

When the policewoman was out of sight, Desirée slipped through the cavern between the two buildings and hurried down the street, her dark clothing blending into the shadows.

Jackie stood by the side of the house looking up at the weathered shingles around the dormer. The Ident technicians had scoured the place for clues and looked in every conceivable hiding place for a double-bladed knife, but they'd found nothing. Within a day or two the house would be released to Stan Lewis, who was still waiting anxiously to move in.

She dug in her pocket for the tagged key, then moved down the back walk toward the gate, peering into shrubs and hedges as she went, kicking through piles of leaves along the path. All the grounds had been searched, as well, by police teams using dogs and metal detectors; the murder weapon wasn't in this yard. Still, she found herself staring at the shrubbery with fierce intensity as if she could somehow will the knife into existence.

The back fence was made of tall slabs, badly in need of paint. A couple of them hung loose from the stringers, floating and creaking in the breeze. Jackie looked at the boards absently, then opened a wire gate and went out into the alley.

She walked down the narrow graveled expanse, over weeds and loose pebbles, then back again, lost in thought.

The house loomed before her, dark and withdrawn, its upper windows staring vacantly. She frowned at them, trying to remember the interior layout. One of the windows looked out from Maribel's bedroom, while the smaller one was the bathroom where the woman had died. Above them the roof was steeply pitched, broken by a stone chimney and a barred vent in the attic. The dormer jutted on the other side, facing away from her to the west.

A lot of loose shingles up there, Jackie thought idly. Stan Lewis was going to have a ton of work if he intended to get the place back in shape. Still, he seemed eager to take possession.

She moved down the alley once more, then turned and approached the house again, wondering what was bothering her. Something seemed wrong, but she couldn't put her finger on it.

Wardlow often laughed at these feelings of hers, calling them women's intuition or "Kaminsky's secret weapon." But Jackie suspected that all good investigators relied on their gut instincts to a certain extent. It was something you acquired after years on the job, a kind of free association, the ability to let your mind drift in and out of various dimensions, weighing and considering the evidence without conscious input.

This ability was probably the reason so many police officers were superstitious. She'd known hard-boiled detectives who routinely consulted psychics for help with their cases, and seasoned patrol officers who didn't feel safe unless they followed exactly the same ritual every night before going out on shift.

Back at the rear gate, Jackie stood and looked up at the house, searching her mind again. But the bothersome detail, whatever it was, wouldn't surface. At last she gave up, opened the gate and approached the house, rummaging in her pocket again for the key.

She opened the back door and stepped into the porch. "Hello?" she called. "Anyone here?"

The house was silent. Jackie moved past an old wicker armchair to examine one of the porch windows, where a piece of plywood was tacked over a broken pane. She recognized it as the window used by an intruder to gain entry the night the house had been trashed and that strange picture left up in the attic.

Just over a week ago, she thought. God, it seems like months.

She stared around the chilly porch, willing the place to give up its secrets.

Who had broken that pane of glass, sneaked into the house and cut photographs of Stan and Chris Lewis from Maribel's albums? Why had they pasted the pictures over that ugly bit of pornography and left it in the attic where it was certain to be found?

She still wasn't sure if the killer had done those things, or if the deeds were separate and unrelated.

Jackie shook her head and went into the kitchen. Already the place had a stale unused smell. The countertops and door handles were black with fingerprint powder and the floor was dirty from the passage of many feet.

She walked through the hallway on the lower floor and climbed the stairs to the upper-level bathroom. The door was closed. Jackie opened it and peered inside.

Most of the bloody symbols had been washed from walls and mirrors, and the tub was empty and scrubbed. But she fancied that the odor still hung in the air, dark and metallic.

There'd been such a lot of blood....

Suddenly the hairs prickled on the back of her neck. She raised her head, listening, then reached under her blazer to release the strap on her holster.

She couldn't tell what she'd heard. A breath of sound, a creaking floorboard somewhere below her, the whisper of a presence....

Jackie drew her gun and edged back on the landing to peer over the staircase. Nobody was in sight, and the lower floor appeared silent and empty.

She crept down the stairs, planting her feet cautiously. She could hear more clearly now, and she knew it wasn't just her imagination. Somebody was in the house, moving through the rooms.

Maybe it was one of the Ident technicians coming back to pick up a piece of forgotten equipment or finish some task. But any police personnel would have called out when they entered the house.

She reached the midpoint on the stairs and paused to flatten herself against the wall, peering down through the archway into the living room. A shadow drifted past, falling briefly onto the hardwood floor. Jackie took a deep breath and moved lower again. When she rested her weight on a bottom step, the old oak creaked like a gunshot in the stillness.

She whirled to face the archway, but there was no time to brace herself. A dark figure erupted through the arched door, knocking her aside. She stumbled and lost her footing, while her elbow banged hard against the carved newel post.

Numbing pain shot up her arm and the gun dangled uselessly for a moment. By the time she could grip the weapon again she heard the back door open and close.

"Shit!" she yelled as she sprinted through the house, tearing out onto the porch. "Stop! Police!"

Her quarry was already vanishing through the rear gate, heading down the alley. Jackie lifted her gun and set off in pursuit, pelting down the graveled alley. She called once more, then ran in grim earnest, conserving her breath for the chase.

17

It had been years since Jackie had pursued anyone on foot. Her final stint in uniform had been spent on vehicle patrol, and the promotion to detective put her behind a desk for most of her working hours. She'd forgotten the sharp panic, the feeling of agonized breathlessness, the sense that her heart was going to swell and explode inside her chest.

While she ran, still clutching her gun, she had time to think about a lot of things. It was bizarre the way her mind kept processing and cataloging information while her body hurtled through the spring afternoon between the hedges and back fences.

She could see the person she was chasing, but wasn't able to tell if it was male or female. Slender and wiry, dressed in dark jeans, jacket and a black cap, running like hell...

"Stop!" she shouted again, gasping. "Police!"

Her quarry tossed a glance backward, then speeded up. Jackie swore and increased her pace, taking a moment to be grateful for all those morning workout sessions in the gym during the past winter. If she hadn't been in shape, she'd probably be on the ground by now.

Another part of her mind was trying to analyze the situation.

Could this be the killer, returning to the crime scene for another thrill? If so, everything depended on her ability to maintain contact with her prey.

She couldn't risk the time to dig through her shoulder bag for the cell phone. By the time she found it and called for backup, that dark figure could have ducked into a yard or down a side street and vanished.

Jackie prayed for someone or something to help her, a passerby or a neighborhood dog, anything to break the wild momentum of their flight. They'd gone a couple of blocks by now, maintaining a distance between them of about fifty feet. She tried to increase her speed, feeling as if her lungs would burst.

At the bottom of the next block, the alley opened out into a park, silent and deserted in the afternoon stillness.

Go for the park, Jackie urged silently. *Don't turn down one of these side streets. Keep heading for the park where I can see you.*

"Yes!" she muttered aloud when the dark figure burst out of the alley and tore off across the grass.

As they sped over level ground, Jackie realized she was gaining a little. With a final agonizing thrust of effort she hurtled herself forward, closing the gap to twenty feet, then ten. At last she was almost near enough to touch the running person, to smell the fear and panic.

But she couldn't find the breath to speak. Instead, she gathered her muscles and leaped, knocking her quarry to the ground and rolling on top of the wiry body.

"Police," she gasped, pressing her gun against the black jacket. "Gun. Don't move."

The heaving form tensed beneath her, then col-

lapsed again. They lay together on the ground, both coughing and taking in huge gulps of air.

Jackie felt light-headed and a little nauseated. Finally she rolled over and struggled to her feet, pointing her gun at the trembling figure on the ground. "Stand up," she panted. "Move slowly. And keep your hands...where I can see them."

The other got up onto all fours, still moaning and gasping, then stood erect and turned.

Jackie looked at the man in utter astonishment. It was Charlie Roarke, the young stable hand who worked with Christine Lewis. He dropped his chin to his chest, then turned his face away, furtive and obviously terrified.

Jackie held the gun on him while she fumbled in the pouch at her waist, searching for a pair of handcuffs. "Put your hands behind you," she said.

"You don't need...to cuff me," he gasped. "I'm not gonna...do anything."

"That's for damn sure," she said grimly, still breathing heavily. "You've done enough already. Practically killed me, making me run that hard."

But she wavered a little, watching him closely. Charlie's handsome face was pale and blotchy, his lips blue-tinged. He sank to his knees on the grass and leaned forward, still fighting for breath.

Charlie Roarke certainly didn't look like a man about to attempt another escape.

"How can you...stand there like that?" he asked. "I can't...even breathe."

"You're in pretty bad shape, all right. I'll bet you're a smoker."

Jackie abandoned her search for the handcuffs but kept her gun drawn, lowering it unobtrusively to her

side as a young woman crossed the park with a couple
of little girls and a baby stroller.

When they were gone, she moved closer to the
gasping man.

"Why were you in that house, Charlie?"

He cast a frightened glance up at her and shook his
head.

"Come on," Jackie said impatiently. "There's no
point in stalling. We both know you were there. I can
book you on break-and-enter charges right now if
that's how you're going to play it. You'd probably
go away for another couple of years. Is that what you
want?"

"I didn't break in," he said sullenly. "I have a
key." He got up and stood facing her, still trembling
and unsteady on his feet.

Jackie was convinced by now that the man posed
no threat. She holstered her gun and indicated a park
bench near the path. "Okay. Let's sit down and have
a little talk, shall we? We'll both move nice and
slow."

He preceded her to the bench and lowered himself
gingerly onto the wooden planks, looking across the
grass with a trapped unhappy expression.

Jackie sat on the other end of the bench, still watching him closely. "Show me the house key, Charlie.
And no tricks, okay?"

He dug in his jacket pocket and extended a house
key on a leather tab.

She took out her own tagged key and compared
them, then pocketed both keys. "Where did you get
it?"

"I used to live there, remember? When I moved

away, I had a couple of extras made before I gave the keys back to Maribel.''

Jackie watched him thoughtfully. His color had improved a little, but he was still shaky, breathing heavily through his mouth, and probably too frightened and exhausted to lie.

"So when did you get there? Were you inside the house when I came in?''

He looked away with a jerky nod, then swallowed hard and spoke. "I was in the den. I heard you open the door and go upstairs. I thought maybe I could get back through the house and slip out the door before you came back down, but I guess you heard me.''

"Why were you there?''

He shook his head, gazing stubbornly at the patch of blue sky between the trees.

Jackie sighed. "Look, Charlie, I already warned you what's going to happen if you don't cooperate. Do you want to go to jail again? Was it really so much fun the last time?''

"I was looking for something that belongs to me,'' he muttered.

She relaxed a little. "Ah. And what's that?''

His face contorted and he hung his head. "I don't want to talk about it.''

"Sorry, but I don't think you have much choice.''

He licked his lips and cast a quick glance at her. Jackie touched the handle of her gun.

"Don't get any ideas,'' she told him softly. "We already know I can outrun you, and I'll shoot if I have to.''

Charlie slouched back on the bench. Tears glistened in his eyes and began to trickle down his cheeks. He brushed at them with the sleeve of his jacket.

"God, it's so awful," he whispered. "It's been a nightmare for years."

Jackie remained silent, waiting for him to go on.

"Maribel, she's...she was such a bitch."

"What did she do to you?"

"She had...something."

Jackie watched him thoughtfully. "Let's go back to the beginning," she suggested. "You lived in Maribel's house for a while, right? How long ago was that?"

"Three years ago."

"And while you were there, she got hold of something that belonged to you, but you can't tell me what it was?"

He licked his lips again. "It wasn't...anything illegal."

"So tell me what it was."

"I'd rather die," he said recklessly. "I don't care what you do to me."

"Oh, Charlie, that's not true. I think you care a whole lot."

She could see him wavering, arguing with himself. His jaw set stubbornly and he shook his head, staring at the distant trees.

Jackie sighed, pondering her next move.

Deals with known and suspected criminals, though unsavory, were an integral part of police work. Plea bargains kept an overburdened justice system from collapsing under its own weight, and promises of immunity brought forward information that could never be gained otherwise.

But the fine art of the deal was also a land mine

that could blow up in a detective's face with horrifying consequences....

"Tell me what you were looking for," she said at last, "and I won't charge you for being unlawfully inside a restricted crime scene."

"If you charge me, what happens?"

"I think you know what happens, Charlie."

He wrung his hands together in his lap. "If I tell you, will you find my stuff and get it out of there before Stan moves in?"

"Absolutely."

"You'd have to do it right away. Stan's moving into the house in a day or two. He'll find them if he looks through Maribel's stuff."

"Find what?"

Charlie sighed heavily. "Some...pictures."

Jackie looked at him, baffled, thinking about all those scattered albums on Maribel's living-room floor after the housebreaking. "Photographs, you mean?"

"Yeah."

"What kind of photos?"

"Pictures of...of me," Charlie whispered. "I was trying to find them. That's what I was doing in the house today when you came."

A light began to dawn. "Was Maribel Lewis blackmailing you, Charlie?"

He nodded miserably. "She had these pictures. She said she'd show them to everybody if I didn't give her two hundred bucks a month. She said she kept them in her purse. I've been paying that bitch for almost three years."

"What kind of pictures were they?"

He gripped his hands together and huddled on the bench, refusing to answer.

"We'll go back right now," Jackie promised. "You'll wait outside, Charlie, and I'll keep looking till I find them. But I need to know what I'm looking for."

He hesitated a moment longer, then nodded reluctantly. "It was just after I went to live there," he said at last. "I was new to the city, and real lonely."

He fell silent, twisting his hands together.

Jackie waited again, sensing he could talk more easily if she didn't press him.

"I met somebody in a bar," he said. "Somebody I really liked."

"And Maribel knew about it?" she said when he paused again.

"I don't know how she found out. It was just a couple of nights, and we sneaked into the house after everybody was asleep. I thought that bitch was at work."

"So you met a woman and took her back to Maribel's house?"

He looked up, his eyes dark with pain. "Sort of."

"And what happened?"

"Somehow Maribel knew we were there. She came downstairs and took pictures of us while we were... while we were sleeping in bed. She showed me the—"

His voice broke. To Jackie's alarm he began to cry, his body shaking with ragged sobs.

Jackie moved closer and put a sympathetic arm around him. "Look, I don't see why that's so awful. Maribel took some naughty photos of you sleeping with a woman. Taking those pictures was definitely a gross thing to do, but why would you pay her money to keep them secret?"

He looked up, his face still streaming with tears. "It wasn't a woman," he whispered.

"Ah." Jackie sat back, her arm still resting across his shoulders.

Maribel Lewis had certainly been a sweetheart, Jackie thought grimly. What else was she going to learn about this murder victim before the case was solved?

"Charlie," she said gently, "it's no shame to be homosexual. People are a lot more understanding nowadays, you know."

He quivered under her touch. "I don't know if I...." He gulped and wiped an arm across his eyes again.

"You don't know if you are?" she guessed. "This guy in the bar—it was just an experiment?"

"Sort of. I always had these...feelings, but I wasn't sure if they were real. I'm still not sure."

"How about Chris Lewis?" Jackie asked. "Was that an experiment, too?"

"Yeah, I guess it was." He looked down miserably at the cinder path next to the bench. "I've known Chris a long time, and I really like her. We were both lonely. I thought maybe it could work out."

"And did it?"

He shook his head. "I couldn't do it. We tried twice, but nothing happened." His face reddened with shame and embarrassment. "Chris—she was real nice about it. She said maybe it was because Stan was my friend that I couldn't do anything."

"So nobody knows about this other part of your life," Jackie suggested, "and you don't want them to know, because you're still not sure about things yourself. Is that right?"

"I'd die if anybody found out. I got sick to my stomach when Maribel showed me the pictures."

"So you've been paying her for three years to keep your secret?"

He buried his face in his hands.

"Did you hate Maribel enough to kill her, Charlie?" she asked softly.

"No way!" He raised his head, looking terrified again. "I could never kill anybody."

"But you were obviously happy when I told you she was dead."

"Damn right I was happy about it. I could hardly believe what you were saying."

"Did you break into her house at night a while ago, looking for those pictures?"

He shook his head vehemently. "Until today, I haven't been inside the place since I left three years ago. I hate that goddamn house."

Jackie sat on the bench beside him for a while, thinking. At last she patted Charlie's shoulder and got to her feet.

"Let's go back and find the pictures," she said.

Charlie sat outside, handcuffed to a railing on the small veranda at the back of the house while Jackie went in to search. The cuffing was just a precaution, probably not necessary. Since his confession, all the fight had gone out of him. He huddled on the steps, head hanging disconsolately.

Jackie checked on him through a rear window, then went into the kitchen.

All of Maribel's drawers and closets had been searched since the murder, but Maribel could have so carefully hidden pictures she was using for blackmail

that a police search might well have left them undis-
covered.

Jackie stood for a while in the lower hallway of
the old house, pondering the problem. Maribel had
told Charlie the pictures were in her purse. But that
was probably just to discourage him from breaking
into the house while she was at work.

She pretended she was Maribel, holding the envelope in her hands, and tried to think how she would
have felt about the pictures and where to hide them.
But in many ways, Maribel was still a mystery to her.

How would her own grandmother have reacted in
this situation?

Jackie visualized Irene Kaminsky with an envelope
full of shocking pictures that represented cold, hard
cash, money for liquor and gambling.

Shameful pictures. Sexy. Hidden and secret. Not
very nice, but extremely valuable.

Jackie moved upstairs with sudden decision and
headed for Maribel's bedroom and her scarred ma-
hogany dresser. A gold-framed picture, presumably of
Stanley Lewis, stood on the dresser in a gritty drift
of fingerprint powder. He was about three years old
in the picture, wearing short knitted pants and a blue
sweater with rows of pearl buttons on the shoulders.

Even at three, Stanley had looked a little sneaky.
Jackie studied the image for a moment, then began
opening various drawers until she found the one with
Maribel's underwear.

With a brief shiver of reluctance, she dug into the
tangle of panties and bras. Maribel had been careless
about her intimate garments. Most of the panties were
worn and stretched, torn away from their elastic
waistbands in places or repaired with safety pins, and
the bras were stained gray at the underarms.

Under the paper liner at the bottom of the drawer she found a plain white envelope, sealed and unmarked. *Yes!* She ran her key under the flap and eased it open, removing a handful of black-and-white snapshots and a strip of negatives.

The pictures showed a very different Charlie Roarke from the terrified young man in the park. He lay in a rumpled bed with a slim blond youth, their naked bodies intertwined.

Both boys were asleep. Jackie looked at the pictures with a lump in her throat, unexpectedly moved. Their eyelashes cast dark childlike fans on their cheeks and they looked joyously fulfilled, their sleeping faces curved in identical smiles of peaceful contentment.

Jackie swallowed hard, staring at the photographs. "Oh, Maribel," she whispered aloud. "You really were a bitch, weren't you?"

At last she put the photos back in the envelope and tucked it into her bag. She went downstairs and locked the door behind her, then escorted Charlie into her car and headed to the substation.

Lew Michelson sat behind his desk, examining the photographs in silence while Jackie leaned against the door frame. Charlie Roarke was still downstairs in an interrogation room where he'd spent a couple of hours being questioned—and been reduced several times to messy tears.

"Okay," the sergeant said at last, looking up without expression. "Seal and mark them, file the paperwork and take the envelope down to an evidence locker. Good work, Jackie. And book the guy for unlawful presence. We don't want him going anywhere."

She stared at her supervisor, then took a few steps forward. "Book him? But, Sarge...I can't do that."

Michelson's usual good cheer had been replaced of late by a weary preoccupied look. He passed a hand over his forehead, sighing, then picked up a pen. "What did you say?"

"I promised him I wouldn't charge him if he told me about the pictures."

"Well, that was a pretty stupid thing to promise, right? Now go and book him. I've got a ton of personnel evaluations to get through before I leave."

Jackie's stomach tightened and her heart began to pound. She approached the desk, took the envelope of pictures and sat on the edge of a vinyl chair, leaning forward.

"Look, Sarge," she said earnestly, "I gave my word. Maybe it was overstepping my authority in this case, but I still made a deal with Roarke. If he told me the truth, he wouldn't be charged for being inside the house. Don't make me break my promise to this poor guy. He's already been through hell."

Michelson sighed and leaned back, pushing the stack of papers away from him. His face was pale, and dark circles ringed his eyes.

"Detective Kaminsky, I don't give a goddamn about your promise, even if you crossed your heart and hoped to die. We're investigating a brutal homicide. We've got some kind of nutcase out there sending threatening letters, and we could have more bodies turning up at any moment. Isn't that right?"

She met his gaze unwillingly.

"Am I right, Jackie?"

"Yes," she muttered, looking down at the envelope in her hands. "You're right."

"And here we've got someone with motive, opportunity—a key to the house, for God's sake—and no alibi. And you want to turn him loose when we've got grounds for an arrest, because you gave your word? Is that what you're saying, Detective?''

Jackie looked up at him again. "Yes, that's what I'm saying."

"For Christ's sake..." Michelson leaned back in the chair and his stomach rumbled noisily. "I can't let you do it," he said. "We have to hang on to Roarke. I'm sorry about what you promised him, but that's how it's going to be. After you've had a bit more experience in homicide—"

"Look," Jackie interrupted furiously, "don't patronize me. I'm not a ten-year-old and I'm certainly not an idiot. I've been working hard and getting extra training for years, and the guys uptown have trusted me with this homicide because they know I'm good. Do you think I can't handle the case?"

She looked steadily at Michelson, who glanced down at the papers on his desk. "I never said that, Jackie."

She waved her arm in the general direction of the other door. "Well, I made a deal with Roarke in good faith. Besides, we've been talking to him for almost two hours, and I don't think he's a killer. What's more, you don't think so, either."

"Oh, I see. And how do you know that? Women's intuition?"

"Bullshit!" Jackie sprang to her feet, outraged, and slammed the flat of her hand on the sergeant's desk. "Look, don't *ever* say that to me again!"

Her voice was loud enough to be heard through the closed door. Faces turned as people in the squad room stared curiously at the wavy greenish glass of Michelson's office window.

The sergeant watched Jackie in thoughtful silence and said nothing.

She sank into the chair again, breathing raggedly while she struggled to get herself back under control.

"Sorry about that, Sarge," she muttered. "I shouldn't have yelled at you. It was out of line."

Michelson shifted in his chair. "Okay, Jackie. I probably shouldn't have made the crack about women's intuition."

Jackie bit her tongue but kept silent.

"So," he said at last, "why are you so sure he isn't the killer?"

"Because he got one of the threatening letters," Jackie said.

"Didn't we all agree the killer would probably send a letter to himself just to deflect suspicion?"

"But that's not the point. Do you remember what Charlie was threatened with?"

Michelson pondered for a moment. Suddenly his face paled, making the freckles more prominent.

"Yes," she said softly. "I can see that you remember."

"Jesus." Michelson licked his lips nervously.

"If Charlie Roarke was a murderer, he might have killed Maribel to get her off his back, after sending threatening letters all over the place to cover his tracks," Jackie said, "but he would never threaten himself with castration. I mean, that's something a man would never do, right? Look at you," she added. "You can hardly even stand to *think* about it."

"Maybe he's crazy," Michelson said stubbornly. "I've heard of prisoners who tried to castrate themselves with broken soup spoons."

"So have I, but Charlie Roarke's not crazy. He's just a poor mixed-up guy who got caught and was being brutally manipulated. I don't think he's even bright enough to organize this whole scam." Jackie got up and headed for the door. "And I'm letting him go."

"Over my direct orders?" Michelson asked. His voice sounded mild, but his eyes were cold and watchful.

"Yes." Jackie turned to face her sergeant. "If that's the way it's going to be."

"And what if I tell you that's not an option?"

She took a deep breath. "Then I'll quit."

"You'll *what?*"

"I'll quit. My badge will be on your desk in the morning."

"For God's sake, Kaminsky," he said. "Don't be such a fool. You'd throw away your career over a two-bit stable hand who spends his days shoveling horseshit and his nights at a gay bar?"

"It's nothing to do with Charlie," Jackie said tightly. "It's more about what kind of job I'm allowed to do, and how much of my own judgment I get to exercise during an investigation."

"And you'd really quit?"

She lifted her chin. "Yes. I'll quit if you force me to arrest Roarke after I gave my word I wouldn't."

"Goddammit, Jackie…"

She stood tensely in the doorway while Michelson leafed through the stacks of papers on his desk.

He leaned back, thinking. "Look," he said at last. "We've got these pictures entered into evidence, and your sworn testimony that you caught Roarke at the crime scene. Right?"

"Yes."

"And if he disappears in the next few days, we should be able to find him?"

"I'm sure of it."

"And if our boy made a run for it, that would be a pretty fair admission of guilt, right?"

"I suppose it would."

There was a long tense silence.

"You know, I've lost eight pounds," he said out of the blue.

"That's...good news, Sarge." Puzzled, she gripped the envelope with nervous fingers.

Again seemingly out of the blue he asked, "Are you seeing Paul this weekend?"

"Yes. We have a date on Friday night." She smiled. "A real dress-up, going-out-for-dinner kind of date. He'll go back to the ranch on Saturday."

"Good. Maybe you'll feel better after that."

"What are you saying?" she asked, angry again. Was he implying that she needed regular sex to do her job properly?

"I'm sorry, Jackie." He smiled sheepishly. "I didn't mean that the way it sounded. I'm only saying I'm glad you're taking some time off for yourself. There's nothing like being with the person you love."

Jackie nodded in confused agreement, still waiting for his final word on the subject of Charlie and her promise.

At last Michelson heaved a sigh and said, "Could we at least keep a real close eye on this kid? Have Wardlow stop by his place once a day?"

She hesitated briefly. "Sure. No problem." Then she got up, the envelope in her hand, and left the office.

18

Jackie paused in the foyer of the restaurant and handed her coat to the hostess. "I'm meeting someone," she said. "I think he's most likely here already, because I'm a bit late."

"What's the name, please?"

"Paul Arnussen. He's tall and blond, probably wearing a—"

"Yes, he's here." The hostess gave Jackie a reassuring smile. "He's been waiting just about ten minutes, that's all."

"Okay. Then I think I'll duck into the ladies' room for a second."

"All right. Your friend is seated down that way, in the third alcove on your right if I'm not here when you come back."

The hostess smiled again and disappeared with Jackie's coat.

Jackie paused for a moment next to a small forest of potted palms, then turned and hurried into the washroom. She stood in front of a full-length mirror and smoothed the skirt over her hips, studying her reflection.

She wore a black jersey dress with a halter top and softly draped skirt, and a pair of dangling copper earrings that gave her a sultry exotic look. Her bare shoulders gleamed and she was wearing more makeup than usual, even some mascara.

An older woman paused beside her, looking in the mirror as she touched a comb to her stiff gray curls.

Jackie licked her lips and tugged at the halter strap of her dress. "I hardly ever dress up like this," she said ruefully.

"Well, you look lovely. Such beautiful skin and hair."

Jackie smiled, encouraged by the woman's warmth. "Thank you."

"My daughter has hair like that." The woman dabbed lipstick on her mouth. "She got it from Harry—that's my husband. Not that Harry has much hair left nowadays. But mine was drab and mousey before it turned gray."

"It's really pretty now," Jackie said. "I love silver hair."

She crossed the room to wash her hands, moving carefully in the unfamiliar high heels, conscious of her black skirt swirling around her legs. Briefly she wondered why she felt so self-conscious, so...naked.

Because I don't have my gun, she realized in astonishment. *I'm out in public without a gun.*

It was an odd sensation, this vulnerability, and strangely exciting. She felt like a different person, a woman with slim legs and shining hazel eyes, with bare shoulders and dangling earrings and a lover waiting for her beyond the gold damask walls of the ladies' room.

"Now, you be sure to have a real nice evening," the older woman told her with a smile as they left the room together.

"Thanks," Jackie said. "You, too."

She clutched her black velvet evening bag and moved through the soft candlelight of the dining room toward the alcoves along the wall.

Paul sat in one of the enclosures at a round linen-draped table, wearing a tweed sport jacket over jeans and an open-necked white shirt. His tanned cheekbones glistened in the soft light, and his hair was like polished gold.

"Hi," she murmured, sitting down across from him on the leather banquette. "Sorry I'm late."

The hard planes of his face softened. "Jackie," he breathed. "My God, you're gorgeous."

Nobody had ever looked at her the way Paul did. His dark eyes seemed to devour her, to gaze into the very center of her heart.

"Don't," she said awkwardly, touching her hair.

"Don't what?"

"Don't keep staring at me. I feel so self-conscious tonight."

"Why?" he asked. "Because you're beautiful?"

"Because I'm wearing makeup and silk stockings and I don't have a gun."

Paul laughed and poured wine into her glass. "We should do this more often." He glanced at his watch. "About four hours ago I was stitching a calf that got tangled up in barbed wire. Now I'm sitting in a restaurant with the most beautiful woman in the world, drinking wine by candlelight."

"How's the calf?" she asked, lifting her wineglass. "Is he going to be okay?"

"I think so. It was pretty amateur surgery, but it seemed to do the job. How was your week?"

Jackie glanced at him in surprise. "Surely it hasn't been a whole week since we talked?"

"Not quite. We had lunch on Tuesday, and I drove into Reardan to call you late that same night. Remember?"

She shook her head. "The days all seem to be running together. I'm working so hard, Paul. This case is making me crazy."

"Any breaks yet?"

Jackie thought about Charlie Roarke creeping through Maribel's house in search of those embarrassing photographs, about Fiona Morgan and her disturbing stories, and Laney Symons with the pentagram tattooed on her shoulder, about Desirée Moreau's strange religion, and Stan Lewis packing to move into his mother's house…

"All kinds of things have been happening," she said. "But nothing we can make any sense of yet. Tell me about the ranch."

"Well, we have thirty-six calves now, and two foals."

"Two foals? Baby horses, you mean?"

Paul smiled and reached out to squeeze her hand. "That's right, sweetheart. Baby horses."

"No kidding. I didn't even know any of your horses were pregnant."

"I wasn't sure, either, but both mares foaled this week. One's a little sorrel filly and the other's a black colt with white stockings."

"Oh, my goodness," she whispered, enchanted. "I can hardly wait to see them."

The waitress arrived to take their orders. They were silent until she left, smiling at each other across the table.

"I can't get over how beautiful you look," he murmured. "I'd like to forget about the damned meal and take you home right now."

"What a big waste of all this trouble. Putting on a dress and high heels, fussing with makeup. If we were just going to stay for ten minutes, I could have worn jeans."

He gave her a wolfish grin. "No way. I like the dress. It's going to be so much fun taking it off."

A deep sexual thrill stabbed through her. "Paul..." she whispered.

"You'd better not look at me like that, sweetheart—" his voice was husky "—or I'm never going to make it through dinner."

The waitress arrived just then with a napkin-covered basket, and the tension fled.

"Here," he told Jackie, offering the basket. "Have some bread."

She selected one of the warm rolls, broke it open on her plate and buttered it. "I almost resigned on Wednesday."

"You did what?" he asked, startled.

"I threatened to quit. Told Michelson I'd have my badge on his desk the next day."

"Well, now, that sounds like a hell of a good idea. In fact, the best suggestion I've heard all week. More butter?"

She shook her head and nibbled the roll.

He opened the folds of the napkin to peer inside the basket. "What made you get so mad at your poor old sergeant?"

"It was a philosophical difference," she said. "I felt he was overriding my authority."

"How?"

Jackie shrugged. "I made a promise to somebody

who provided evidence in the case. Michelson threatened ʒ break my promise without giving me any say in the matter. It was really upsetting.''

"Are you still upset?"

"Sort of, but not for the same reason." Jackie moved her hands restlessly on the tablecloth. "I won the argument, but ever since, I've been lying awake at night wondering if maybe Sarge was right, after all."

He looked at her intently, his dark eyes so probing she began to feel uncomfortable again.

"What?" she asked.

He looked down at the crusty roll in his hands, then up again. "You seem really obsessed about all this," he said. "I know it's a big case for you, but I hate to see it taking so much out of you."

"The sarge is concerned about me, too." She took another bite from the roll, realizing for the first time that she was famished. "But he seems to think I just need some loving." She shook her head and smiled, recalling the weird conversation with Michelson.

Paul's dark eyes sparkled with amusement. "Well, then, I guess I'll have to do my civic duty, won't I? After all, somebody's got to keep the police happy."

She smiled back at him. "And you're just the man to do it."

"Damn right I am." Under the table he put a hand on her knee, then slid it up under her skirt to stroke her silk-clad thigh.

She shivered at his touch and bit her lip. "If you keep doing that," she warned, "we'll be making love on the table in about five minutes."

"That might be interesting."

"It would certainly be interesting to the other patrons."

His hand stroked gently, edged higher. "Is there a garter belt?" he whispered.

"Paul, don't..."

He removed his hand, smoothed the skirt back over her knees and smiled blandly at the waitress as she delivered their salads.

Jackie's cheeks burned. She felt such a fierce wave of yearning that it was all she could do to concentrate on the plate of greens.

"When I get you home," she muttered after a moment, "you're going to pay for all this teasing."

He sobered and his voice was husky. "I'm not teasing," he said. "Not at all, sweetheart."

Jackie began to eat automatically, forgetting about her dress, her earrings, the wine and candlelight, even the fact that she'd left her gun at home, locked in the bedside table.

She wanted only to finish this meal, get away from the restaurant and be alone with him, and it was practically killing her to wait.

They hurried through the lobby of Jackie's apartment building and headed for the elevator, so wrapped up in each other that they were hardly aware of anything else.

"Just a second," she murmured, rummaging in her evening bag for the keys. "I haven't picked up my mail since yesterday."

He hugged her and kissed her cheek. "Are you planning to pay some bills tonight?"

Jackie laughed, pulling away from him. "Just waiting for a letter from my grandmother. She promised to send pictures of Angela's new baby.''

"Angela has another baby?"

"A little girl, born last month. Paul, I told you all about the baby."

"Probably, but it's not easy to keep track of your cousins."

She took a bundle of letters and flyers from the mailbox, then reached up to kiss his neck. "Okay. Let's go home, cowboy."

Two other couples were using the elevator. Jackie stood close to Paul while he wrapped his arms around her from behind, resting his chin on top of her head. She felt warmed and safe, and she tingled with anticipation.

They got off at her floor and started down the hall, leaning against each other and kissing, lost in their own world. Inside the apartment he stripped off his jacket, then strode to the fridge, opened it and took out a bottle.

Jackie's eyebrows shot up. "Champagne? In *my* fridge?"

"I stopped by earlier and laid in some supplies in case we got snowbound or something."

"Snowbound in this city?" She chuckled.

"Stranger things have happened," he said.

"Well...snowbound with you." Jackie sighed and looked up from her bundle of mail, gazing at the window. "Wouldn't that be lovely?"

He took a couple of wineglasses from the cupboard and popped the cork on the champagne bottle, trapping it expertly in his hand. "All we have to do is draw the drapes, take the phone off the hook and pretend it's snowing."

"Okay." She smiled at him, slitted an envelope and shook the letter out.

He crossed the room to offer her a glass of wine, then stopped and looked at her. "Jackie, is something wrong? You've gone white as a sheet."

"Jesus," she whispered, staring at a typewritten page with a hand-drawn star in the lower corner.

"What is it?" he asked, setting the glasses down on the counter and reaching for the letter. "What's going on?"

"Don't touch it!"

Jackie dropped the sheet of paper onto the table with shaking hands. Both she and Paul stared at it.

The letter read:

Dear Bitch-Cop,

You think you're so smart. You think you know so much, but you don't know anything. The Divine One is more powerful than you can imagine. You will die by your own gun, bitch. Your blood and brains will be splattered on the ground.

Unlike the other two letters Jackie had seen, this one had a brief postscript at the bottom of the page near the pentagram.

Just thought you'd like to know, bitch, that somebody else is going to die soon. By the time you read this letter the Divine One's blood lust will be satisfied, but only for a little while. Keep looking over your shoulder.

She took a knife from one of the kitchen drawers and used it to flip the envelope over. The letter had been posted in Spokane the previous day. Jackie stared at the envelope, her heart pounding, so absorbed she was hardly conscious of Paul until he grabbed her arm and shook her.

"What the hell does this mean? Is it some kind of joke?"

She looked up at his tense angry face. "I don't think it's a joke."

"Then what is it?"

"It's part of the case I'm working on. A lot of the witnesses have received letters like this." She looked around the room. "I need to find a couple of evidence folders. I think my briefcase is in the bedroom, but my other—"

He caught her shoulder as she started for the door. "Jackie, talk to me, for God's sake! Is this guy crazy, or what?"

"We don't even *know* if it's a guy. The FBI psychologist in Portland thinks it's more likely a woman, because women tend to be the ones who send threatening letters. Look, Paul, I really have to get these things into folders."

"You're not going anywhere until you tell me what this is about."

She sank into a chair, averting her eyes from the letter on the table, and told him the details of the case. He listened in growing horror.

"You mean this creep has already killed somebody?" His eyes narrowed and he leaned forward intently. "It was the woman at the autopsy, right? That's why you were so upset on Tuesday."

"That's right."

"And now *you're* being threatened?" His hands

clenched into fists. He stared down at them, flexing his fingers. "I can't stand this, Jackie."

"Please," she begged, "don't react that way. I need you to support me."

"*Support* you? When some nutcase is sending death threats?"

She shook her head and got up. "I have to find an evidence folder. Nobody's touched this but me, so we might be able to lift some decent prints."

"Don't talk to me about fingerprints!"

Reluctantly she sank back into the chair and looked at him. "What can I tell you, Paul? This is my job. We need to catch this weirdo before somebody else gets hurt. Lots of people have gotten letters like this, you know. I'm not the only one."

"Well, you're the only one I care about," he said bitterly. "Are they going to give you some kind of protection?"

"Who?"

"Who do you think? The police force. Are they going to make sure you're safe?"

"I *am* the police," she said, trying to smile. "When people need protection, I'm who they call."

"You know what I mean." He gestured at the letter. "What are they going to do about this?"

"I don't know. What can anybody do? I'll just have to make sure I'm armed all the time and be really careful. But I don't think this guy is coming after me."

"Why not?"

"Because I'm not part of the group. I'm an outsider. Whatever weird psychosexual thing is going on with this bunch of people, I'm only a bystander."

"If you were just a bystander, you wouldn't be

getting letters threatening to blow your brains out. My God...'' He dropped his face into his hands and sat slumped at the table, his shoulders quivering.

"Paul.'' She reached out to touch him. "Darling, please don't be so upset. I know how to take care of myself.''

He looked up, his face pale and haggard. "How can you protect yourself against a crazy person? Somebody could be out on the balcony right now, waiting for a chance to get you alone.''

"So I'll be sure to check the balcony every time I come home. It's my job, Paul,'' she told him earnestly. "I'm trained to deal with situations like this.''

He shook his head and got up to prowl restlessly around the room. "From now on I won't stay out at the ranch overnight,'' he said. "I'll drive back and forth every day so you won't be alone at night.''

His obvious fear was beginning to make her, too, feel tense and edgy.

"Look, I don't want you to do that,'' she told him. "You need to be there at night for the rest of the calving. Besides, why should you drive all those miles at the end of a long day? I can look after myself.''

He whirled to stare at her in disbelief. "You must be kidding. Do you honestly think I could sleep out there knowing you're here alone and some maniac is stalking you?''

"Nobody's stalking me!'' she said sharply. "This is just harassment. In fact, it's probably an encouraging sign,'' she added, trying to convince herself, as well as him. "If we're drawing this kind of reaction, we must be getting close. We're about to flush somebody out into the open.''

"Encouraging,'' he muttered, leaning over the sink

to stare out the window. He gripped the counter tightly, his broad shoulders tense under the white shirt. "How did they get your home address? You're not in the book anymore."

"No, but I used to be until you started making such a fuss about it. Anybody who wanted to get my address could look it up in an old phone book. It doesn't necessarily mean anything."

"So you don't believe there's going to be another murder?" he asked. "Even though that's what the goddamn letter says, right?"

"I think it's just posturing," she said. "It's somebody craving attention, that's all."

At that moment the phone rang, sounding shrill and harsh. They exchanged a glance while Jackie reached for the receiver.

"Hello?" she said tensely.

"Jackie? Michelson here."

"Hi, Sarge." Her heart began to pound again. "What's up?"

"We've got another one. I need you over here right away."

She bit her lip and glanced nervously at Paul. "Who is it?"

"Stan Lewis. And it's really ugly. We're out in the Valley at the mill where he worked. Bring Wardlow if you can get hold of him."

Paul's eyes rested on her with burning intensity. Jackie turned away and gripped the phone. "I'm on my way," she said. "I'll be there in half an hour."

19

Jackie parked at the curb outside Wardlow's apartment and waited while he came striding down to the car. He got in, looking annoyed.

"I was halfway through 'NYPD Blue,'" he complained. "This better be good, Kaminsky."

She put the car into gear and headed out through the sparse nighttime traffic. "Oh, it's good," she said grimly. "It's just terrific."

"So what's the deal?" he asked, the scowl fading.

"Our killer just got to Stan Lewis. Sarge called me from the feed mill."

"You mean he was killed at work?"

"Apparently. I don't know any details except that Sarge says it's ugly."

Neither said anything for a long moment.

"What exactly did Stan's letter say?" Wardlow asked at last. "I've got it in my notes but I can't remember offhand."

"We didn't see it, remember—Stan threw it out—but he told me it said he deserved punishment for fornicating with two women, and he was going to die a thousand deaths."

"A thousand deaths," Wardlow repeated. "So what are we going to be looking at, do you suppose? Torture and dismemberment?"

Jackie shook her head. They both fell silent again. Eventually Jackie spoke.

"You know what this means, don't you, Brian?"

"It means we're dealing with a serial killer. From now on we'll have all kinds of resources at our disposal, including the FBI profiler."

"You sound so cheerful."

"It's going to be nice to get some help with this case. I'm sick of going over and over the same evidence, and everybody pointing fingers at Chris when we should be looking for the real killer."

"Have you…" Jackie frowned at a passing car that swerved back into the outside lane just ahead of her unmarked vehicle, peppering the windshield with grit left over from a long winter of street sanding. "Have you talked to her lately?"

"I stopped by their place this afternoon to see how Gordie was doing."

"And how was he?"

"Kind of strange. Really quiet and withdrawn. I think all this stuff is beginning to get to him. God knows how the poor kid's going to react now when we have to tell him about his father."

"Was anyone else there?"

"No. Desirée wasn't around, and when I asked Gordie, he just shrugged and said she was usually out somewhere." Wardlow watched the vanishing taillights ahead of them. "Can't say as I was sorry to miss her."

Jackie glanced at him. "What time was this?"

"Five o'clock, just after I got off shift. Chris wasn't back from the ranch when I got there. Did Sarge give you an approximate time of death?"

"He didn't tell me a thing except that it was an ugly scene."

"Well, Chris got home while I was talking to Gordie. She was worn-out, said she planned to grab something to eat and go to bed early."

"How long did you stay after she got there?"

"Not long. You know," he added moodily, "I'll be glad when we catch this son of a bitch so I can start living like a normal human being again."

Jackie glanced at him. "What's happening with the divorce?" she asked. "Have you reached a settlement?"

"Finally there's some good news. The lawyers negotiated a hefty lump-sum payment that's going to clean out all my savings."

Her eyes widened in disbelief. "And that's good news?"

"To get the money, Sarah has to sign off on any future claim for spousal support or a share of my pension."

"And she's agreed?"

He nodded. "She's not happy about it, but apparently she and her boyfriend need the cash."

"Then it's really good news, isn't it?" Jackie said. "At least your future's safe now."

"I guess so. And my current lifestyle is cheap enough that I can start building some savings again if I don't have to worry about Sarah draining my income every month."

"So what's the problem?"

"I just don't know…"

"What?"

He drummed his fingers nervously on the armrest.

"I don't know if I'm ever going to *have* a future. At least, not the kind of future I want."

"Oh, come on," she scoffed, trying to lighten his bleak mood. "That's pretty defeatist. There are lots of nice women out there, Brian."

"Sure." He stared out the window. "Some of them are even suspected of murder."

Jackie cast him another glance. "You're talking about Chris Lewis."

"Right. And Chris Lewis is no killer."

Jackie gripped the wheel in frustration, and her patience snapped. "Well, great. Hold on to your starry-eyed convictions. Just don't go around saying them out loud to anybody else, okay? Because if there's even a whiff of police bias in this case, you could jeopardize the whole investigation."

"I know that. What do you think I am, some kind of idiot?" He turned to look at her. "Hey, why are you so tense and snappy tonight?"

"Because we're driving across town to look at another god-awful corpse that's the remains of a person I used to know, and we can't seem to do a single thing to stop the killing."

He reached over and gripped her shoulder. "Paul was coming in tonight, wasn't he? I guess this probably spoiled your evening."

"Our evening was spoiled before I ever got the call from Sarge," she said bitterly.

"How come? You guys fighting again?"

"Not at first. We were having such a beautiful evening," Jackie said. "We met at the Coach House for dinner. I was all decked out in this great new dress, high heels, dangly earrings—the works."

Her partner gave a teasing wolf whistle. "I wish I could have seen you."

"And we had wine and poached salmon—a really lovely meal." Jackie sighed, remembering. "You know, it felt so strange to be out in public in a dress and high heels—and with no gun."

"Yeah, I can imagine."

"We were both feeling pretty romantic by the time we got home," Jackie went on. "Paul even had some champagne tucked away in the fridge. I'd picked up my mail on the way upstairs. I opened the letters, hoping for a card from my grandmother."

Something in her voice caught his attention. He looked at her quickly while she stared straight ahead, nearing the feed mill where she'd first talked with Stanley Lewis.

"Kaminsky?" he asked. "What is it?"

She gestured over her shoulder at the briefcase in the back seat. "Take out the top evidence folder."

He unfastened his seat belt to reach back for the briefcase, unfastened it and drew out a clear plastic folder.

Jackie switched on the interior light and pulled up in front of the mill, parking among a crowd of police cars and emergency vehicles.

Wardlow peered down at the folder with a puzzled frown. "It's from our guy, all right, but which letter is it? Who got this one, Kaminsky?"

"*I* did."

He stared at her, his boyish face taut with alarm. "*You* got this letter? At your apartment?"

"It was in my letter box tonight when I picked up my mail after having dinner with Paul. You can just imagine how much it added to the romantic mood."

"How did Paul react?" Wardlow looked again at the letter beneath its protective shield of plastic, then read it carefully while Jackie watched.

"He went nuts," she said. "But Sarge called about that time and I had to change and get over here, so Paul and I didn't have much chance to talk about the letter."

"The *bastard*." Wardlow stared at the hand-drawn pentagram. "When we get hold of this scumbag, I'd like to kill him with my bare hands. It'd be a pleasure."

"You'd better watch out," she said dryly. "Keep talking like that, and you could be the next one to get a note from our friend."

"Look," her partner said urgently, restraining her as she reached for the door handle. "What are you going to do about this?"

She took the folder from him and stored it in her briefcase again. "I'm going to have the thing dusted for prints and entered into evidence."

"Come on, you know what I mean. You're alone at home during the week while Paul's away, right?"

She sighed. "He plans to drive back and forth all those miles, every single day, and neglect his new-born calves so I won't be alone at night. But I can imagine how pleasant those evenings will be. I'll have to work late most nights, and by the time I finally get home he'll be so worried and upset we'll spend the whole time fighting with each other."

"I could stay with you this week," Wardlow offered. "Let me move in and sleep on your couch for a while, just till we catch this guy. Then Paul won't have to worry about you."

Jackie hesitated, then shook her head. "It's not a

solution, Brian. Now that we've apparently got another murder, neither of us will be home much for the next few days. Like I told Paul, I'll just be really careful to carry my gun and watch my back."

He climbed out of the car. "I don't like it, Kaminsky. Will you be showing this letter to Michelson?"

"Of course."

"Good." He fell into step beside her as they approached the mill, dark and towering against the nighttime sky. "Maybe he'll have some ideas on how to protect you."

"Look, I don't need…"

But they both stopped talking as they stepped over the lines of police tape, passed through the big front doors and went into the musty interior of the mill.

The scene that greeted them was eerie, almost surreal. Beams of yellow light glowed from the floor and ceiling, filled with dust motes swirling out of the chilly darkness. The machinery was stilled and footsteps echoed hollowly as people moved across the rough concrete floor laden with cameras and equipment.

Lew Michelson approached them, carrying a couple of file folders. He wore jeans and a windbreaker, and his face was grim.

"Hi, Sarge," Wardlow said.

"Hi, kids. This isn't a pretty scene. We're keeping everybody away from the body until we've had time to check for footwear impressions. There's a lot of dust on this floor."

"Are they finding anything?" Jackie asked.

"A few partials, but nothing definitive so far." Michelson jerked his thumb at a push broom leaning against the wall near the open door of the office.

"Looks like our killer did some housecleaning after the crime, just like he did at that first scene up in the attic. We're hoping maybe he missed a couple this time."

"Who found the body?" Wardlow asked.

"One of the mill supervisors stopped by after supper to make a few computer entries. He called it in right away."

Jackie looked at the chunky man being interviewed by a couple of uniformed officers inside the glass-walled office. He sat with his hands gripped tightly together on the desktop, looking pale and sick.

"I recognize him," she said. "He's the guy I talked to when I came over here to see Stan Lewis after the break-in at Maribel's house."

"Well," Michelson said grimly, "you'll need to talk to him again. But first you'd better have a look at this. Keep between the tapes, okay?"

He led the way down a narrow path lined with yellow plastic tape, heading toward a hopper at the rear of the mill. It was a huge shallow bin about forty feet in diameter, rising more than ten feet above the level of the floor and sloping to a cone-shaped bottom.

"As near as we can figure, Lewis must've brought somebody up here to look in the hopper. When they were on the walkway, the other person pushed him and he fell through the railing."

Wardlow tested the railing, then shook it and knelt to study the broken portion.

"How do you know there was anybody else?" he asked, glancing up at Michelson over his shoulder. "That stuff in the bin's so fine and dusty, it's like quicksand, right? If he fell in from up here, he'd probably drown while he was trying to get out.''

"The grain isn't what killed him," Michelson said grimly. "He bled to death."

"Blood?" Jackie looked blankly at the huge bin and the body of a man caught in its center, upright among the grain and dust. Her eyes widened in horror. "Jesus," she whispered. "You don't mean…"

"Oh, yeah. We're dealing with a real sweetheart here," Michelson said.

Wardlow looked from Jackie to Michelson. "Am I missing something?" he asked.

"This is a gravity bin," Jackie told her partner. "I watched it in operation for a few minutes when I was here last time. The screenings are fed down onto an auger. You know what that is."

He smiled without humor. "You tell me, Kaminsky. You're the farmer."

"It's a series of whirling metal blades like a long corkscrew that carries the stuff up a shaft to the yard outside the mill."

Wardlow looked at the rigid figure in the spotlight. "My God," he breathed in sudden understanding. "That's awful."

"You're not kidding. The supervisor says the bin was almost full when they went off shift at five o'clock," Michelson said. "Now about half the screenings are piled on the ground outside, along with bits and pieces of Stan Lewis."

"So Stan comes up here onto the catwalk with somebody," Wardlow said slowly. "They're looking at the bin. This somebody pushes him over the railing, then goes back downstairs while Stan's flailing around, trying to get out of the hopper."

"But meantime," Michelson said, "our killer runs over and flips the switch to turn on the auger. Stan Lewis doesn't have a chance. That's how we know there was a second person involved, you see? The auger had to be activated while Stan was already on the catwalk, because there's an automatic gate that prevents anybody from entering the walkway once the auger's running."

Jackie and Wardlow both nodded.

"So," Michelson said, "the auger starts sucking the grain down onto those blades, carrying him with it."

"Was the auger still running when the supervisor got here?" Jackie asked.

Michelson shook his head. "It was switched on, but the motor wasn't working. The blades chewed up his feet and boots, then stalled when they got jammed on the heavier bones in his legs."

"So what alerted the supervisor there was anything inside the bin?"

"He saw some lights that weren't supposed to be turned on, then noticed the railing was broken on the catwalk and the auger switch had been activated. He turned it off, climbed the stairs and saw what you're looking at." Michelson waved his hand at the grotesque figure in the hopper.

"What did he do next?" Jackie asked.

"He dropped into the screenings bin, which was only half-full by then, and waded over to the body. But as soon as he got there he could tell that Stan was dead, and that most of his lower legs were gone. He climbed back out and placed the call."

Jackie looked down at the dusty catwalk under her

feet. "Then a lot of these footprints must belong to the supervisor."

"We've got his footwear for elimination," Michelson said. "But there's no doubt he obscured most of whatever might have been here. Not that we could get decent impressions off this stuff, anyhow." He kicked at the stamped metal surface.

Wardlow frowned. "I'm still wondering why Lewis would come out here after work."

"You'd better come down and talk to the supervisor now, okay?"

Wardlow turned to follow the sergeant back down the walkway. Jackie lingered, staring at the man in the bin with his grain-filled eyes and mouth, his frozen scream of anguish.

He was drowning in grain while the auger blades chopped his legs off, she realized. And all the time, he knew exactly what was happening to him....

Wardlow turned back to watch her. "What are you thinking, Kaminsky?"

Jackie looked at the two men. "This wasn't quick or easy. It must have taken a long time and been absolutely horrible." She paused, then continued slowly, "I'm thinking Stan Lewis died a thousand deaths, just like the letter said."

20

"So let's go over this one more time." Lew Michelson leaned back wearily in his chair and stretched his arms over his head, then lowered them to grip both hands together on the desk.

The members of the task force watched in silence. It was now Monday morning and the group had been expanded to include six more uniformed officers, as well as homicide detectives Leiter and Kellerman from the downtown office. They were working with Jackie and Wardlow on the second murder.

Captain Alvarez sat at the front of the room next to Lieutenant Travers, his handsome face looking tired and strained.

"Could we review this whole thing one more time?" he asked. "How many anonymous letters were received in all?"

"Six," Jackie said. "To Maribel Lewis, Stan Lewis, Chris Lewis, Desirée Moreau and Charlie Roarke."

"And you." The captain watched her closely.

"Yes," Jackie said. "I got a letter, too, just before the murder on Friday."

"And we now have...what? Three of them in our possession?"

"That's right," Wardlow said. "Maribel's, Chris's and Jackie's."

"Has the lab been able to do anything with these letters?" Travers asked.

Michelson shook his head and consulted some notes on his desk.

"Not even a bit of trace evidence. The letters and addresses were done on a laser printer. The hand-drawn star was done with some kind of ordinary ball-point pen, probably the kind you buy in multipacks at the grocery store. The papers and envelopes have no prints at all except those already eliminated to the recipients and others who handled them."

"So our guy's been using gloves all the way?" Leiter asked.

Michelson nodded at Sergeant Welsh, a slim blond woman in her forties who worked in Identification.

"Probably thin surgical gloves," she said. "Even fuming with cyanoacrylate, we can't seem to pick up any palm or finger smudges except for those we've already eliminated."

"What's cyanoacrylate?" Officer Howe asked.

Sergeant Welsh smiled at the younger woman. "You've probably used it at home," she said. "The patented name is Crazy Glue."

"Crazy Glue?" Brenda repeated, wide-eyed. "No kidding. You guys use that in the lab?"

"The fumes are used routinely for highlighting ridge detail and smudges not readily visible by any other means," Welsh said. "But even that process isn't helping us with these letters."

"We sent the envelopes away to the FBI," Michelson said. "Our lab was hoping the feds might be able to find some DNA in the saliva on the envelope flap, but there wasn't any. The glue was apparently moistened with plain water.''

"Six letters," Alvarez said grimly, "all threatening death. And two of the recipients are now dead. This killer means business.''

"Only five of them actually threaten death." Jackie consulted her notes. "The text of Chris Lewis's letter mentions torture and suffering, but not death. All the others not only threaten death but are pretty specific about how it's going to be accomplished.''

Everybody in the room turned to look at the blowup of Jackie's letter, mounted on an easel at the front of the room.

"Your blood and brains will be splattered on the ground,'' it said.

Wardlow slammed his fist angrily on the desktop. No one spoke for a minute, the lengthening silence taut and strained. Somebody coughed, while another sighed and shuffled his feet.

"Could you review the procedures we've got in place to protect the other letter recipients?'' the captain asked, clearing his throat.

"Charlie Roarke's moved in with a friend for a couple of weeks,'' Wardlow said. "I went over and talked with him yesterday afternoon while he was packing to leave his apartment.''

"Did he object at all about having to move?'' Jackie asked.

"No. He seemed really scared.''

"How about you, Detective?'' The captain turned to Jackie. "What measures are being taken to ensure your safety?''

"Paul's driving into the city every night so I won't

be alone when I'm off shift. The rest of the time I'm just paying extra-close attention to everything I do."

"I'm staying with her as much as possible, Captain," Wardlow added. "We don't make single calls these days if we can help it."

"Good," Alvarez said. "That's one of the reasons Leiter and Kellerman have been assigned to the case, just so you can double up with Kaminsky. We don't want her out there alone."

Jackie opened her mouth to protest but saw the captain's shrewd dark eyes resting on her and thought better of it.

"Two of the people who received letters are Desirée and Chris, and they live in the same house," she said, instead. "We've assigned a couple of patrol cars to take turns sitting outside their place all night. If anybody tries to get in, we're going to know about it."

Officer Pringle shuffled his feet and spoke up for the first time. "I'm one of the guys sitting out there," he said. "And I keep wondering, what if I'm watching this place and the killer's already inside?"

"You mean, one of those two women could have killed both Stan and Maribel Lewis?" Jackie asked.

"It's definitely a possibility, right?" Pringle said. "And they're both locked up together inside the house with that little kid. I wonder sometimes if I'm watching the henhouse while the fox is in there killing chickens. It's a scary feeling."

"I don't think you have to worry," Wardlow said. "They know you're out there and nobody else could get in without being seen. Desirée would have to be pretty bold to kill her sister or nephew under those circumstances, knowing she'd be caught for sure."

"Bold?" Pringle looked skeptical. "Crazy, maybe."

Jackie thought about Maribel's limp body in the bloody tub, and Stan Lewis's grain-filled mouth, his frozen scream of agony.

She leafed quickly through her notes. "Look, can we talk for a few minutes about suspects and alibis? We've got so many people out there doing interviews I'm not even sure I've got the information all up to date in my case file."

Detective Kellerman spoke up now. "Leiter and I did the neighborhood around the mill. Mostly it's a light industrial area with just a few houses. Nobody saw anything unusual at the mill on Friday night, except that some of the lights were on after dark."

"Nobody coming or going?" Wardlow asked. "No vehicles or foot traffic?"

"Not a thing."

"That mill's a long way out," Jackie said. "Way off the beaten track." She frowned at her notes and tapped her pen on the paper.

Alvarez leaned forward. "What are you thinking, Detective?"

"I'm wondering about Desirée. She doesn't drive, so if she went out there to kill Stan Lewis, she'd have to hitchhike or ride the bus, in which case somebody might remember her. She's pretty hard to overlook."

Brenda Howe made a note in her book. "I'll check with all the bus drivers as soon as we get out of here."

"But it's probably going to be a dead end," Michelson said. "Stan Lewis wouldn't have walked up on that catwalk except to show the mill workings to somebody. He was pushed over the railing by somebody he trusted. I think it's more likely he took the killer out to the mill with him on Friday night.''

"Not necessarily," Wardlow said. "Somebody could've been holding a weapon on him and made him climb the catwalk.''

"But in that case it'd have to be somebody who knew how the mill operated and what was in the bottom of that screenings bin. How would they know, unless Stanley had explained it to them?''

Kellerman looked around thoughtfully, tapping his fingers on the desk. "All right, so he's taking a friend for a tour of the mill, a little sight-seeing after hours. He suggests they climb up and look into the screenings bin, because it's really neat how the mill cleans and disposes of this stuff. Up they go, and while they're on the catwalk Stanley gets pushed over the edge.''

Jackie nodded. "Desirée or Laney Symons could easily have familiarized themselves with how a screenings bin operates, and Chris Lewis and Charlie Roarke would probably know already, in connection with their jobs.''

"Good point. So when are we going to take a closer look at Charlie Roarke?" Leiter asked.

"And there's another person we haven't thought of,'' Travers said.

"Who's that, Lieutenant?" Michelson turned to glance at his superior officer.

"The little kid. Lewis's son.''

A stunned silence fell. The police officers exchanged uneasy glances.

"He's twelve years old and big for his age, right?" Alvarez said.

"Not really big," Wardlow said. "Just kind of chubby."

"And this is the sort of thing a divorced father does with his kid on a Friday night. He takes him to the job site after hours, shows him around, brags a bit about where Dad works. He takes his son up onto the catwalk and shows him the screenings bin, and says they have to be really careful because if a guy falls in while the auger's switched on, he'll be sucked right onto those sharp blades and cut to pieces."

The officers listened, appalled.

"Gordie's mad at Dad for leaving Mommy and not paying enough attention to him," Alvarez went on. "He gives Daddy a push and watches him flounder in the grain, then runs downstairs to flip the switch."

"But..." Jackie looked from the captain to Lieutenant Travers. "The kid would have to be a monster to do something like that."

"It wouldn't be the first time we've run into a kid who's a monster," Michelson said grimly. "In fact, they're getting to be pretty damn common these days."

"But that means he would have killed his grandmother, too," Wardlow argued. "Stabbed her right in her own bathtub."

"And sent all the anonymous letters," Jackie added. "Is Gordie even old enough to type those letters? I can't remember how much a kid's learned by sixth or seventh grade."

"Where was Gordie Lewis on Friday night?" Leiter asked. "Has anybody checked?"

"I was at their place around five on Friday," Wardlow said. "Gordie was home, but Desirée wasn't. He had no idea where she was. Chris got home just after I arrived, said she planned to spend the evening there.''

"Did she?"

Jackie glanced at her partner, who nodded.

"She says she did. I went back on Saturday to tell them about Stan and checked on their activities the night before.'' Wardlow looked down at his notes. "Chris said she was worn out from working all week with the horses. She had a hot bath and went to bed about seven-thirty, read and watched television in her room for a couple of hours and fell asleep.''

"Did she see her son during that time?"

"No, but Gordie says he was in the living room watching television and playing video games. When he peeked in to say good-night around ten o'clock, his mother was asleep so he made himself a snack in the kitchen and went to bed.''

"What do they say about Desirée's whereabouts?" Jackie asked.

"They didn't see her at all on Friday night, but that's not unusual. Apparently Desirée comes and goes according to her own schedule. Chris has given up trying to control her.''

"What was the reaction when you told them about Stan?" Michelson asked.

"It was pretty strange,'' Wardlow said reluctantly. "Both of them seemed kind of frozen. When I told Gordie about his grandmother last week, he fell to pieces. But this time he just sat still for a while, then walked into his room and closed the door.''

"How about Christine?" Michelson asked. "What did she do?"

"Pretty much the same thing. She turned a little pale and looked sick, but she seemed more concerned about Gordie. I think she was anxious for me to leave so she could go and comfort him.''

"Did she ask any questions about what happened?" Travers asked.

"Nothing beyond the ordinary. Like I said, she seemed mostly concerned about Gordie. She kept looking at the door to his room. Finally I went away so she could deal with the kid.''

"Who spoke to Desirée?" Michelson asked.

"I did.'' Jackie shook her head ruefully. "By now, I should be really good friends with Desirée. We've talked often enough.''

"What's her alibi?" Leiter asked.

"She says she was down at the Shining Eye, looking for a book.''

"The Shining Eye?"

"It's a little place downtown, sort of a combination bookstore and espresso shop. They sell stuff on satanism, mysticism, all kinds of erotica and weird religions. Apparently Desirée's a regular there. Doesn't just drop in and leave, but hangs around.''

"Have you been able to confirm the alibi?" Kellerman asked.

Jackie nodded. "She was there, all right. The clerk remembers seeing her and selling her a book, but he can't remember what time she arrived or left. It seems Friday nights are really busy down at the Shining Eye.''

"How about Laney Symons and Charlie Roarke?" Brenda asked.

"That's another weird story," Wardlow said. "They're actually providing alibis for each other. Charlie was at the Bum Steer on Friday night listening to Laney while she sang. She confirms that he was in the bar for all of her first set, which runs from eight o'clock until sometime after nine.''

"But the murder could have happened earlier, right?"

Wardlow looked at his notes. "The medical examiner places it around eight, but admits he could be off by as much as an hour."

"So where were Charlie and Laney before then?"

"Charlie says he was on the way to the club. Laney was in the back room practicing for her set. At least that's what her pal Archie says."

"The skinny dude with the ponytail and leather vest?" Jackie asked.

"That's the guy. Archie's not exactly the most reliable witness I've ever dealt with," Wardlow told her with a brief grin.

"How did Laney take the news about her boyfriend?" Kellerman asked.

"That was the strangest reaction of all," Wardlow said, his grin fading. "When I told her, she stared at me for a while like I was out of my mind, then threw her coffee mug on the floor and smashed it. She started to cry and scream, went right out of control. Her mascara was smeared all over her cheeks. After about ten minutes she calmed down and asked me when the will would be read."

"The will?" Travers said.

"Apparently Stanley made a will leaving everything to Laney."

"So she gets Maribel's house?" Leiter asked in surprise.

"That's right. There's a small life-insurance policy for Gordie, but the rest of Stan's estate goes to Laney Symons. When I asked her why it wouldn't go to

Gordie, she asked what a little kid would need with
a big old house like that.''

"Interesting," Leiter murmured. "Very interesting.
This house has changed hands twice in the past
week.''

A knock sounded on the door. Jackie got up to
answer it, drawing the newcomer into the squad room.

"This is Agent Baumann from the FBI office in
Portland," she told the group. "A lot of you have
met him before. For those who haven't, Agent Baumann is a forensic psychologist, and he's been kind
enough to fly over here this morning to give us his
insights on our anonymous letter-writer.''

Agent Baumann marched to the front of the room
and set his briefcase on the desk next to Captain Alvarez. He was small and nattily dressed in pleated
slacks, vest and bow tie, with steel-rimmed spectacles
and a fringe of dark hair around a smooth bald pate.

"Good morning, folks," he said. "From what Detective Kaminsky tells me, you're dealing with some
ugly business here.''

He opened the briefcase and took out a handful of
photocopied sheets, arranging them neatly on the desk
while the police officers watched.

"I have copies of the letters you've managed to
recover," he said, "plus notes on the contents of
other letters that have been reported by the recipients.
I also have case summaries on your two murders, and
I've spent the weekend analyzing all this material.''
He glanced at Jackie. "Detective Kaminsky, if you
would, please?''

Jackie wheeled an overhead projector into position
and walked to the front of the room to pull down a
screen, then returned to her desk.

Baumann moved across the room to stand by the projector, still addressing the group. "This isn't by any means a detailed profile. It's merely my cautious opinion on your letter-writer. A full psychological profile requires a major commitment of time and personnel."

The psychologist flipped a page of statistics onto the projector.

"Each year in America we deal with approximately 7,688 unsolved murders. Of these, we only have time to work up full profiles on eight hundred of the most dangerous killers. Current budget cutbacks will further curtail our profiling services. I believe Detective Kaminsky has already explained some of this to you."

He glanced at Jackie, who nodded.

"Having said that," he went on, "an initial examination of the letters shows me a number of interesting elements. First, I'd guess your killer is probably female, though I'm not saying this with any degree of certainty and I'd need to do a lot more work before I'd commit to the opinion."

"Why do you think so?" Michelson asked.

"Because the murders conform to a female pattern. Statistically women tend to use knives in murders more often than men and to push people from high places. Also, there's an element in the letters of powerful sensuality, which could possibly be the result of repressed lesbianism."

"Lesbianism?" Jackie looked up in surprise as Maribel's letter flashed onto the screen, followed by Chris Lewis's, then her own.

"The females are all referred to as bitches or goddesses," Baumann said. "Every letter mentions sexual matters, usually shameful ones. I sense a strong undercurrent of unresolved sexuality, as we tend to find in people like latent homosexuals who are frightened or repelled by their own impulses. There's also the emasculation theme in Charlie Roarke's letter. I find that quite intriguing.''

"What about the references to satanism?" Michelson asked.

"That could be a blind, or it could be genuine. It's hard to tell in such a brief text. I'm much more interested in the killer's sexual impulses, where the letters and the murders both offer some interesting contradictions. In the letters, for instance, we have words like *whoring* and *fornicating*, which are rather old-fashioned terms, no longer in general use. This would indicate an older person as the writer.''

Baumann put another transparency on the projector. This one listed suspects and victims, along with a brief description of each murder.

"And we also have a couple of very well-organized crimes," he went on. "Considering the nature of the threats in the letters, you might even say these crimes were orchestrated. This is also an attribute of maturity. Young people are much more likely to commit messy impulsive crimes.''

"So we're looking for an older killer?" Michelson said.

"Not necessarily. That's the puzzling thing about these letters. Despite the mature deliberate nature of both murders, the sexual undertone is so intense that it seems almost adolescent. Human sex drive is never as strong and compelling as during adolescence.''

"So what's the bottom line?" Alvarez asked while the other officers watched the screen in fascination.

"The bottom line is that we have a very disturbed individual here. I would look for somebody with obsessive-compulsive tendencies, intense but repressed sexuality and an intellect high enough to create an impression of calm maturity even though the psyche is raging with unresolved conflicts."

"So how can we recognize this person?" Wardlow asked.

"That's the problem. Your suspect will likely be difficult to identify or pick out of a group. The person who wrote these letters will seem like an ordinary person to the casual onlooker. I would suggest a well-socialized individual who keeps these psychotic tendencies carefully concealed."

"Well, that certainly rules out Desirée," Jackie murmured.

Baumann shook his head. "Bear in mind, Detective, that this is a very limited analysis and should be taken with a hefty grain of salt. A proper psychological profile takes much longer to develop."

"Could the killer be a twelve-year-old boy?" Travers asked.

Baumann looked at the lieutenant. "You're thinking about the son and grandson of the victims?"

Travers shifted in his chair. "Just one of the thoughts we've been kicking around."

"It's a bit of a stretch, but I wouldn't rule it out," the psychologist said thoughtfully. "If the child were bright enough to compose these letters, their content and the nature of the crimes probably wouldn't be beyond his capabilities, though on the surface he doesn't fit the psychological profile. Of course," he added, "I'd have to interview the child to determine that."

"We probably don't have time for that." Michelson stared at the screen. "We've already had two murders. I'm scared as hell there's going to be another one soon."

"In fact, that's another thing I wanted to point out." Baumann placed a final transparency on the tray. "We had a gap of over a month between receipt of the letters and the first murder, but the second murder occurred within a very short time after that. The killer has been emboldened by success and is following some kind of well-thought-out plan. I'd look for another attack very soon." He paused. "I would also predict that the next victim will be either a child or a female."

"Why?" Jackie asked.

"Because we have an orderly killer here, a person who seems fond of patterns. We had an older female victim followed by a mature male. Depending on the pattern being developed, we'll either have a young victim or another female, possibly both."

"But the killer seems to know a lot about this group of people," Michelson said. "He or she could be following some kind of pattern all his own, something we're not even aware of."

"That's entirely likely," Baumann agreed. "It could be a generational thing within this particular family, in which case Gordie Lewis would be the next target—except, of course, he didn't receive a letter, so that probably cancels him out as a potential victim. Or we might simply be witnessing escalation of risk and excitement. The first victim was relatively helpless, the second considerably more able."

A few of the police officers exchanged nervous glances, but the room was silent.

"All things considered," Baumann said, fingering his bow tie, "I believe there are two people who should be given special protection."

"Who are they?" Jackie asked.

"One of them is Desirée Moreau."

Wardlow shook his head. "I think she's the killer," he said. "I've thought so, almost from the beginning."

Baumann regarded him mildly. "You could well be right, Detective. She certainly fulfills a number of the criteria I've developed for this suspect. I'm merely giving you my opinion."

"Who's the other person at risk?" Michelson asked.

Baumann glanced around the room soberly. "I believe," he said, "that at this moment, Detective Kaminsky is in very grave danger."

21

The meeting dispersed and Agent Baumann left the room with Captain Alvarez, Sergeant Michelson and the lieutenant. Wardlow hesitated, then came over to Jackie's desk.

"So what's next?" he asked her with forced casualness, flipping through some of the papers stacked near her computer.

"Lunch, I guess. And after that I think we should go ahead with our plan."

"You mean getting everybody down here at the same time?"

Jackie nodded. "It's worth trying. We've never had all these people sitting around a table together. With so many undercurrents and weird dynamics in this group, it might be productive to watch them interact. Especially," she said, "if we have the meeting here at the station and they're all a little tense about it."

"If one of them's the killer," Wardlow suggested, "he or she will be really tense."

"That's what I think. Agent Baumann believes it's a good idea."

Wardlow gave her a keen glance. "Not entirely. He says it might jar something loose, but it could also be really dangerous to panic the killer."

"Brian, what choice do we have?" Jackie gathered

up her briefcase and shoulder bag. "Everybody agrees there'll be another killing soon if we don't catch this person. We have to do something."

"Okay." He shoved the papers aside and perched on the corner of her desk. "Brenda and I can make the calls this afternoon and schedule the meeting for tomorrow."

"Couldn't we still organize it for later this afternoon?"

Wardlow shook his head. "Stan Lewis's funeral is at three o'clock, and they'll all be there. We can't do it today."

"Shit, I forgot." Jackie shouldered her bag and started for the door. "Well, I'll see you in an hour or so, then."

He reached out to grab her sleeve. "Where are you going, Kaminsky?"

She gave him a level glance. "I'm going home for lunch."

"Is Paul going to be there?"

"Of course not. He won't get there until after dark tonight."

Wardlow continued to hold her jacket. "Let's go out for burgers."

"My head's aching. I want to go home for a while. Besides, I left a file there and I need to pick it up."

"We can swing by your place on our way over to the restaurant."

Jackie shook her head. "I'm going home." She turned to look directly at her partner. "I can't let this get to me, Brian. I have to keep living a normal life. If I panic and start running scared, I'll be even more of a target. You know that."

"I really don't like the idea of you going home to an empty apartment."

She freed her sleeve from his grasp and started to move away. "I live on the second floor behind a set of security doors. How could anybody get into my place in broad daylight?"

He slid off the desk and followed her to the door. "Just be careful, Kaminsky, okay?"

"I'm always careful."

She gave him a brief smile and hurried out to the parking lot to find her car. But as she drove the few blocks to her apartment, the psychologist's words kept ringing in her mind.

Very grave danger...

Jackie shivered and clutched the wheel, glancing nervously in the rearview mirror.

The threat of danger was nothing unusual to her. Most officers on the beat put themselves at risk every day of their lives, though the vast majority of shifts turned out to be uneventful, even boring.

The most terrifying thing about this situation was not having any idea where the danger lay. In the past when she'd been called to a domestic conflict or a robbery in progress, she knew what to expect and how to protect herself. But the killer who stalked her now could be somebody she'd met and spoken with, a person she hadn't even suspected.

It could be anybody.

She unlocked the front door of her building and rode upstairs in the elevator, pausing at her floor to unfasten the flap on her holster. After a glance up and down the empty hallway, she walked toward her apartment, wishing she'd thought to leave something on the latch, a strand of hair or a tiny strip of plastic to show if the door had been opened after she left.

But that was ridiculous, she reminded herself. It was the same kind of paranoia she'd told Wardlow she wanted to avoid. Her door was locked with a dead bolt, fully secure. Nobody else had a key except Paul.

She opened the door and stepped inside the apartment, reaching automatically for the handle of her gun. The rooms were silent and still in the muted light that filtered through closed drapes.

Suddenly the hair prickled on the back of her neck. *Somebody's here,* she thought, and her throat went dry.

A scent seemed to hang on the air, a trace of alien presence, a whiff of evil.

She felt a shudder of pure terror and an urgent desire to turn and run. Instead, she forced herself to check the front closet, then moved down the hall and into the bathroom, pulling aside the shower curtain to look at the empty tub. She let the curtain fall and edged into the bedroom, her heart pounding.

Moving quickly, Jackie bent to look under the bed, then took a deep breath and opened the closet doors where her clothes hung quietly next to Paul's.

After a moment she shut the closet and edged back down the hall to the living room, standing tensely in the doorway and looking around at the tidy area, the sofa and chairs, the coffee table she'd built, her flute in its leather case and the afghans her grandmother had knitted.

Her heartbeat slowed a little and her breath began to come more easily.

That eerie sense of an intruder in the apartment had

been simply the work of an overwrought imagination, she told herself.

Nobody was here.

She moved across the living room and pulled the drapes aside to look at the covered balcony, empty except for a few pieces of outdoor furniture.

Soon after they'd met, Paul had built her a couple of cedar chairs and a roomy cushioned lounge where they liked to curl up together with their wineglasses to enjoy the mild prairie evenings.

Suddenly Jackie's heart began to hammer again. She could see a piece of colored paper lying in the middle of the lounge, fluttering gently in the spring breeze.

She pulled the glass door aside and stepped out onto the carpeted balcony. First, touching her gun handle, she peered over the railing at the grass below, where a few green shoots were beginning to appear through the withered growth. The apartment building was silent in the midday brightness. Nobody was in sight, and there was no indication of how anybody could have reached her balcony.

Either they used a ladder, she thought, *or they came through my apartment.*

Unless…

She craned her neck to peer upward, wondering how easily somebody could reach the roof of the building and work their way down to the balcony. It was only a three-story building, but the sides were smooth brick with no visible footholds except for the windowsills.

Finally she gave up and turned to look at the paper on the cushioned lounge. It was weighted down with a couple of stones, and Jackie studied it for a moment, then went inside to get an evidence folder.

Not as if there'll be anything to find on the damned thing, she thought bitterly as she eased the paper into the plastic folder, then carried it inside and put it down on the kitchen table. *This killer doesn't leave fingerprints.*

The paper had been torn from the same kind of magazine as that picture left up in Maribel's attic. It featured a voluptuous female body, naked except for a police jacket hanging open over huge, dark-nippled breasts. The woman had a big silver badge pinned to her jacket and carried a nightstick, rubbing it against her crotch in a lewd manner.

Her head had been obliterated from the image, replaced by a photograph of Jackie's face on grainy newsprint. She recognized the picture as one that had appeared in a local paper when she'd solved the kidnapping case involving Harlan and Adrienne Calder's little nephew.

Jackie looked at the photo in growing confusion.

That article had been in the newspaper almost a year ago. It was highly improbable that somebody had been stalking her all this time, collecting pictures of her and keeping them. More likely they'd gone to the trouble of leafing through every issue in the newspaper morgue to find one that carried her picture.

In that case, she thought with a quick surge of excitement, there could be a good chance of finding who'd done this. The clerk in the newspaper office might well remember somebody who'd come in recently to look at a lot of back issues, then purchased a copy from the previous summer.

Forcing herself to overcome her revulsion, she held

the folder up to the light. There was something so hideously distasteful about her own features superimposed on that pornographic image.

A pentagram was hand-drawn on the corner of the image, next to a few globs of a dark waxy substance. Jackie recognized them as the same thing she'd found on the wood floorboards in Maribel's attic. The lab had confirmed that the substance was composed of drippings from an ordinary black candle, the kind that could be purchased in any novelty store.

She wondered if some kind of ceremony had been conducted around this image, and shuddered again. What incantations had been muttered, what darkly sexual rituals carried out over her photograph?

She dropped the folder onto the table, feeling revolted and sick.

Abruptly she turned and went back down the hall to the bedroom, opening the closet door. With a great surge of longing she reached out to grasp one of Paul's cotton shirts, holding it against her face and breathing deeply of its clean fragrance.

Maybe I should quit my job, she thought, surprising herself by actually considering it for the first time. *If I don't, I'm going to lose him.*

The thought of life without him made her feel empty and bereft. But leaving her job was also a frightening prospect. After thirteen years in the police force she didn't know how to be anything else, and she didn't want to learn.

Of course, a happy relationship with the man she loved meant far more than any job. But a deep stubborn part of her was angry with him for making this demand, for refusing to be close to her unless she could somehow guarantee her own safety.

When she looked deep inside herself, Jackie knew this was what she hated most about her current situation. She was impatient with Paul's fears, but bitterly angry with the unseen killer for being clever and ruthless enough to ferret out the one source of conflict between herself and her lover, then use it to manipulate both of them into this monstrous state of affairs.

"You *bastard*," she muttered aloud, flooded suddenly by cold outrage as she clutched the soft white cotton of the shirt. She turned to face the empty bedroom. "I'm going to make you pay for this. Come on, asshole. Why don't you come after me and see what happens?"

At that moment her telephone began to ring, shattering the afternoon stillness.

She crossed the bedroom to lift the receiver, taking a deep breath and forcing her voice to sound normal. "Hello?"

"Is this Detective Kaminsky?" a female voice asked.

"Yes, it is."

"I have to tell you something. I need to see you right away."

"Who is this?" Jackie asked, gripping the phone.

"It's Desirée Moreau."

Jackie called in a brief radio message for Wardlow, notifying him of her location, then parked at the curb in front of the school.

After a few minutes Desirée came hurrying down the walk, glancing nervously over her shoulder, and went around the car to climb into the passenger seat.

Jackie looked over at the girl who huddled nervously by the window. Desirée rocked forward and hugged her knees, raising her booted feet to rest them on the vinyl upholstery where they left smears of dirt.

"Put your feet down," Jackie said automatically. "You're getting mud all over my car."

Desirée cast her a glance of undisguised contempt. "Can we just get out of here?"

Alarm bells began to ring in Jackie's head. "Where do you want to go?"

"Anywhere. Just away from here." The girl buried her face against her knees, still ignoring Jackie's request to remove the muddy boots from the seat.

Jackie looked at her passenger with thoughtful caution. Desirée seemed thinner and more ethereal than ever, and her dark hair hung down in ragged strings to obscure her cheeks. She wore something resembling a black caftan belted with coarse rope, long enough to be soiled and muddy around the hem. The garment was huge, certainly loose enough to conceal a weapon.

Jackie picked up her radio and called Wardlow again. "Leaving the school," she said. "Heading up the next block toward Corbin Park. I'll stop on the east side, under the trees."

"I'll be there in five," he said promptly, then ended the connection.

Desirée rolled her head on her knees to stare at Jackie with those pale eyes. The irises were such a light gray that their margins were almost invisible.

"Are you scared of me?" she asked.

Jackie drove down the street and turned toward Corbin Park. "Should I be?"

"Of course not. I've told you before, I'm wiccan. We believe in peace and healing."

"But maybe you have your own way of achieving those things."

Desirée laughed unexpectedly, a harsh, almost manic sound that made Jackie's skin crawl. "Maybe I do," she said.

After driving a few blocks in tense silence, Jackie pulled up and parked under a row of trees just starting to bud.

She shifted the car out of gear but left it running, then turned to face her passenger. "Well, here we are," she said. "What did you want to talk about?"

The girl fingered her smooth golden nose ring. "The person who's been doing all this...stuff," she said at last. "What'll happen to them if you catch them?"

Jackie considered her answer carefully. "We'll talk to them and find out as much as we can about what's been going on. We'll make sure they have a good lawyer and any other help they need."

"What kind of help?"

"Medical help, counseling, whatever seems to be necessary."

Desirée flashed another of those disconcerting pale glances. "Do you think this person is crazy?"

"Two people have been brutally murdered and a lot of others have been threatened. That's not exactly sane behavior, is it?"

"But if this person is crazy, or...sick," Desirée said with obvious reluctance, "then they wouldn't have to go to jail, right? They'd just go to a hospital or something for a while until they're better, and then be able to go home again."

"What are you saying?" Jackie asked gently. "Do you want to tell me something about these murders?"

"I just wondered if…"

In the rearview mirror, Jackie saw Wardlow pull up and drift to a stop behind them. Desirée caught the direction of her glance and whirled to look back at the other police car. Her pupils dilated with panic.

"I have to go," she muttered.

Jackie put a restraining hand on the girl's arm under the coarse black wool of her robe.

"Don't run away, Desirée. Stay and talk to me. That's just my partner back there," she continued in a soothing monotone, trying to hold the girl with her voice. "His name's Detective Wardlow, and he's been at your place quite a few times in the past couple of weeks. He's really fond of Gordie."

"Gordie?" Desirée flung her head up wildly. "What did you say about Gordie?"

"Nothing. I just mentioned that Detective Wardlow had been—"

"I'm afraid," Desirée whispered, clutching her stone amulet, "Gordie will be next."

Jackie tensed. "Why are you afraid? What makes you think Gordie's in danger?"

"Because he saw something. He doesn't even realize it yet, but he won't be allowed to live after what he saw. He'll have to be killed."

"Who's going to kill him?"

"Satan," the girl whispered, her face turning even paler under the greasy strands of hair. "Satan will kill him. Poor little Gordie, he'll have to be sacrificed on the sacred altar."

The words had a familiar ring. After a moment's thought, Jackie realized they were almost identical to the threat Desirée had reported from her own anonymous letter. She watched the girl with narrowed eyes, wondering what to do next.

"Look, Desirée," she said at last, "if you're really concerned about your nephew, you should help us protect him. Tell me what you know about everything, and we'll promise to help you."

"How can you help?" the girl said, her voice low and toneless. "Nobody can stop Satan."

"Of course we can help. If you'll just..."

A few groups of students began to straggle through the park, their arms laden with books, laughing and talking as they headed for school. Desirée glanced at them wildly, then hunched down in the seat and hid her face against her knees.

Suddenly she opened the door and bolted from the police car, heading across the withered grass of the park at a tight run. Her hair streamed in the wind and the black robe flapped around her skinny body, making her look like a ragged crow.

22

"We should find some excuse to detain her," Wardlow said, pacing restlessly around Michelson's office. "If we don't, somebody else is going to get killed."

"We can't detain her." The sergeant sat behind his desk, looking irritably at a page full of notes. "Legally we can't even *question* her without the permission and presence of her legal guardian."

"Chris Lewis is her legal guardian," Jackie said. "I'm sure she'd give permission."

"If she doesn't, we could apply to Social Services for the appointment of a guardian," Michelson said. "The paperwork would take some time, though. Maybe more than we've got."

"Yeah, and what happens then?" Detective Leiter, hastily summoned from the downtown office, looked at the other three police officers in the room. "Even if we do bring the kid in and question her, we've got nothing to hold her. Not even a bit of circumstantial evidence. We've got her own admission that she follows some weird religion, nothing more. We probably couldn't keep her for twenty-four hours."

"At least it'd be twenty-four hours where we wouldn't have any bodies turning up," Wardlow muttered. "I hate to think of her spending the night in that basement suite with Chris and Gordie."

"The place is under surveillance all night," Leiter said.

Wardlow sprawled in one of the chairs. "So what? Pringle's right. Having an officer sitting outside that house overnight is like watching the henhouse while the fox is inside."

Michelson turned to Jackie. "What do you think? Is this girl a killer?"

"I don't know." Jackie frowned thoughtfully and began to tick items off on her fingers. "First, it seems like every time there's some kind of incident, she's the first one I see afterward. She's connected to all the people involved. She fits the profile. And she's a very spooky person. But—" Jackie dropped her hand "—Baumann seems convinced Desirée's likely to be the next victim, not the killer."

"Based on what?" Wardlow asked. "Personally I'm not all that impressed by this profiling stuff. It seems a lot like reading tea leaves. I'd rather deal with hard evidence."

"Well, now, if we had some, that would be great," Leiter said dryly. "I've never seen a couple of homicides with so little evidence. We have two brutal murders and no witnesses, no traces left at the scene, nothing at all to go on. Kellerman and I have been beating the bushes since Friday night, following up every lead we could think of. We have six uniforms helping us full-time. And we've still got zip."

Michelson looked up from his page. "So what are you saying? Do you think the kid's right? It's Satan himself committing these murders and nobody can ever stop him?"

"That's not altogether true. We have a witness for the first murder," Jackie said quietly. "Almost a witness, at least. Fiona Morgan saw Chris Lewis parked outside the house while Maribel was being killed."

"So you think Desirée knows her sister committed these murders and she's trying to find a way to tell you about it?" Leiter asked.

"Maybe. And that could explain her concern about what's going to happen to the killer after we make the arrest."

"But there's a couple of things wrong with that picture," Wardlow said. "One, Desirée hates Chris, right? So why should she be worried about her welfare? Desirée would be more likely to enjoy turning her in."

"Good point," Michelson said. "What's the other problem?"

"From what she told Kaminsky, Desirée seems to think Gordie's in danger. If Chris Lewis is the killer, that means she'd have to be capable of murdering her own son. I just can't see it."

He looked around at the others, who watched him silently.

"Kaminsky," Wardlow said, "you've met the woman and talked to her. Do you honestly think she could kill her own kid?"

"I don't know what to think." Jackie opened her briefcase and took out the plastic folder, tossing it onto Michelson's desk. "This was on my balcony today when I went home for lunch."

The sergeant looked down at the folder. His broad face drained of color. "Jesus," he muttered, glancing up at the others.

The two detectives got up to peer over his shoulder.

Leiter turned and looked sharply at Jackie. "Any sign of forced entry at your apartment?"

She shook her head. "I should have left something on the latch, but I didn't want to be completely paranoid. Besides, Paul fitted the door with a dead bolt on the weekend. I don't see how it could be forced."

"So how did they access the balcony?"

All three men watched her tensely while she considered.

"I guess there are a couple of options," she said. "The balconies are joined from above by upright columns. Somebody could have sneaked up onto the roof, then shinnied down to my place. But they'd have to be pretty athletic, and they'd still risk being seen from the third-floor apartment."

"What's the other option?"

"The super's been washing windows as part of his spring cleanup," Jackie said. "I went around back and found a metal ladder stored against the wall. Somebody could have used it to get up to my balcony, then put it back."

"In broad daylight, without being seen?"

"I don't know if this thing was left outside in broad daylight. Paul and I didn't use the balcony all weekend. That picture could have been out there for days."

"We'll send a couple of uniforms over to your building right away to ask if anybody saw anything," Michelson said. "And *this*—" he touched the folder with a grimace of distaste "—we'll shoot over to the lab, but they're not going to find anything," he said flatly. "Not a goddamn thing." He rubbed a hand through his thinning hair and tossed an antacid tablet into his mouth. "Christ, sometimes I hate this job."

Wardlow got up and began to pace again. "What

else can we do?'' He turned to the detective from downtown. ''Leiter, you're supposed to be the hotshot homicide guy. Don't you and Kellerman have any ideas?''

Leiter shook his head. ''We both figure the best approach is to go ahead with the meeting, like Jackie suggested. We get everybody together here at the station and grill them for a few hours, ask lots of questions and watch their reactions. Personally I'd like the chance to see Laney Symons and Chris Lewis in the same room.''

''You really think this whole thing is some kind of squabble over a man?'' Jackie asked.

''Maybe. It all seems to be based on sex.''

''But if they've been fighting over Stan Lewis, he's dead now,'' Michelson said. ''And I don't think this thing is over. In fact, I have an ugly feeling something's going to happen real soon.'' He looked soberly at Jackie. ''I'm worried about you.''

Wardlow gestured toward the folder. ''Have you told Paul about this?''

''No way,'' she said. ''And I'm not going to. Paul's already upset about the whole thing. This would freak him out completely.''

''Don't you think he has a right to know?'' Michelson asked. ''If somebody was threatening my wife like this, I'd want to know about it.''

''I'm not telling him,'' Jackie said coldly. ''And I don't want anybody else telling him, either.''

The other policemen exchanged frowning glances. Michelson seemed on the point of objecting further when there was a knock on the door and one of the secretaries poked her head in.

''Jackie?'' she said. ''Can you take a call?''

"Who is it?"

"Adrienne Calder."

"Okay. Excuse me a minute, guys. I'll be right back." She left the sergeant's office to take the call at her own desk in the squad room.

"Hi, Jackie," Adrienne said. "I'm really sorry to bother you at work, but Harlan needs to know what time to pick you up tomorrow, and we can never get hold of you at home these days."

"Pick me up?" Jackie asked.

"Oh, hell, I was right," Adrienne said cheerfully. "You've forgotten all about it, haven't you?"

Jackie searched her mind, trying to recall an appointment with her friends.

"The school orchestra is playing tomorrow night at a benefit concert, and Alex has a flute solo," Adrienne said. "I made all these arrangements with you last week. We were going to go out for dinner together before the concert, remember?"

Jackie slapped her forehead. "Oh, I'm sorry! I've been so busy."

"That's okay. Can you make it?"

"I don't think so. I'm in the middle of something at work, and I'm just snowed under."

"It's these awful murders, right? Are you working on that, too?"

"Actually one of them is my case."

"Well, I know you can't talk about it," Adrienne said. "I'll tell Alex you're busy and you'll make it next time. Okay?"

"I'm sorry, Adrienne. I feel so awful."

Jackie gripped the phone, trying to remember a time when she wasn't working on these murders, when she'd had a happy teasing relationship with Paul and done pleasant things with her friends.

It had only been two weeks, but it seemed like years.

"Will Alex be really disappointed?" she asked.

Adrienne chuckled. "Not as much as she would have been a few weeks ago. Actually she's going to the concert with Joel. It's their first real nighttime date. They're so cute, Jackie. You should see them together. Alex is a different girl."

Jackie smiled. "Well, that's good news."

"One of those murders happened over in Joel's neighborhood, didn't it? You know, I had no idea he was Fiona Morgan's son until Alex visited their house."

"Do you know her?" Jackie asked.

"A little. Actually Harlan knows her better than I do. They've worked together on various environmental committees over the years. Harlan says she's a formidable woman."

"She seemed pretty formidable when I spoke to her," Jackie said.

"Harlan thinks she could run the city council all by herself. He's had a couple of clashes with her and come out on the short end. But then—" Adrienne chuckled "—Harlan's such a pussycat. He can't fight with a woman."

"No kidding." Jackie toyed thoughtfully with the phone cord. "Maybe I'll have a talk with him if I get a chance. Is he really busy these days?"

"Never too busy for you, sweetie. Don't work too hard, you hear?"

Jackie smiled bleakly. "I hear."

"And bring Paul around for dinner sometime. I haven't seen that gorgeous man for ages."

"I don't see him much, either."

"Hey, what's up?" Adrienne asked with quick concern. "Is something wrong?"

"No, everything's fine. I'm just busy. Look, I have to go now. I'm in the middle of a meeting."

"Okay. Call me on the weekend, all right? Maybe we can go out shopping for our spring wardrobes and have some girl talk."

"I'd like that," Jackie said wistfully. "I really would."

She hung up the phone and looked at it for a few minutes, then went back into Michelson's office where the other officers were planning questions and strategy for their group interview the following day.

On Tuesday afternoon, Wardlow strolled into the squad room about two o'clock and paused by Jackie's desk.

"Well, our little party's ready to begin," he told her. "Bring your coffee and join us."

"Is everybody here?" Jackie gathered some files from the desk and stood up.

"Everybody except Desirée. Chris says the kid knew about the meeting this morning and promised to come, but you know our little Desirée. She's not exactly the most reliable girl in the world."

"I'll call the school," Jackie said. "If she's there, I'm going right over to get her. She's not ducking out of this."

But Desirée wasn't in class and hadn't been at home-room period. The school listed her as officially absent and was checking on her whereabouts.

"If you find her, could you call me right away?" Jackie asked the high-school secretary. "It's very important."

"Sure thing, Detective," the young woman said.

Jackie pictured the secretary sitting at her desk next to the principal's office, chewing gum and examining her fingernails.

She sighed and went down the hall to the conference room.

Seven people sat around the table in uneasy silence, drinking coffee from plastic cups. Leiter, Kellerman, Wardlow and Michelson were already there, facing Elaine Symons, Christine Lewis and Charlie Roarke. Two empty chairs stood at the table.

Jackie slid into one of them and lowered her briefcase to the floor. "Desirée's absent from school," she said. "I assume she'll turn up here soon."

"Shall we get started?" Michelson asked, peering over the top of his reading glasses.

"I think this is a crock," Elaine Symons said abruptly. "You can't bring us down here and harass us. I want a lawyer."

"So get one," Leiter said mildly. "We'll wait while you make the call."

Laney stared at him with cold belligerence. "Screw you," she said rudely.

Jackie watched them with interest. Leiter and Kellerman had been managing the investigation for the Stan Lewis murder, and much of their attention had been focused on Laney Symons. It appeared the relationship was deteriorating rapidly.

Careful makeup couldn't hide the fact that Laney's face was blotchy, her eyes red and sore-looking, as if she'd been crying all night. She wore a white shirt with the sleeves rolled up and the hem tied in a knot under her lush breasts.

"This was Stan's shirt," she muttered when she noticed Jackie's eyes on her. She hugged herself and looked down at the white cotton covering her breasts. "It makes him feel a little closer."

Jackie felt a touch of sympathy, along with a conviction that Laney's suffering was genuine.

Chris Lewis also seemed moved by the other woman's misery. She reached out a small work-roughened hand to touch Laney's arm, murmuring something. But Laney shook the hand away as if it were a snake, then turned to Detective Kellerman.

"So you don't think I need a lawyer. I thought you were supposed to be able to have a lawyer before you talked to the police. I thought it was the law."

Kellerman had a thin hawklike face and predatory gray eyes. He leaned forward and smiled, though the expression in his eyes didn't change. "Of course you can have an attorney present if you wish, Laney. We've already told you, feel free to go and call one right now. We'll wait."

She glanced around the room suspiciously. "What about the others here? What about Charlie?" she asked, clearly refusing to acknowledge Chris's presence by name. "Shouldn't Charlie have a lawyer, too?"

Michelson lowered his glasses and spoke gently. "You don't seem to understand what's going on here today, Ms. Symons," he said. "Maybe the officers didn't explain it to you carefully enough. What we're doing is simply having a brief exchange of ideas to

help us get at the truth about who's been threatening
you people and causing all this trouble.''

"An exchange of ideas," Laney repeated.

Charlie Roarke sat next to Laney, glancing at
Jackie from time to time with a look of mute appeal.
She made notes in her book and watched him co-
vertly.

Charlie seemed to be under terrible stress. His
handsome face was pale and his hands twitched as he
gripped the coffee mug. There were bluish circles under his eyes, and his pupils were so dilated she wondered if he was on something.

Only Chris Lewis seemed composed. Her face was
calm, her hands still. She looked from one police officer to the other with quiet courtesy, waiting to be
told what to do. At one point her gaze caught Wardlow's and she smiled with shy warmth.

He smiled back, then glanced at Jackie quickly and
cleared his throat.

"That's right," Michelson told Laney in a soothing
tone. "We're having a little chat to see if we can help
each other. Nobody in the room is a target of our
investigation at this point, and we have no specific
evidence to incriminate any of you."

Except for the fact that Chris Lewis was witnessed
at the scene during the time of the first murder, Jackie
thought. But she knows we're aware of that.

"So nobody needs a lawyer right now," Michelson
continued, "though all of you are certainly free to
retain counsel whenever you choose. If one of you
becomes a suspect during the course of our investi-
gations, you'll be notified immediately and advised of
your right to hire an attorney." He gave a slight
smile. "So now, is that understood?"

The sergeant's comfortable manner seemed to set all of them a little more at ease. They nodded, glancing warily around the table.

"Detective Kaminsky?" Michelson asked, leaning back in his chair. "Would you like to begin?"

She opened one of the files on her desk. "I really wish Desirée was here," she said. "But until she arrives, I guess we'll just have to do the best we can without her."

Laney glared and shifted angrily in her chair, Chris met Jackie's eyes with calm interest, and Charlie stared down at his hands, a lock of dark hair falling over his forehead.

"I'm investigating the murder of Maribel Lewis," Jackie said. "Maribel, like her son, received an anonymous threatening letter, and so did two of you who are here today."

Charlie's hand tightened on his cup and he muttered something under his breath. Chris made no response.

"Laney, you never got a letter, did you?" Leiter asked.

The woman shook her head, setting the long blond hair swinging.

"Did you know that Stanley got one?" Jackie asked.

"He did?" Laney asked, clearly surprised. "*Stan* got one of the letters? I never knew that. What did it say?"

The police officers all watched her closely. Kellerman leaned forward a little. "The letter said he was going to die a thousand deaths. He was going to be punished by Satan because he'd fornicated with two women at the same time."

"Two women?" Laney looked around in confusion, licking her lips.

Either she was innocent, Jackie thought, or she was a hell of an actress. Of course, maybe acting ability went along with being a singer. Laney was certainly used to being onstage.

"Your letter said something similar, Chris," Jackie went on. "It said you were going to be tortured and punished for whoring after two men."

Chris's delicate features turned pink with embarrassment. She folded her hands tightly together on the desktop, but looked at Jackie without wavering. "Yes, that's what it said."

"For God's sake," Charlie muttered, squirming miserably on the hard wooden chair. "Do we really have to go into all this?"

"Two men? Two women?" Laney looked around with angry belligerence. "What the fuck is going on here?"

Chris shifted her gaze to the other woman. "I'm sorry, Laney. I slept with Stan a couple of times during the Christmas holidays. We were hoping maybe we could get back together for Gordie's sake." Her flush deepened, spreading to her neck under the collar of her denim shirt. "But I was also sleeping with Charlie at the same time."

Laney stared, openmouthed. Suddenly she let out a cry of rage and lunged sideways with her painted fingernails curled like talons, aiming for the other woman's face.

"You *bitch!*" she screamed. "You goddamn *whore*, with your goody-goody smile and your cutesy little blue jeans. God, I should just…"

Wardlow restrained the woman, holding her firmly

by the upper arms until she subsided, glaring and muttering.

"Okay," Michelson said briskly. "Let's all get a grip on ourselves, shall we?" He glanced at Jackie, who gestured silently toward Kellerman.

"Let's move away from the letters for a minute," Kellerman said, obviously sticking with their initial plan to keep the discussion wide-ranging so nobody could prepare for their questions. "I want to know what all of you were doing the night of Stan's death."

"I was home in bed before eight o'clock," Chris said after a brief silence. "Gordie was there, too."

"And you, Charlie?" Leiter asked.

"I was on my way over to the Bum Steer. I spent the evening there, drinking and listening to Laney sing."

Kellerman turned to Laney. "Were you at the club all evening, too?"

She glared at him. "I've told you this shit about a thousand times."

"Could you tell me once more," he suggested patiently, "for the officers who haven't heard it?"

She shifted restlessly in the chair, rubbing her cheek absently, curling a bright strand of hair around her finger. "I went home from work to bathe and dress, then drove over to the club just before eight to practice some songs with Archie. I waited all night for Stan to show up. He was supposed to be there at the beginning of my first set. Around ten-thirty the cops came to tell me about..." Her voice broke and she covered her face with both hands.

"Could each of you tell me the last time you saw Stan Lewis alive?" Kellerman asked.

Charlie glanced around, then cleared his throat. "I

saw him at the Bum Steer on Wednesday night. That was the last time I saw him."

"We had lunch on Friday, the day he died," Laney said, rubbing her tear-streaked face. "We were celebrating because we were going to move into the house and start living a decent life for a change."

"But you're still moving in, aren't you, Laney?" Kellerman asked. "You've inherited the house from Stan, right?"

Jackie saw the way Chris's eyes narrowed and her eyes focused on Laney Symons with hard dislike. "That house should belong to Gordie," she said. "He was the only beneficiary in Stan's will."

"Not anymore," Laney told the other woman with cold smugness, though her face was still blotchy from crying. "Stan changed his will before he died, bitch. That man loved me."

Chris met the woman's eyes steadily, her face unreadable. Laney was the first to look away, muttering something under her breath.

"Chris?" Wardlow asked. "When did you last see Stan Lewis alive?"

"On Friday evening around five o'clock," Chris said. "Right after Detective Wardlow left, I went up to Maribel's house with Gordie for a few minutes."

"Why?" Jackie asked.

"Stan was cleaning up the yard, burning leaves and raking dead grass out of the lawn. He'd hired Joel Morgan, and Gordie wanted to go up and help them, mostly because he worships Joel, I think."

"So the three of them were working in the yard?"

Chris nodded. "I left Gordie there for a while and went back home to tidy up and have a bath. Gordie came in about an hour later, saying his father had to leave because he was going home to clean up, then over to Laney's club. I was still in the tub, so Gordie talked to me through the door.''

"Did you see Gordie again that night?" Leiter asked. Chris shook her head.

"I went straight to bed after my bath. I think he was in the living room most of the evening, playing video games."

"Where was Desirée?" Jackie asked.

"I don't know. I didn't see her all evening."

"Was that unusual?" Michelson asked.

"Not at all," Chris said. "I have no control over her anymore. I don't even try, because it makes her so angry I'm afraid she'll…" Chris's words trailed off.

"What are you afraid of?" Kellerman asked. Chris looked up reluctantly.

"That she'll hurt me or Gordie if she gets too angry."

The police officers exchanged brief glances. "What frame of mind was Stan in while he was doing his yard work on Friday evening?" Wardlow asked.

"He seemed really happy," Chris murmured. "He said…" She glanced quickly at Laney, then looked away. "He kept saying it was the beginning of a whole new life for him."

23

After the meeting dispersed, Wardlow paced the floor of the squad room while Jackie and the other two detectives sat watching him. He was in shirt-sleeves, his leather shoulder holster strapped under his arm.

"Well, that was a real waste of time," he said. "We don't know anything we didn't know before except that Chris Lewis is actually *afraid* of Desirée and that Laney Symons hates Chris enough to attack her physically."

"I believe Chris hates Laney just as much," Leiter said. "For such a gentle little person, Chris Lewis seemed pretty damned cold when she looked at that woman."

"She was upset on her kid's behalf," Kellerman argued. "You know, not getting his rightful inheritance. Even nice women can get vicious when there's a threat to their kids."

Jackie doodled on a notepad next to her computer, her brow creased in a frown.

"Jackie?" Leiter asked. "Any thoughts?"

She shook herself and looked up. "Pardon?"

Wardlow paused by her desk. "Did you get anything out of that meeting?"

She looked down at the squiggles on her paper. "A

couple of things. For one, I'm beginning to get a handle c.. Chris Lewis. I think she's a kind of catalyst.''

The three men turned to stare at her.

''She's one of those people who brings out emotions in a really strong way,'' Jackie said. ''Men are protective of her, while women seem to hate her and feel passionately jealous of her. But I'm not sure even Chris is aware of the effect she has on people. And I've been wondering...''

''What?'' Kellerman prompted.

Jackie shook her head. ''I don't have any answers. Just some things that struck me as odd. I really want to talk to Desirée.''

''Don't we all,'' Wardlow said grimly.

Jackie got up with sudden decision and gathered her things. ''I'm going out to look for her. By now, I think I know most of her hangouts.''

Wardlow shrugged into his jacket. ''Okay, I'll come with you.''

Jackie paused by the door. ''I thought you were taking Officer Howe tonight and doing another sweep of the neighborhood around Maribel's house.''

''That was the plan, but I don't want you alone with Desirée.''

''I'll call you right away if I locate her. Look, I really want to know about anything you pick up in the neighborhood.''

Her tone was urgent, and the other three detectives looked at her in surprise. ''Why?'' Kellerman asked.

She hesitated, fingering the doorknob. ''I'd like to know what Stan did on Friday night after he finished cleaning up the yard, and how long Gordie stayed with him before they left.''

Wardlow looked at her sharply. "Are you onto something, Kaminsky?"

"Not really. I just need to find Desirée."

He followed her to the door, looking troubled. "I don't like this."

"I won't be talking to anybody on my own, Brian," Jackie told him. "If I find her, I'll call right away so you and Brenda can come over to give me some backup. Is that okay?"

"Call whether you find her or not. I want to know when you go home, and whether Paul's there."

Jackie sighed and opened the door. "Okay, okay. Don't worry. I'll be fine."

But after she'd driven around for a couple of hours in the spring twilight, she felt considerably less confident. The sun dropped below the horizon and the shadows lengthened, casting long fingers of darkness across yards and curbs, washing the gritty downtown streets in an eerie glow.

There was no sign of Desirée at the Shining Eye or any of the coffeehouses. She wasn't at the basement suite when Jackie called Chris to check, and she apparently hadn't been seen anywhere else since leaving for school on Tuesday morning.

At last Jackie gave up and headed home, pondering her next move. Before driving into her underground parking space she took a swing through the apartment parking lot to see if Paul's truck was there. Suddenly she had no desire to go upstairs to an empty apartment.

It's that damn Wardlow, she thought. He's got me spooked, too.

She felt a flood of relief when she saw the familiar dark blue truck parked at the end of the lot. Her mood lifted as she started to turn around, thinking gratefully about a hot meal and the chance to unwind and talk to Paul.

But as she shifted into Reverse, she caught sight of what appeared to be a ragged bundle of clothing on the pavement near the big garbage container.

It looked like someone had tossed the bundle and missed the bin. But there was something odd about that mound of fabric. Jackie hesitated, then got out of the car, looking around in the deepening twilight at the building and the shadows between the parked vehicles.

Her pace quickened as she approached the bundle on the pavement.

"Oh, *no*," she whispered in horror as she bent over it. "Oh my God..."

Desirée Moreau lay on the pavement, her face and clothes drenched with blood.

Jackie left the hospital room and went back to the reception area where Paul waited. Leiter, Kellerman and Wardlow were with him, along with Michelson, who'd been called from a nephew's wedding and seemed uncomfortable in a suit and tie.

She paused in the doorway to look at them, hidden behind a bank of artificial plants. Paul's blond hair gleamed softly under the fluorescent lights. Even in this setting he seemed larger and more powerful than any of the men around him as he leaned back against the vinyl bench, his arms folded, and stared at the wall.

Jackie watched him for a moment, feeling shaky and miserable. Finally she approached the men and sank into a chair next to Wardlow, who dropped a sympathetic hand on her shoulder.

"It's so awful," she muttered. "They just finished stitching her tongue and treating a punctured lung."

Michelson shook his head. "Amazing those stab wounds didn't kill her."

"An inch to the left and one of them would have pierced her heart. It still did a hell of a lot of damage."

"Can she talk?" Leiter asked.

Wardlow glared. "Her tongue's been cut to ribbons. Whoever did this and dumped her at Kaminsky's apartment building wanted to make it pretty damned clear she won't be talking to the police."

"You know what I mean," Leiter said. "Can she give you any signals? Maybe write the name of the person who did it?"

"She's not conscious yet," Jackie said. "The doctor told me I could check back in a few minutes."

Paul met her eyes, his face taut with concern. "Are you all right?"

"I guess so. But I'll be working late, Paul. You might as well go home."

"Who's going to be with you?" He looked around at the other officers. "I'm not letting you go anywhere by yourself."

"Paul—"

"I'll be with her," Michelson said. "Jackie and I will go back to the office after the kid regains consciousness. Brian, I want you to go over and talk to Chris Lewis right away, then start canvassing the neighborhood around Jackie's apartment to see if anybody saw anything." He turned to Leiter and Kellerman. "You two check out Laney Symons and

Charlie Roarke. Get to them as soon as you can and find out exactly what they did after they left the station today.''

The three detectives got to their feet. Paul hesitated, then stood up, too, looking at Michelson. "You'll be with Jackie the whole time?" he asked. "She won't be alone?"

"Paul…" Jackie said.

"I'll be with her," Michelson promised. "I won't let her go anywhere on her own."

"All right." Paul moved toward the door, half a head taller than any of the men around him. He turned and looked back at Jackie, meeting her eyes steadily.

"I'll be waiting up for you," he said.

"Okay, Paul. I'll see you at home."

The men left and she was alone with Michelson, who watched her quietly.

"He can't take any more of this, Sarge," she said at last. "I don't know what to do."

"Could you stand to give up the job?" Michelson asked.

"I don't want to quit. No matter how I feel about him, he still has no right to force me into a decision like that."

"Then, could you stand to lose him?" Michelson asked. "He's a good man, Jackie. And he loves you."

She felt a flood of sorrow and pain. "I used to think I'd die if I lost him," she murmured, gazing fixedly at the wall. "But sometimes now I…I feel like he's already gone."

Michelson put an awkward arm around her shoulders.

A nurse appeared in the doorway. "Detective Kaminsky? The patient is out of surgery and semiconscious. You can see her now, but just for a couple of minutes.''

Jackie exchanged a glance with her sergeant, then got up and followed the woman down the hall to a surgical recovery room where Desirée lay strapped to an IV unit and a respirator.

''Is she breathing on her own now?'' Jackie whispered, peering in from the doorway.

''Yes,'' the nurse said. ''But we want the respirator available just in case there's a problem. Her tongue's been stitched and she's got a sedative drip in her IV for the pain. You can just stay a couple of minutes.''

''Thank you.'' Jackie turned to Officer Pringle, who sat on a chair in the hallway. ''Will you be here all night, Dave?''

''Until I'm relieved at 4:00 a.m.''

''Good. After I leave, don't let anybody into her room without checking credentials, even the medical staff. We don't want somebody to get a second crack at her.''

''She'll be safe,'' the young officer said.

Jackie nodded, then went into the room and approached the bed. Desirée lay with closed eyes, breathing so shallowly that the movement of the white sheet covering her body was almost imperceptible. Black hair, still matted with blood, fanned across the pillows, and her face was so pale it was almost translucent.

''Desirée,'' Jackie murmured, leaning over the bed. ''Desirée, it's Detective Kaminsky. Can you hear me?''

The light gray eyes opened and gazed up at her drowsily.

''I know you can't talk,'' Jackie said. ''But we

want to know if you saw the person who did this to you.''

Desirée's eyelids drifted shut, then opened again. This time her eyes seemed a little more focused. She tried to speak and winced with pain, lifting a hand awkwardly to her mouth.

"Don't try to talk,'' Jackie said. "Just nod if you can hear me.''

Desirée dipped her chin a fraction, closing her eyes again.

"Good.'' Jackie stared at the pale features. "Did you see the person who hurt you, Desirée?''

The girl's face twisted with fear. She rolled her head against the pillow and tried to lift herself onto her elbows.

"You're safe now,'' Jackie said. "You're in the hospital and there's a policeman sitting right outside the door. Nobody can hurt you.''

Desirée's anxious gaze swung to Jackie. After a moment she settled back against the pillows, shifted restlessly and made a series of unintelligible grunts.

"Don't,'' Jackie said gently. "Your tongue's been stitched up, Desirée. You can't talk now. But if you could just—''

Desirée grabbed Jackie's hand, and with one icy finger scratched something on the palm, looking up at her importunately.

"A star?'' Jackie said.

Desirée nodded and traced another symbol. She frowned, scratching again and again on Jackie's palm.

"A rope?'' Jackie said. "Is that what you mean? A star and a rope?''

Desirée shook her head and formed another symbol.

"A coat hanger?" Jackie said.

Another worried frown, and more symbols. Jackie recognized a star, the shape of a fish, then the curved symbol again.

"A fishhook!" she said. "A star and a fishhook?"

But Desirée was exhausted by her efforts, and the sedative in her IV was clearly beginning to take effect. Her eyes closed and her face grew still.

"She'll probably sleep for a long time now," the nurse whispered, appearing at Jackie's side. "She needs her rest, Detective."

"All right. Thank you for letting me talk to her."

Jackie frequently worked late in the course of her job, but it always felt strange to be in the squad room at night when everybody else had gone home. There was no ringing of phones or clatter of keyboards, no good-natured raillery or sudden tension as an emergency began to develop. The sky beyond the windows glittered with stars, and the streets were silent in the evening calm. The clock above Michelson's door read just after nine—Michelson was behind that door, of course, true to his promise to stay with her—but the hour felt more like two in the morning.

Jackie thought about Paul waiting up for her at home, and the discussion they would no doubt have when she got there.

She could hardly bear the prospect of an argument, of Paul saying goodbye and walking out the door. And yet she acknowledged that a secret cowardly part of her had been expecting this to happen right from the beginning.

He's too good for you, her grandmother's voice kept whispering in her ear. *He's smart and handsome*

and sexy, and what are you? You're Jackie Kaminsky,
plain as porridge, from the wrong side of town....

"Oh, for God's sake," Jackie muttered, ruffling papers in annoyance.

She couldn't believe these thoughts still tormented her after so many years away from Gram, such a long time of being out on her own and working hard to prove her competence.

A lot of the problem was this baffling case, she decided. The murders and violence were undermining her confidence in her own abilities. The killer kept striking right under their noses, almost taunting them. And Jackie couldn't stop the horror from happening, no matter how hard she tried.

She stared moodily at the sheet of paper where she'd been outlining notes, trying to cross-reference alibis and conflicting statements.

At the bottom of the sheet she drew a pentagram, then sketched a fishhook beside it, pondering their significance. Desirée had seemed so insistent about the two symbols. But the poor girl was in shock and heavily sedated, not to mention a pretty strange person to begin with.

At last Jackie pushed the sheet aside, still preoccupied, and lifted some papers from her "in" basket. They were reports with witness interviews filed by Wardlow, requiring her authorization before being passed on to Michelson.

Jackie went through them, scribbling her initials at the bottom of each page and tossing them into the other basket. Suddenly she stopped and sat rigidly erect, staring at one of the papers.

Her hands grew clammy and her breath caught in her throat. "Jesus," she whispered, her head spinning. "Oh, Jesus... How could I have been so *blind?*"

She got up and hurried over to Michelson's door. He sat wearily at the desk with his tie slung over a chair back, the suit jacket tossed on another chair and his sleeves rolled up. As she entered the room, he replaced the telephone receiver.

"Kellerman and Leiter have finished with Charlie," he told her. "Zero on that one. They're heading for Laney Symon's place right now, but—" He stopped abruptly. "Jackie, what is it? You look like you've just seen a ghost."

She swallowed nervously and took a deep breath. "We need to get hold of a judge right away. We need a warrant to search and seize."

Almost fifteen minutes later they were still arguing, but Jackie was starting to make some headway.

"Come on, Sarge, we have to do this," she pleaded. "We can't let it go another day. The situation's too dangerous. Look, we've already got two bodies and a poor kid who's been disfigured for life. What's going to happen to the next victim if we don't move now?"

He shifted uncomfortably in his chair and took a couple of antacid tablets. "You realize that if you're wrong, serving this warrant could cost us our jobs? Both of us?"

Jackie met his gaze steadily. "I know you've got a lot more of a career to lose than I do, but I'm willing to take the chance. Besides, the ICU nurse says Desirée's been slipping in and out of consciousness again. We can stop by there for confirmation before we get the warrant."

"If she's capable of giving you any confirmation. And if it means anything, considering the state she's in. Oh, hell." He passed a hand over his hair. "Of all the people in the city, why does it have to be *that* woman?"

Jackie watched him and said nothing.

Michelson pushed back his chair with a sigh. "She'll eat us alive, Jackie."

"Not if we're right."

"And you're certain of this?"

"As certain as I can be, given that we have almost no evidence apart from Desirée."

"Jackie, I still don't believe we can get enough from the girl to justify a warrant."

"If it's challenged," Jackie said stubbornly, "we'll have to deal with that problem when we come to it. But I'm the investigating officer, and I think we've got enough. I just have to convince the judge."

"Okay, outline it for me again. Tell me everything you've got."

Patiently Jackie went through the case one more time, laying out all the facts in the light of her new conviction.

When she finished, the sergeant nodded reluctantly and picked up the phone.

"Judge Schellbeck?" he said after a moment. "This is Sergeant Lew Michelson from the northwest substation. I'm really sorry to bother you so late at night, but we need a warrant to search and seize. I'll be over in a few minutes, if that's all right with you."

Michelson glanced up at Jackie while he listened to the other end of the conversation.

"I'll have one of my detectives with me to outline the case. We're serving the warrant tonight. Oh, and

Judge,'' he added with a grimace at Jackie, ''you're
not going to be very happy when I tell you whose
house we're searching.''

Michelson said the name and listened to another
stream of conversation.

''I know all that,'' he said wearily. ''But my detective is convinced this is valid, and I support her
judgment.'' He took a deep nervous breath. ''So we'll
be over as soon as we can, Judge. We just need to
make a little stop at the hospital first.''

Michelson hung up and looked soberly at Jackie.

''Well, here goes,'' he said. ''I hope you know
what you're doing.''

An hour later, armed with their warrant, they drove
down the street past Maribel's house.

''Just a minute,'' Jackie said on impulse. ''Let's
take a turn into the alleyway and drive down it.''

At the wheel, Michelson gave her a wry glance.
''Trying to postpone the agony?''

''No,'' she said with growing excitement. ''I just
want to look at something.''

He glanced over at her, then made the turn and
headed slowly down the alley. As they passed the rear
of Maribel's house, Jackie took a good look.

''I was right!'' she said in triumph. ''You can't see
the attic dormer from here. *Damn*,'' she added as her
elation ebbed away. ''I should have thought about it
long ago. When I handcuffed Charlie Roarke out here
that day, something struck me as funny but I couldn't
put my finger on it.''

Michelson stopped in the alley right behind Maribel's house and looked up at its darkened bulk against
the stars. ''I'll be damned,'' he muttered. ''You're

right. Well, I guess that settles it." He turned to her with a bleak smile. "Into the lion's den."

He drove back down the alley, turned onto the street and parked in front of an imposing brick house illuminated by discreet spotlights, its well-tended lawns and shrubs decked out in the fresh green of spring.

A patrol car pulled up and stopped behind them. Jackie went back to confer briefly with the two uniformed officers, who waited in their car. Then she followed the sergeant up the walk, nervously clutching her search warrant.

Too late, she realized that Fiona Morgan probably wouldn't even be home tonight. She'd be downtown, watching Joel as he played in the school concert along with Alex and the other students.

But a few muted lights glowed from the lower floor behind damask draperies. As soon as Michelson rang the doorbell, they could hear rapid footsteps approaching from within. Fiona Morgan answered the door, wearing a green velour bathrobe with a white towel wrapped turban-style around her head.

On any other woman, Jackie thought, the outfit would probably be dowdy. But Fiona Morgan looked like a member of some exotic royal family in cape and headdress.

She peered out at them, her eyebrows rising slightly when she recognized Jackie.

"Hello, Detective," she said with more than the usual trace of her Scottish brogue. "Isn't it rather late in the evening for a social call?"

"This is Sergeant Michelson," Jackie said, indicating her companion.

"We need to come into your house and look around a bit, ma'am," Michelson told the woman.

Fiona stared at him. "Whatever for?"

"In conjunction with our investigation of the murders in the Lewis family."

"But I don't see why…"

Michelson moved closer to the door. "If you'd just allow us to do our job, ma'am, we'll try to cause you as little inconvenience as possible."

Fiona appeared to be recovering from her original shock. "Well, you'll certainly not set one foot inside my house without a warrant, Sergeant," she said crisply. "And you know it as well as I do."

"We have a warrant, ma'am." The sergeant offered her the paper with its official seal.

Fiona took the warrant and read through it, then looked up with an angry frown. "This is ludicrous. There's no reason for you to be in my house. None at all."

"Then it won't take long for us to get out of here," Michelson said. "Come on, Detective," he added, taking Jackie's arm. "Let's get started."

"I want both your badge numbers." Fiona backed across the foyer as they came in. "I intend to call Chief Parker immediately and lodge a formal protest. This is simply outrageous!"

Jackie exchanged a glance with her sergeant. She wondered whether Michelson felt as terrified as she did. If so, he was doing a good job of concealing his emotion.

"I think," he told the councillor stoically, "we'd like to begin upstairs, if that's all right with you, Mrs. Morgan."

Two red spots burned in her cheeks. "Begin wherever you choose," she snapped. "I'm going right now to telephone my lawyer, then the chief of police."

She strode out of the room in a swirl of velvet, leaving Jackie and Michelson exchanging a look of deep resignation before they turned and trudged up the stairs.

The old house was lovely, with dark oak moldings, heavy Berber carpets, and artwork lining the upper hall above the wainscoting. At the far end of the corridor Jackie peeked into a room papered in ivory damask. A rosewood writing desk and a graceful Queen Anne couch sat along one wall.

"That must be Fiona's," she muttered to the sergeant. "Let's try the other one."

"We're drawing a total blank up here," he said, looking increasingly worried.

"Then we'll have to check the attic and the cellar." Jackie tested a brass knob on the door opposite Fiona's dressing room. "It's locked," she said.

Michelson was moving along the hall, checking other doors. He returned to Jackie's side, looking intently at the glossy panels of raised oak.

"Terrific," he muttered. "This is probably the one we want."

"I'll do it." Jackie moved over to the landing. "Mrs. Morgan?" she called. "There's a door up here that seems to be locked. Could you bring us the key, please?"

Fiona appeared in the lower foyer, clutching the newel post while she glared up at them. "That locked room belongs to my son. I certainly have no intention of violating his privacy.''

Michelson came to stand behind Jackie, and she was grateful for his square stolid presence. ''We have a legal search warrant, Mrs. Morgan. We're authorized to enter any room in the house.''

''That may well be,'' she said icily. ''But I myself haven't set foot in my son's room for more than three years. He cleans and maintains the room himself, and guards his privacy. Perhaps a little more than most young people do, but I have chosen to respect it. In fact, I don't even have a key.''

''If you can't unlock it for us,'' Jackie said, ''we'll have to break it down.''

''Go ahead,'' Fiona said bitterly. ''The police force is nothing but a squad of bullies, anyway.'' She began to walk away, then whirled to glare up at them again. ''And be assured I will bill your department for any damage done to my house.''

Jackie and her sergeant exchanged another resigned glance and went back down the hall to the closed door.

''How much do you figure a door like this would cost?'' he asked, testing its strength gingerly with his shoulder.

''I'd have to ask Paul, but I'm betting it's more than a week's pay. Can you manage on your own?''

''Not likely. I wish I had some tools with me. This sucker's really solid.''

The sergeant stood back slightly and delivered a well-placed kick to the door. It shivered but held.

Jackie studied the latch. ''It'll give next time, Sarge.''

Again he kicked. The latch ripped from its casing

and the door swung inward, hanging crookedly on bent hinges. A breath of musty stale air greeted them, along with utter blackness.

Jackie fumbled for the switch for the overhead light and turned it on. It was a globe veiled by some kind of black scarf pierced with cutout stars and a crescent moon. She reached up to pull down the scarf and the room was flooded with garish light.

"Oh my God," Michelson breathed, looking around in hushed awe. Joel Morgan's room was like no other teenage boy's they'd ever seen.

This place was a sorcerer's cave, dark and sinister, filled with objects and images so terrible that even a couple of hardened police officers found them difficult to look at. Black hooded robes hung along the wall, and cabalistic symbols dangled from hooks in the ceiling, rotating slowly in the gust of fresh air that accompanied the door's opening.

An array of ceremonial daggers hung in a curved pattern on one wall, two of them stained with a dark flaking substance. Pornographic images were plastered everywhere, depicting sodomy, bestiality and the subjugation and torture of women, many of them scenes so unspeakably brutal that Jackie felt the bile rising in her throat.

Michelson stood next to her, staring at the covered window where a wooden altar was flanked by tiers of unlit candles.

"Look, Jackie," he said in a horrified whisper.

She followed his gaze and moved closer. The altar was also a shrine, covered with photographs of a woman, locks of hair, torn bits of clothing and other souvenirs.

The woman was Christine Lewis.

Michelson knelt beside Jackie, holding his flashlight on the pictures. "These are Polaroids," he muttered. "I'll bet she never knew they were being taken."

Most of the photographs showed Chris Lewis suntanning in the backyard of Maribel's house, concealed in the alcove behind the porch. They had apparently been taken through a hole in the fence. In one of them, enlarged so much that it was grainy and blurred, Chris was topless. Her small pink-nippled breasts flattened against her chest as she lay faceup on the blanket.

There were other pictures of Chris, as well, undressing in her basement room, looking at her naked body in a full-length mirror, lying in a rumpled bed with her ex-husband and with Charlie Roarke. Most of the images were hazy, as if they'd been photographed through a layer of gauze.

Among the pictures of Chris were three others, candid shots of Maribel, Stan and Desirée. All three images had been smeared with blood and slashed to ribbons.

"He's obsessed with her," Jackie whispered. "It's been all about Chris right from the start. He wanted to kill her enemies and all the men who'd ever been close to her. Those were the people who got threatening letters."

"But Chris got a letter, too," Michelson said.

"She wasn't threatened with death, remember? Just punishment for her sins. He said he'd take great pleasure in punishing her. And he probably would have," Jackie added grimly. "The sick little bastard."

A sound behind them made both police officers turn, then rise hastily to their feet. Fiona Morgan stood in the doorway, still looking regal in her robe and turban. But her face was ghastly pale, her eyes dark with alarm as she glanced nervously at the pornographic images and sinister contents of the room.

"It's just…it must be some kind of dreadful phase he's going through," she said at last, giving Jackie a look of desperate appeal. "Joel's always been such a nice boy. Everybody says so. This is all some kind of boyish nonsense, nothing more."

Jackie waved her hand at the two bloodstained daggers on the wall. "Are you sure?" she asked quietly.

Fiona stared at the daggers in horror, covering her mouth with both hands, then looked back at the two officers. "But surely you don't think…"

Michelson stepped forward. "Where is your son right now, Mrs. Morgan?"

"He's playing his clarinet at a school concert. I let him take the Mercedes so he could drive his date home afterward. I believe they're planning to go out somewhere for ice cream when the concert's over."

Jackie felt a chill run down her spine. "Who's his date?"

Fiona turned to her. "You know—that little girl you mentioned when you were here before. Alexandra."

"Oh my God." Jackie stared at the woman, then at Michelson. "His date…it's *Alex*. Sarge," she said urgently. "We have to get to them right away. We can't let him be alone with her. I think he…"

"What?" Michelson asked when she paused.

"I think he probably cultivated Alex right from the beginning," Jackie said slowly. "He knew she was my friend, and he decided she might be useful later on if he needed to put some pressure on me." Her hands began to tremble. "If anything happens to that girl…"

Michelson got the license-plate number of the Mercedes from Fiona, then reached for his cell phone and called the dispatcher at the downtown station. He explained their situation and asked for backup at the school, as well as some technicians at the Morgan house to photograph and collect evidence from Joel's room.

"Keep it as quiet as you can," Michelson told the dispatcher urgently. "Secured phone lines, unmarked cars, nobody running around on the streets near the school. We can't risk getting this kid spooked." He glanced at Jackie. "Anything you want?"

"I'd like Wardlow to be over there, if he's available."

Michelson spoke into the phone again, then called the officers waiting in the car below, instructing them to enter the house and guard the contents of Joel's room until the technicians arrived.

Finally he gripped Jackie's arm. "We'd better get going."

"Officer, stop." Fiona Morgan turned to face the sergeant, blocking the door.

"Ma'am, this is urgent. I'm sorry about your son, but there's a good chance he's already killed two people and seriously injured a third. We have to apprehend him before anything else happens."

"That's…" Fiona choked. "That's what I'm trying to tell you."

Jackie moved forward slowly. "What, Mrs. Morgan?"

Fiona indicated a small leather case lined with dark blue velvet, lying open on the bed. "That contained a revolver belonging to my husband. Two years ago it went missing. I reported the gun stolen from my house, but it was never recovered.''

The two police officers looked at her tensely. ''You think Joel took it?'' Jackie said.

''Now I know he did. I recognize the case. My husband's initials are monogrammed on the lid.''

Michelson looked at the empty case, then the opened boxes of nine-millimeter shells on a black table near the door.

''Oh, hell,'' he muttered, hastily picking up the phone again to call the dispatcher. ''Here's an update on the Wilcox School situation,'' he said into the receiver. ''The kid's probably armed with a concealed handgun. He's in an auditorium with a whole crowd of other kids and their parents, and he'll have a girl with him when he leaves the building. She could be at risk. We need a special team dispatched, but everybody has to proceed with extreme caution. And I want as many people in plain clothes as you can find.''

He listened to the phone for a moment.

''Okay,'' he said. ''If the concert's still under way and they're inside the school, I'll want to meet with our people at the front entrance. If the public is already exiting the building, nobody moves until we've coordinated some kind of plan. Remember to keep it low-key and maintain contact by land-line only. No radios, okay?''

As he was speaking, the two uniformed officers climbed the stairs and stood in the doorway, looking curiously around Joel's bedroom.

Michelson and Jackie exchanged a few words with them, then hurried out, leaving Fiona Morgan watching them from the upper landing like a figure in some medieval tragedy.

Jackie glanced at Michelson as they drove to the school. His jaw was rigid, the freckled cheeks pale with tension.

"Was there any way we could've seen this earlier?" he asked.

"I've been wondering the same thing myself. I was completely taken in by him, and so was everybody else. He's such a nice well-mannered kid and he's also really smart. I don't think he left any clues, Sarge. There's nothing we overlooked."

"Except that he's a homicidal maniac, and he was right under our noses the whole time."

Jackie nodded, grimly staring at the darkened streets.

"Well," Michelson said heavily, "there's nothing we can do about it now except try to keep anybody else from getting hurt."

She clenched her hands into fists. "I hate to think of him with a loaded gun in that whole crowd of people. God knows what he'll do if he gets spooked."

"We have to get him isolated somehow so we can move in. No point in doing anything when the girl's with him, sure as hell we're going to have a hostage situation on our hands."

Jackie thought about Alex with her gentle nature, her sweetness and shy humor.

And Harlan and Adrienne sitting together in that crowded school auditorium, watching proudly as their daughter played her flute solo…

Michelson cast her a quick glance. "We'll get him, Jackie. Just stay cool."

"I'm trying." Jackie shifted restlessly in the passenger seat and peered out the window again as they approached the school. "I hope Brian's here."

"I see his car over there." Michelson gestured at one of the vehicles double-parked in the school's parking lot.

Dark figures were moving toward the front of the school, gathering in a little knot outside the door. One of them hurried over to Jackie and Michelson as they ran up the walk.

"Brian," Jackie said with relief. "What's happening inside, do you know?"

"The concert has about ten minutes to go. There's a violin duet and an ensemble piece for the conclusion."

"Has anybody in there been alerted?" Michelson asked.

Wardlow shook his head. "We've been waiting for you."

"Okay." Michelson approached the group by the door. "I want some of you at every exit. Are there five people here in street clothes?"

He glanced around at the other police officers. A few men and women moved forward, most of them wearing jeans or sweatpants.

"Come with me," he told them. "We'll slip inside the door and the detectives can show you what this kid looks like. Separate as much as you can and try to stay inconspicuous. Then I want one of you at each door along with the uniforms so they know who to look for. Above all, we want to make sure he doesn't get into his car with the girl."

Jackie hesitated. "I can't go inside. He'll recognize me right away."

"Somebody has to cover the car," Wardlow said, touching her arm. "You know what it looks like?"

She scanned the student parking lot and immediately spotted a late-model yellow Mercedes, conspicuous among the rows of rusty vans and muscle cars.

"There it is," she said. "I'll wait till you come out, then head over there."

Tensely she stood and watched through the big glass windows as Michelson and the plainclothes officers moved into the school, crossing the foyer to the auditorium entrance. Others dispersed and fanned out around the building, heading for the exits.

The night was dark and brilliant with stars. A cold wind tugged at her hair and slipped icy fingers inside her collar.

After a few moments Wardlow came running back out, looking pale and shaken. "Shit, the kid recognized me!" he told Jackie. "He's been watching you for days, so he must have seen me at some point."

"What happened?" she asked.

"He was really cool. When he saw us from the stage, he leaned over and whispered to the girl, then took her backstage somewhere. Nobody in the crowd knows what's going on. We have people at every exit watching for him, but they're not going to make a move as long as the girl's with him."

"Oh, hell. Come on, Brian. We have to get to his car."

Jackie and her partner ran across the grass to the parking lot and stationed themselves behind the rear fenders of the Mercedes, crouching low on the pavement with their guns drawn.

"Are you okay, Kaminsky?" he muttered in the darkness.

"I'm fine." She pressed her cheek against the cold metal, trying to see the school building.

"What finally made you tumble to him?"

Jackie rocked on her heels, considering. "It's always bothered me somewhere at the back of my mind, the way he told us he'd seen lights up in Maribel's attic that first night, but I wasn't consciously aware of the discrepancy until tonight when I realized you can't see the dormer clearly from the back alley. Still, I had the feeling something was wrong."

"What else? That's not enough to get a warrant."

"Well, the investigative manuals tell you not to overlook the obvious, right? And Joel Morgan was always there, right on the spot after every crime. But I didn't actually think much about him until tonight, after Desirée scratched something on my hand. I thought it was a star and a fishhook, but then I realized it wasn't a fishhook at all." Jackie sketched a figure on his arm in the darkness. "It was the letter *J*. I finally realized it when I was putting my own initials on some file reports back at the office. Can you see anything yet, Brian?"

"Not yet. I've got the rear of the building in sight, but nobody's leaving. How about you?"

"My sight line's blocked by this van next to us. Do you think—"

"One of the side doors just opened." Wardlow leaned forward tensely. "It's him. He's got the girl with him."

"Do you see a gun?"

"No, but he must have said something, because our guys are standing back to let him pass. Nobody's moving."

"How does Alex look?"

"She's terrified. Shh," Wardlow whispered urgently. "They're heading this way."

The night was so quiet Jackie could hear the footsteps of the young people as they approached, and Wardlow's ragged breathing nearby.

"I see you," Joel's voice called out suddenly. "Behind the car! Whoever's there, stand up and come out slowly or I'm going to kill her."

Jackie and her partner stood up. Joel Morgan faced them, his square face burnished by the moonlight. Alex was next to him, wide-eyed with terror. The boy held her with one hand, brandishing a gun in the other.

"It's loaded," he said, pointing the gun at Alex's head. "Should I blow her away, Jackie? I'll do it if you want me to. I'd enjoy blowing her head off."

Jackie lowered her gun and stood facing him tensely.

"Let her go," she said, moving around the car. "Come on, Joel. You can't accomplish anything by hurting her."

"Don't come any closer!" the boy shouted, his face contorted with panic. "You—" he gestured at Wardlow with the gun "—get out of here. I'm not interested in you."

Wardlow glanced at Jackie.

"Go!" Joel said.

"It's okay, Brian," she murmured. "Do what he says."

Wardlow turned reluctantly and started across the parking lot toward a group of officers standing at a careful distance.

Jackie faced Joel Morgan and his terrified hostage. "Let her go, Joel," she said again. "She's never done anything to hurt you. Take me, instead." She dropped her gun onto the grass, then opened her jacket to show the empty holster. "I'm unarmed, and the police won't hurt you as long as I'm with you."

He laughed suddenly, a wild manic sound in the hushed stillness. "Oh, I'm planning to take you with me, all right, Jackie," he said. "It's going to be lots of fun. In fact, I'm taking both of you."

He shoved the gun against Alex's neck, keeping his eyes on Jackie.

"Get in the car," he told the girl, reaching into his pocket to click the automatic door lock. "Passenger-side front seat. Open the window."

With a beseeching glance at Jackie, Alex scrambled into the car and lowered the window. Joel moved closer, holding the gun close to her blond head.

"Now, let me tell you what's going to happen," he said to Jackie. "I'll get in the back seat and keep the gun on her. You're going to drive. If you do anything stupid, her brains are all over the car. You got it, pig lady? You think you can handle this?"

"I've got it," Jackie said steadily. "I'll do exactly as you say."

"That's a really good girl. Don't move until I tell you."

She cast a warning glance at the group of police officers watching silently from the lawn. Joel climbed into the back seat of the car, keeping his gun trained on Alex's head. With the other hand, he tossed a set of keys into the driver's seat.

"Okay," he called. "Get in and drive. Alex, close the window."

Jackie took a deep breath, opened the door and slid behind the wheel. She had an incongruous flash of surprise at the luxurious interior and the richness of the tan leather seats, then a vague sense of amazement that she could even notice such things.

"Don't worry, sweetie," she murmured to Alex. "Everything's going to be okay."

"Shut up!" the boy said tightly from the back seat. "Don't talk to her."

Jackie turned the key in the ignition and the powerful engine hummed to life. She shifted into Drive.

"Okay," she said without looking back. "Where to?"

People began to exit the school building, moving in pairs and groups toward the parking lot. A few of them paused to look at the group of armed police officers on the lawn below them, then exchanged puzzled glances and stood uneasily in the moonlight.

"I want to go to Riverfront Park," Joel said from the back seat. "I want to take a ride on the carousel. Just drive nice and easy, Jackie, and don't try anything dumb, or your little friend here won't be so pretty anymore."

25

They drove through the sleepy moonlit neighborhoods, in and out of the wash of street lamps. Alex stared blindly out the window, twisting her hands together in her lap. Jackie could see tears shining on the girl's cheeks, but didn't dare touch her or speak to her.

Hold on, kid, she urged silently. *Hold on, and I'll try to get you out of this.*

But she knew all too well how dangerous their situation was. When somebody went on a killing rampage like Joel Morgan's, the outcome was almost always suicide.

Jackie wondered if that was why he'd armed himself with the handgun tonight. His weapons of choice for other people had involved knives.

And if he planned to commit suicide, he'd certainly have no compunction about taking a couple more victims with him.

She considered crashing the car, even began looking around for an appropriate location, then decided against the plan. A minor crash would just panic him and get both her and Alex killed. Anything more serious might defeat the purpose, since the car had no passenger air bag and Joel hadn't allowed them to buckle their seat belts.

As she drove, Jackie struggled to remember her

training, all those psychology and human-behavior classes about the safest methods for negotiating with a desperate criminal.

She glanced at him in the rearview mirror, surprised and a little unnerved by his calm. Joel Morgan held the gun steadily and met her gaze without expression, as handsome and pleasant-looking as ever.

Except for his eyes, she realized with a shiver. Those eyes were like windows into a world of madness, and as cold and merciless as the pale orbs of a shark.

"You did really well, Joel," she told him, struggling to sound casual. "We didn't even—"

"Shut up." He waved the gun tensely. "Don't talk, just drive."

She considered, then decided to risk it again. "But I'm just telling you how smart you are. We would never have suspected you if Desirée Moreau had died, and she almost did."

He opened his mouth to protest, then met Jackie's gaze in the mirror. "Yeah?"

It's working, she thought. *Thank God.*

She gripped the wheel, feeling like somebody about to creep through a minefield, and chose her next words with infinite care.

"That was certainly the most clever series of crimes we've ever investigated. You had all of us completely fooled."

A smile tugged at his mouth. "It was easy killing the old lady. She didn't even know what hit her," he said casually. "And she deserved it, too," he added, stroking the barrel of his gun. "Treating Chris the way she did all the time."

"But killing Maribel wasn't the hardest part. Sending all those letters, even finding out the information to put in them—that certainly couldn't have been easy."

He shrugged and peered at her face in the mirror again. "It's easy to find stuff out. I've got books on investigative procedures. You just need to know how to shadow people and eavesdrop on conversations, things like that. I'd have made a good cop, Jackie."

She was disturbed by the way he spoke in the past tense, as if his life was over. Definitely not a good sign.

"You'd make a great cop, Joel," she said, hoping she wasn't laying it on too thick. "You'll be great at anything you do, because you're so smart."

"Yeah, well, my mother's never thought so. She makes it her business to let me know that nothing I ever do is going to be good enough." He sprawled back in his seat, vanishing from the mirror. *"Nothing!"* he added bitterly, and began to swear under his breath, an incoherent stream of curses.

Jackie knew she wasn't qualified to delve into the relationship between this troubled boy and his mother. Her amateur efforts at psychology might well do more harm than good. But she needed to keep him talking if she and Alex were to have any chance at all of surviving the next few hours.

"How about Stan Lewis?" she asked. "How did you manage that one?"

"It was a little harder. First I had to come up with an excuse to get him alone somewhere. While we were raking leaves that day, I told Stan I was thinking of applying for a summer job at the mill where he worked, and asked if he'd mind taking me out to have a look around. After we got there, he started showing off all the machinery and stuff, telling me how everything worked. When I saw those auger blades, I knew exactly how I wanted him to die.''

"Why did he need to die, Joel?''

"Because he started touching her again,'' the boy muttered. "She got away from him and then he started hanging around again. Him and that other guy, both slobbering over her and pawing at her. I hated them so much I'd have liked to kill them a hundred times, but they had to wait their turn.''

"Their turn?''

"Roarke was going to be next.'' He licked his lips. "But then Desirée started talking to you and I had to shut her up. Desirée's been watching me for years. I was afraid she might know something.''

"So it was all about Chris? This whole thing was about Chris Lewis?''

"I love her,'' he said hoarsely. "I've loved her from the first time she ever talked to me. She's a goddess.''

"Did she—''

"The woman's not human, you know.'' He was speaking louder now, more rapidly, his face glistening with sweat. "She has rare powers. She's the only one who can lift me out of the pit I've fallen into. I wanted to go into her room and lie on top of her like a vampire to draw the powers from her, but I never could.''

"Why not?''

"I couldn't get close to her. All those other people were always around. Especially Desirée, who had some stupid crush on me and hated Chris because she could see how I felt about the goddess. I had to get rid of all those other people so Chris and I could finally be alone together in peace.''

Alex cast Jackie a brief agonized glance. Jackie gave her a fleeting smile in return, trying to look reassuring. She turned onto Riverfront Drive, pulling to a stop near the deserted carousel.

This was one of the most appealing locations in a city filled with beautiful places. The carousel was at least fifty or sixty feet in diameter. Its antique hand-carved horses and animals had been lovingly restored, then installed in a wooden gazebo overlooking the park and the Spokane River.

"Get out of the car, pig," Joel said, gesturing briefly with the gun before leveling it at Alex's head again. "Move around the front and stop where I can see you."

Jackie obeyed, walking around the car on the darkened pavement, conscious of the vehicles that began to converge all along the drive. Policemen slipped out and melted into the shadows, taking up distant locations among the trees and shrubbery.

Joel flung himself from the back seat and fired a couple of shots into the darkness. "Back off!" he shouted. "Keep your distance or I'll kill both of them!"

He gestured for Alex to get out of the car.

"Go stand with your pig friend," he said. "Stay close together. Walk toward the carousel. We're all going for a ride."

Jackie paused. "It's closed and locked, Joel. You can't—"

"Don't tell me what I can't do!"

He fired another couple of rounds toward the carousel. The panes of protective glass shivered and some bullet holes showed, but the covers stayed in place.

"People are always telling me what to do," Joel muttered, mostly to himself, digging in his pocket for more ammunition. "My dad was never like that. He

loved me. One day he came down here to the carousel
and rode with me, and we both laughed. I was four
years old.''

Jackie watched closely as he reloaded with prac-
ticed skill, wondering if there was time to launch herself at him. As if reading her thoughts he jerked the
gun upright and fired a shot toward them. Jackie felt
the bullet whistle harshly past her ear.

"Don't even think about it, pig," he said, laughing
loudly. "You can't outsmart me. You've already admitted it.''

"That's true. You're very smart, Joel."

Alex seemed to be on the verge of collapse. Jackie
reached out to put an arm around the girl, but Joel
screamed and waved the gun again.

"Don't touch her! Start walking to the carousel."

Alex turned and stumbled toward the circle of gaily
colored horses behind their bullet-damaged screen.
Jackie followed, trying to keep herself between the
girl's body and the crazed boy with the gun.

On both sides she could sense policemen moving
closer, members of the SWAT team with blackened
faces who crouched low or slithered across the grass
on their bellies. Surely Joel was aware of them, too,
but it seemed he didn't want to be distracted by their
presence. He was concentrating on his two captives,
and on the carousel.

"Can you open the door?" he asked Jackie, crowd-
ing close behind her. She could smell his fear, the
rank scent of his perspiration.

She tugged at the screen of glass and wood while
Alex shivered next to her. "It's locked, Joel."

"Then I'll have to kill you. Come around in front
of me." He maneuvered them until he stood against

the building. Jackie and Alex were fully in the open, standing in a pool of moonlight outside the carousel.

Jackie realized his strategy. Joel was conscious of the policemen hidden in the shrubs all around them. He was using the hostages to screen his body so no sharpshooter could get a clear shot at him without endangering one of the two women.

"That's good," he said. "Stay right there."

He was about ten feet away from them, huddled back into the shadows of the carousel entry while he kept his gun trained on both of them.

"I'm really disappointed in you, Jackie," he said tonelessly. "You're a cop. I thought you could open the carousel and take me for a ride, but you have no power at all. I'm going to kill you now."

Jackie swallowed hard. A memory of Paul drifted into her mind, surprisingly vivid. He was outdoors in the sunlight, kneeling to attach a strand of barbed wire. He was smiling up at her....

She clung to the image, feeling warmed and grateful.

"That's fine, Joel. Kill me if you need to. But let Alex go. She's never done anything to you, and she doesn't even *know* Chris Lewis."

Joel seemed to consider, fondling and stroking the barrel of the gun with his free hand.

"But I think I need to kill her," he said at last. "It's kind of like sacrificing a virgin on the sacred altar. Maybe Satan will give me some points for it."

"You won't have time to kill both of us," Jackie said. "After one shot they'll be all over you."

"Don't give me that crap, Jackie." He sounded bored and annoyed. "Like I said, you really disappoint me." He raised the gun and leveled it at her head. "This is a nine-millimeter semiautomatic. I could kill six of you before any of those goons in the bushes even had time to react.''

She stood uncertainly in the cold darkness, trying to think, struggling to formulate a plan.

''But what I'm going to do,'' he said next, ''is kill her first. I'm going to make you watch her die, Jackie, and give you just a few seconds to realize that it's all your fault. Then I'll blow you away, and your last thought will be what a total fuckup you've been.''

She clenched her hands into fists. When he stopped speaking, the only sound in the park was the lonely chirp of crickets, the cry of a gull over the water and the distant rumble of traffic.

He raised his hand and pointed the gun at Alex, steadying it on his other hand. As he pulled the trigger Jackie flung herself at the girl, driving both of them to the pavement.

She heard the roar of gunfire and felt a circle of heat growing and spreading within her. But it all seemed strangely distant, as if it was happening to somebody else.

Vaguely she was aware of more gunfire, the pounding of feet and shouts that filled the night. Alex was beneath her, lying very still, bright hair spilling across the chilly pavement in a pool of silver.

''Alex,'' Jackie whispered, dry-mouthed with fear. ''Sweetheart, are you okay?''

But there was no reply, and then Jackie couldn't talk anymore.

She'd slid off a cliff into a black void....

26

She saw an opening filled with light, but the brightness hurt her eyes and made them difficult to focus.

She saw a body clothed in white robes. An angel? Then a face appeared suddenly in the square of light. It was a wide dark face with shiny eyeglasses, a gray mustache and a gold front tooth.

A most unlikely angel, Jackie thought in confusion. But then, she had no idea what to expect in this new place.

She blinked and frowned.

"Ah, the lady is awake," her angel murmured in a gentle accented voice. "I am Dr. Rajabali. I am sure you must be very thirsty."

She realized that her mouth was dry and raspy, and her lips felt swollen. The angel lifted her head and placed something between her lips. She sucked a mouthful of delicious cool liquid and marveled at its taste.

But, of course, this was heaven. She must be drinking ambrosia.

"You are a very lucky young woman," he was saying as he stroked her forehead. "The bullet entered here, next to your left kidney." He touched the back of his robe with a brown hand. "The exit wound is here." This time he indicated the front of his garment, which bulged modestly over a rounded abdomen.

Jackie watched him in confusion, barely comprehending the words.

"I am afraid," he went on, "the exit wound was rather messy, but we have stitched it up very carefully and there will be minimal scarring. A loop of the small intestine was pierced and it has also been stitched. You have no other internal injuries, but there was much loss of blood and you will experience pain for several days."

She was beginning to understand the cadence and accent of his voice—she could even make out a few of the words. At last she forced her swollen lips open and muttered something, then tried again.

"You mean...I'm not dead?"

He gave her a sunny white-and-gold smile. "Oh, no, my dear. You are very much alive."

Abruptly he vanished and she was lost in the darkness again. She dreamed that Adrienne came and stood by her bed, holding a tall red amaryllis in a silver pot. Jackie knew it was a dream because Adrienne was crying, her beautiful face streaming with tears, and she couldn't imagine such a thing happening in real life.

Adrienne kissed her cheek and told her that Alex was fine, unhurt. All the kids at her school were impressed by her involvement in the tragedy, Adrienne said. Young people were calling and dropping by the house. It appeared Alex wasn't going to be lonely anymore.

Jackie stirred wistfully in the bed, wishing her dream could be true and Alex was really all right. When she awoke she saw a tall red flower on the windowsill and gazed at it, puzzled.

Then Wardlow and Michelson were in the room, standing next to her bed. Michelson wore his dark blue uniform, but Wardlow was dressed in jeans and an old yellow sweatshirt.

"Am I still dreaming?" Jackie asked her partner, struggling to form the words through dry chapped lips.

He grinned and lifted her water glass, holding the straw to her lips. She drank thirstily.

Michelson moved closer to the bed, clutching a bowl of white roses.

"Is Alex all right?" Jackie asked.

"She's fine," Wardlow said. "Still a little upset, but not a scratch on her. Apparently she's quite a hero to the kids at her school."

Jackie glanced beyond him at the tall red flower on the windowsill, frowning.

Michelson set his bowl of flowers next to the amaryllis, then stood beside Wardlow and looked down at her gravely.

"What about Joel?" she asked them.

Wardlow shook his head. "After he fired and you went down, the kid ran out from his hiding place to get a better shot. At least five of our guys hit him before he could pull the trigger again. He's dead."

She closed her eyes.

"It's for the best, Jackie," Michelson said gently, touching her hand.

She knew what he meant. This way there'd be no trial, no new turmoil within the families. And no individual cop would have to go through the rest of his life knowing he'd fired the shot that killed a seventeen-year-old boy.

But it still hurt like hell.

"I tried so hard," she told Wardlow, blinking back tears. "I did everything I could think of. But he..."

Wardlow patted her arm. "Don't sweat it, Kaminsky. You did great. Nobody could have done better."

"We're all so damned proud of you…" Michelson's voice actually broke.

Jackie blinked in surprise and tried to focus on the sergeant, but he stepped back and vanished into the square of light.

She turned to Wardlow again. "How's Desirée?"

"Getting stronger all the time. Chris and I have been spending a lot of time with her. She's in a room just down the hall. I'm going back there in a minute to take Chris out for lunch."

"Desirée's going to be okay?"

"It looks real good. She can sit up now, and the doctors think she'll be able to talk normally when her tongue heals."

Jackie peered up at her partner's face. "You look so happy."

He smiled and touched her arm again. "Yeah, Kaminsky," he said huskily. "I'm real happy."

She wanted desperately to ask about Paul, but she was afraid of what she might hear.

A nurse came and spoke quietly to the sergeant, who took Wardlow's arm. They turned and started toward the door.

"Hey, Sarge," Jackie called weakly from the bed.

"Yes?"

"I never told you…how good you're looking. So trim and fit."

She closed her eyes in sudden weariness, then opened them and wondered if she was dreaming again, because Michelson's broad face seemed to glisten with tears as he hurried out the door.

The next time she woke Jackie felt a little stronger, more aware of her surroundings. The dazzle of sunlight had faded to a pastel glow, and a man stood silhouetted against the pale silver of the window.

Jackie saw a hard tanned cheek, a white shirt and the collar of a worn leather jacket, a gleam of fading light on golden hair.

Her heart began to pound, and she clenched her hands tightly.

He turned to look at her, then approached the bed. "You're awake."

"Paul," she whispered.

His nearness filled her heart and mind. She ached with love for him, yearned to touch his face, gather him in her arms and hold him for all the days and years of her life.

"I'll quit," she murmured.

"What did you say?" He leaned closer, touching her cheek, stroking the hair gently back from her forehead.

"My job. I'll quit. I can't bear to lose you."

"Oh, Jackie." His face twisted with emotion. He sank onto a chair and buried his face in the pillow next to hers.

She stroked his warm golden hair, content to be near him.

At last he lifted his head and kissed her. "I don't want you to quit."

Jackie watched him in confusion.

"I've been sitting outside that door, thinking about you," he said, "and coming in here whenever they'd let me. And I've been watching all the others, too."

"What others?"

"All those police officers. There's been a steady stream of them coming by, peeking in at you and talking with me. It's like a family."

"Yes," she said. "It really is."

"For the first time I'm beginning to understand how important this job must be to you."

She gazed up at him, trying to comprehend. "How long have I been out of it, Paul?"

"Almost two whole days." He smiled wearily. "I've had a lot of time to think."

"Two days?" she said in astonishment. "Really?"

"The longest two days of my life. I love you so much, sweetheart."

She touched his cheek, ran a lingering hand over the line of his mouth and jaw. Paul took the hand and held it tightly, kissing her fingers, laying her palm against his lips.

"I love you," he repeated. "I love the woman you are, and I've got no right to make you change for my sake. All the time I was sitting out there..."

His voice caught, and it was a moment before he could go on.

"I made a deal," he said huskily. "A bargain with God, or whoever's in charge up there. I said if you could just live, I'd let you be yourself from now on. I wouldn't try to control you anymore."

She considered his words. "You mean...I can have both?" she said at last. "I can have you *and* my job?"

He squeezed her hand again, then bent to kiss her mouth. "You can have anything you want. Anything that's in my power to give you."

She watched him, considering. "Anything?"

"Just name it."

She could feel her heart melting. It warmed and trickled through her body in bright rivers of longing.

"Let's make love," she whispered.

He stared down at her in astonishment, then began to laugh.

She laughed with him for a moment, but it hurt too much, so she had to be satisfied with holding his hand and watching in drowsy contentment as the fading sunlight edged his cheek with gold.

Turn the page for a preview of
Jackie Kaminsky's next exciting case

THIRD CHOICE

by

Margot Dalton

coming December 1998

only from

_____ Third Choice _____

The child bent, puffing, to heave at a ball of snow almost as large as herself. The snow was slightly sticky, heavy and dense, just right for building a snowman.

And it was fun to be outside in the darkness, exciting and a little scary.

Her house stood nearby, big and comforting, glistening with Christmas lights. As she stood erect to tug at one of her damp woolen mittens, the door opened and her father appeared in the glow of the entryway, holding a newspaper.

"Angel, are you okay?" he called into the darkness.

"I'm find, Daddy. I got the whole bottom of my snowman finished and now I'm making his tummy."

"Well, you can't stay out much longer, sweetheart," he said. "It's almost time for bed."

"_No!_" she yelled passionately. "Not bedtime yet, I have to finish my snowman!"

He yielded as she knew he would. "All right," he said. "Just a few more minutes, then. And don't go past the fence."

"Okay, Daddy," she said contentedly, watching him vanish inside the lighted bulk of the house. She lifted a second ball onto the big one, then stood back to admire the effect.

Perfect, she thought.

Now she needed to add the smallest snowball for the head. In a plastic pail next to the fence she already had a carrot to make the nose, one her father's old slouch hats and a lot of...

She looked up, startled. The headlights of a car were bearing down on her, coming closer and closer, so near that their glow almost blinded her.

But that wasn't right, she thought in confusion. The cars were supposed to be on the street driving back and forth. Not here in her yard close to her house, where she was always safe.

Not here...

Belatedly she screamed and tried to jump aside. The car's tires screeched on the ice and a fender grazed the metal fence, then hit her body with a heavy, sickening impact.

She felt the car striking her, felt herself lift and fly through the air like a rag doll to land on the snow in a crumpled heap.

The car's red taillights vanished into the night and the pain began to blossom inside her body. She whimpered and tried to call her father, but her mouth was filled with salty blood and the words wouldn't come.

Gradually the world began to change, as if she were swimming underwater from sunlight into darkness. The windows of the house, the glistening Christmas decorations, the street lamps along the walk, all blurred to a single dazzle of color.

Then, slowly, the colors faded to blackness.